EVIL EMPIRE ™

DIVIDED WE STAND

BOOM!
STUDIOS

EVIL EMPIRE Volume Two, September 2015. Published by BOOM! Studios, a division of Boom Entertainment, Inc. Evil Empire is ™ & © 2015 Boom Entertainment, Inc. Originally published in single magazine form as EVIL EMPIRE No.5-8. ™ & © 2015 Boom Entertainment, Inc. All rights reserved. BOOM! Studios™ and the BOOM! Studios logo are trademarks of Boom Entertainment, Inc., registered in various countries and categories. All characters, events, and institutions depicted herein are fictional. Any similarity between any of the names, characters, persons, events, and/or institutions in this publication to actual names, characters, and persons, whether living or dead, events, and/or institutions is unintended and purely coincidental. BOOM! Studios does not read or accept unsolicited submissions of ideas, stories, or artwork.

A catalog record of this book is available from OCLC and from the BOOM! Studios website, www.boom-studios.com, on the Librarians Page.

BOOM! Studios, 5670 Wilshire Boulevard, Suite 450, Los Angeles, CA 90036-5679. Printed in China. First Printing.

ISBN: 978-1-60886-733-2, eISBN: 978-1-61398-404-8

I'm sure those of you who can't see eye to eye with me are wondering why this is happening. Why the riots? Why the unrest?

exc. 0.0 **Why now?**

CREATED AND WRITTEN BY
MAX BEMIS

ILLUSTRATED BY
JOE EISMA
(CHAPTER FIVE)
AND ANDREA MUTTI
(CHAPTERS SIX THROUGH EIGHT)

COLORED BY
JUAN MANUEL TUMBURÚS
(CHAPTER FIVE)
AND **CHRIS BLYTHE**
(CHAPTERS SIX THROUGH EIGHT)

LETTERED BY
ED DUKESHIRE

COVER BY
JAY SHAW

DESIGNER
SCOTT NEWMAN

ASSOCIATE EDITOR
JASMINE AMIRI

EDITOR
DAFNA PLEBAN

CHAPTER
FIVE
.... *fig. 1*

exc. 1.0 **Every day we allow atrocities and betrayals
of faith to go *unpunished*.**

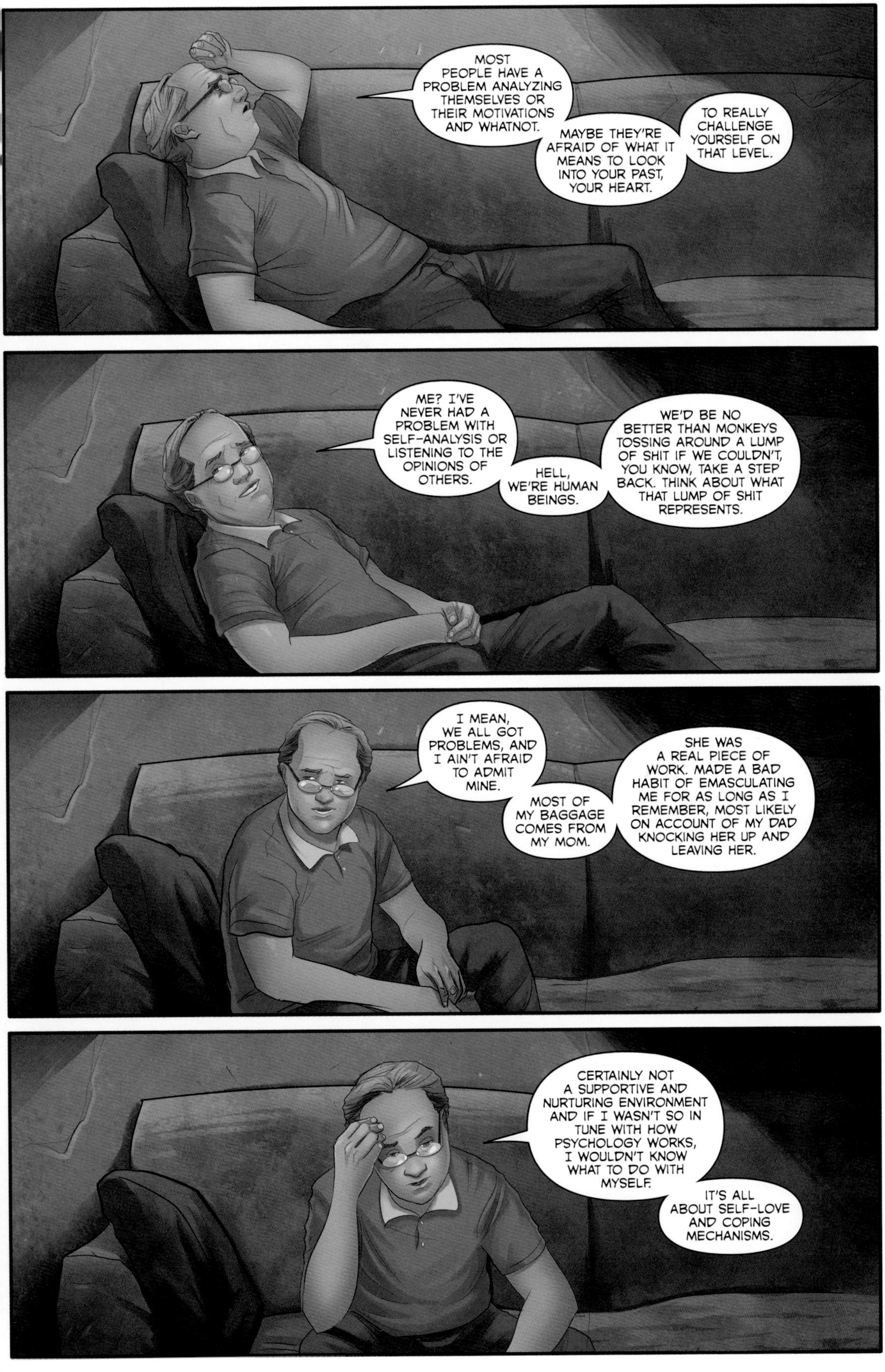
MOST PEOPLE HAVE A PROBLEM ANALYZING THEMSELVES OR THEIR MOTIVATIONS AND WHATNOT.
MAYBE THEY'RE AFRAID OF WHAT IT MEANS TO LOOK INTO YOUR PAST, YOUR HEART.
TO REALLY CHALLENGE YOURSELF ON THAT LEVEL.
ME? I'VE NEVER HAD A PROBLEM WITH SELF-ANALYSIS OR LISTENING TO THE OPINIONS OF OTHERS.
HELL, WE'RE HUMAN BEINGS.
WE'D BE NO BETTER THAN MONKEYS TOSSING AROUND A LUMP OF SHIT IF WE COULDN'T, YOU KNOW, TAKE A STEP BACK. THINK ABOUT WHAT THAT LUMP OF SHIT REPRESENTS.
I MEAN, WE ALL GOT PROBLEMS, AND I AIN'T AFRAID TO ADMIT MINE.
MOST OF MY BAGGAGE COMES FROM MY MOM.
SHE WAS A REAL PIECE OF WORK. MADE A BAD HABIT OF EMASCULATING ME FOR AS LONG AS I REMEMBER, MOST LIKELY ON ACCOUNT OF MY DAD KNOCKING HER UP AND LEAVING HER.
CERTAINLY NOT A SUPPORTIVE AND NURTURING ENVIRONMENT AND IF I WASN'T SO IN TUNE WITH HOW PSYCHOLOGY WORKS, I WOULDN'T KNOW WHAT TO DO WITH MYSELF.
IT'S ALL ABOUT SELF-LOVE AND COPING MECHANISMS.

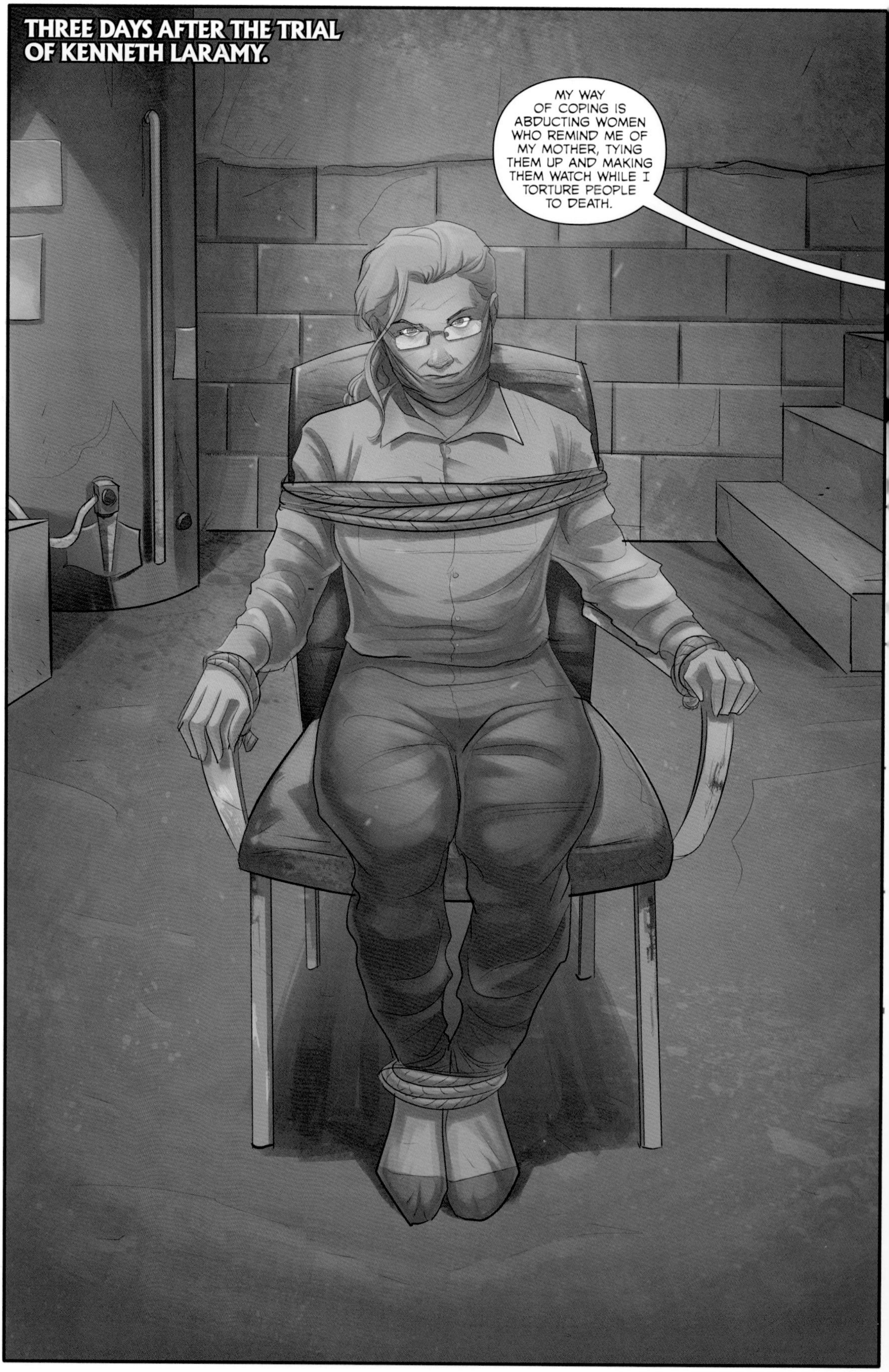
THREE DAYS AFTER THE TRIAL OF KENNETH LARAMY.
MY WAY OF COPING IS ABDUCTING WOMEN WHO REMIND ME OF MY MOTHER, TYING THEM UP AND MAKING THEM WATCH WHILE I TORTURE PEOPLE TO DEATH.

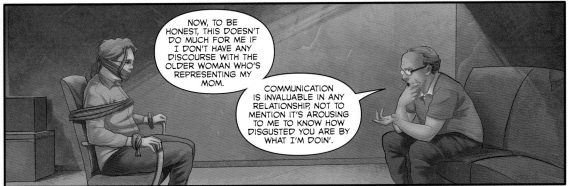

NOW, TO BE HONEST, THIS DOESN'T DO MUCH FOR ME IF I DON'T HAVE ANY DISCOURSE WITH THE OLDER WOMAN WHO'S REPRESENTING MY MOM.

COMMUNICATION IS INVALUABLE IN ANY RELATIONSHIP, NOT TO MENTION IT'S AROUSING TO ME TO KNOW HOW DISGUSTED YOU ARE BY WHAT I'M DOIN'.

THAT BEING SAID, I'M GONNA UN-GAG YOU.

BEFORE I DO, JUST KNOW THIS BASEMENT IS SOUNDPROOFED AS FUCK.

YOU PULLIN' A JAMIE LEE CURTIS IS ONLY GOING TO BE ANNOYING TO ME AND STRENUOUS FOR YOU, WHICH I'M SURE WE'D BOTH LIKE TO AVOID.

CAN YOU NOD IF YOU GET THAT?

THAT'S GOOD, THAT'S GOOD.

THANK YOU.

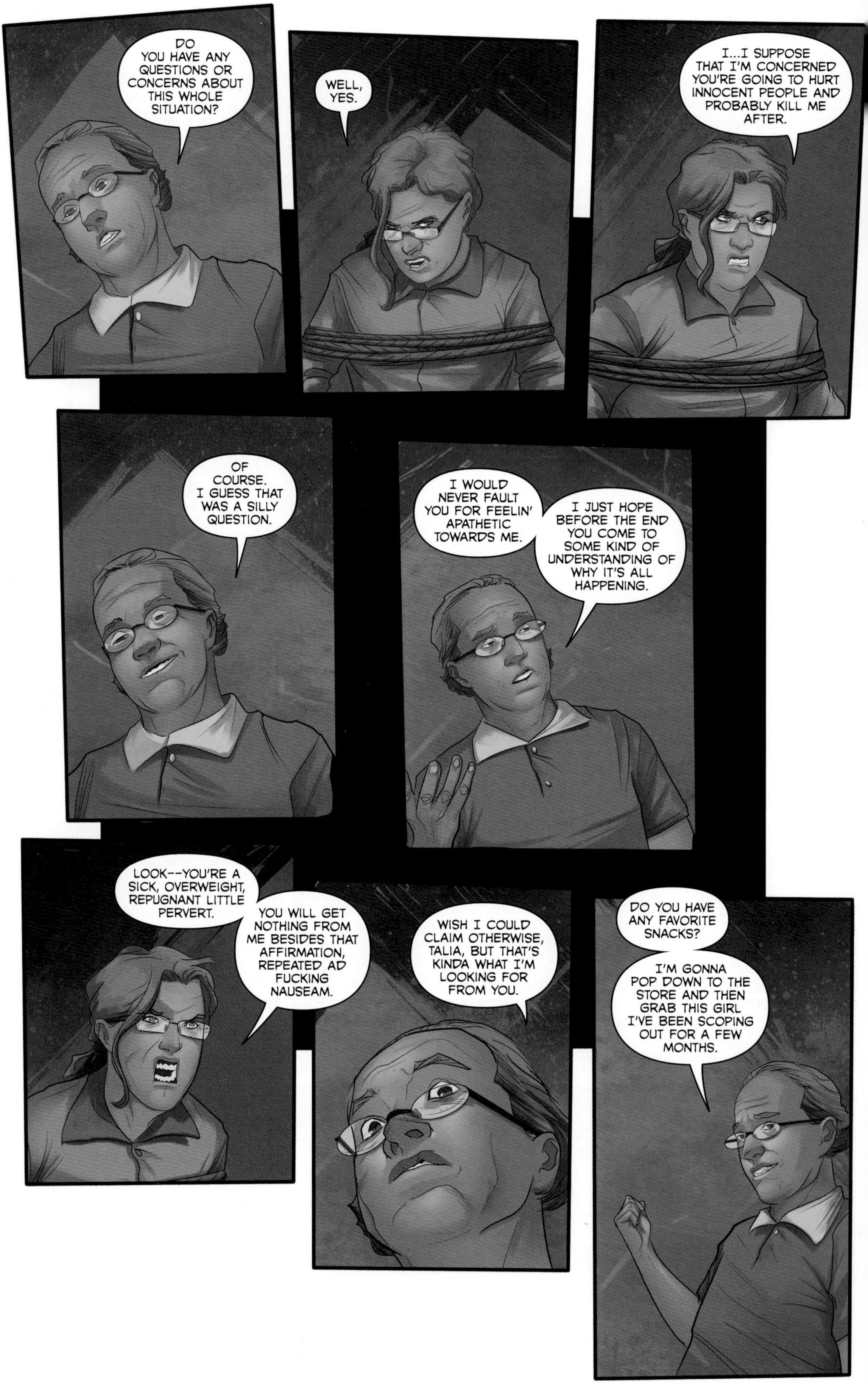
DO YOU HAVE ANY QUESTIONS OR CONCERNS ABOUT THIS WHOLE SITUATION?
WELL, YES.
I...I SUPPOSE THAT I'M CONCERNED YOU'RE GOING TO HURT INNOCENT PEOPLE AND PROBABLY KILL ME AFTER.
OF COURSE. I GUESS THAT WAS A SILLY QUESTION.
I WOULD NEVER FAULT YOU FOR FEELIN' APATHETIC TOWARDS ME.
I JUST HOPE BEFORE THE END YOU COME TO SOME KIND OF UNDERSTANDING OF WHY IT'S ALL HAPPENING.
LOOK--YOU'RE A SICK, OVERWEIGHT, REPUGNANT LITTLE PERVERT.
YOU WILL GET NOTHING FROM ME BESIDES THAT AFFIRMATION, REPEATED AD FUCKING NAUSEAM.
WISH I COULD CLAIM OTHERWISE, TALIA, BUT THAT'S KINDA WHAT I'M LOOKING FOR FROM YOU.
DO YOU HAVE ANY FAVORITE SNACKS?
I'M GONNA POP DOWN TO THE STORE AND THEN GRAB THIS GIRL I'VE BEEN SCOPING OUT FOR A FEW MONTHS.

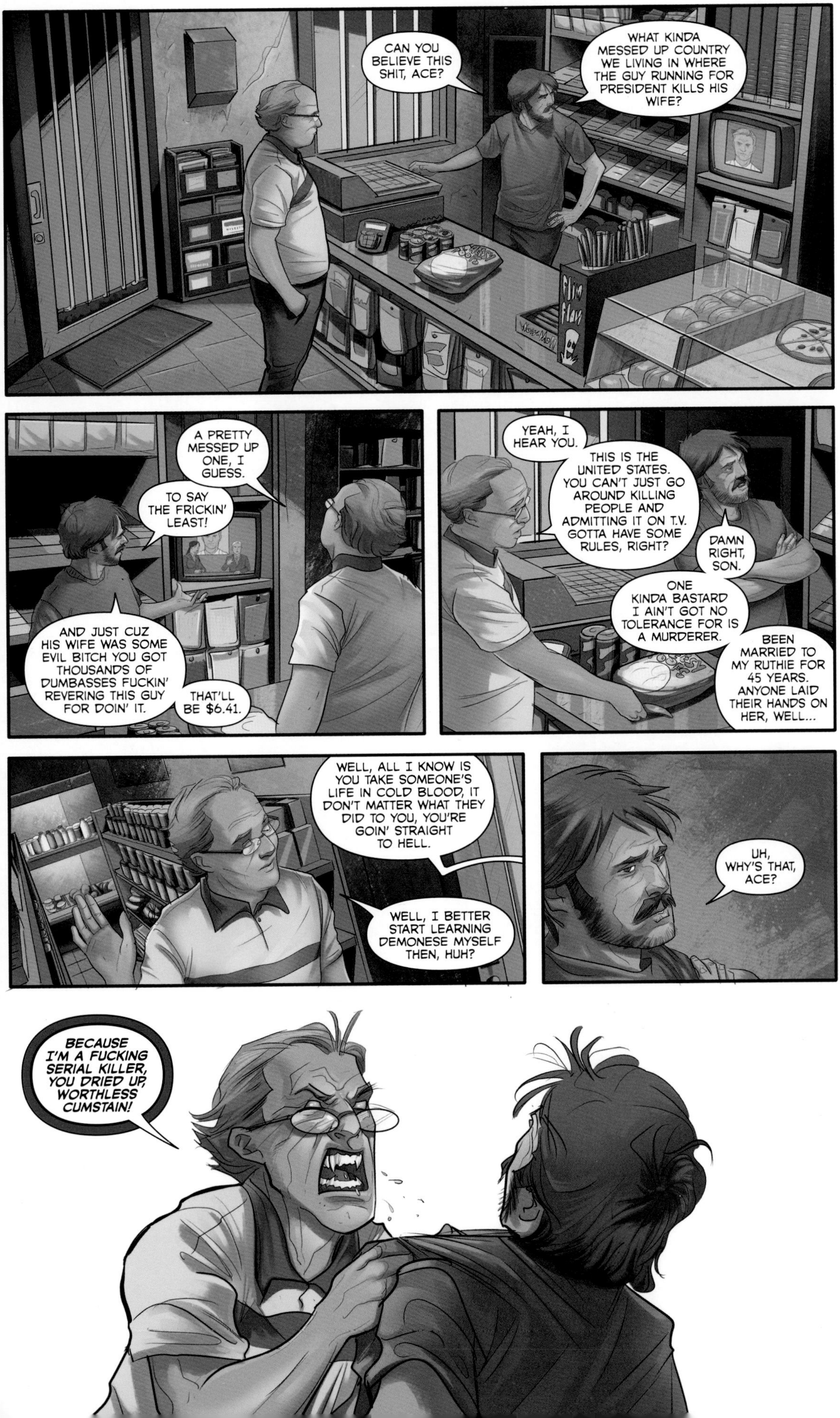
CAN YOU BELIEVE THIS SHIT, ACE?
WHAT KINDA MESSED UP COUNTRY WE LIVING IN WHERE THE GUY RUNNING FOR PRESIDENT KILLS HIS WIFE?
A PRETTY MESSED UP ONE, I GUESS.
TO SAY THE FRICKIN' LEAST!
AND JUST CUZ HIS WIFE WAS SOME EVIL BITCH YOU GOT THOUSANDS OF DUMBASSES FUCKIN' REVERING THIS GUY FOR DOIN' IT.
THAT'LL BE $6.41.
YEAH, I HEAR YOU.
THIS IS THE UNITED STATES. YOU CAN'T JUST GO AROUND KILLING PEOPLE AND ADMITTING IT ON T.V. GOTTA HAVE SOME RULES, RIGHT?
DAMN RIGHT, SON.
ONE KINDA BASTARD I AIN'T GOT NO TOLERANCE FOR IS A MURDERER.
BEEN MARRIED TO MY RUTHIE FOR 45 YEARS. ANYONE LAID THEIR HANDS ON HER, WELL...
WELL, ALL I KNOW IS YOU TAKE SOMEONE'S LIFE IN COLD BLOOD, IT DON'T MATTER WHAT THEY DID TO YOU, YOU'RE GOIN' STRAIGHT TO HELL.
WELL, I BETTER START LEARNING DEMONESE MYSELF THEN, HUH?
UH, WHY'S THAT, ACE?
BECAUSE I'M A FUCKING SERIAL KILLER, YOU DRIED UP, WORTHLESS CUMSTAIN!

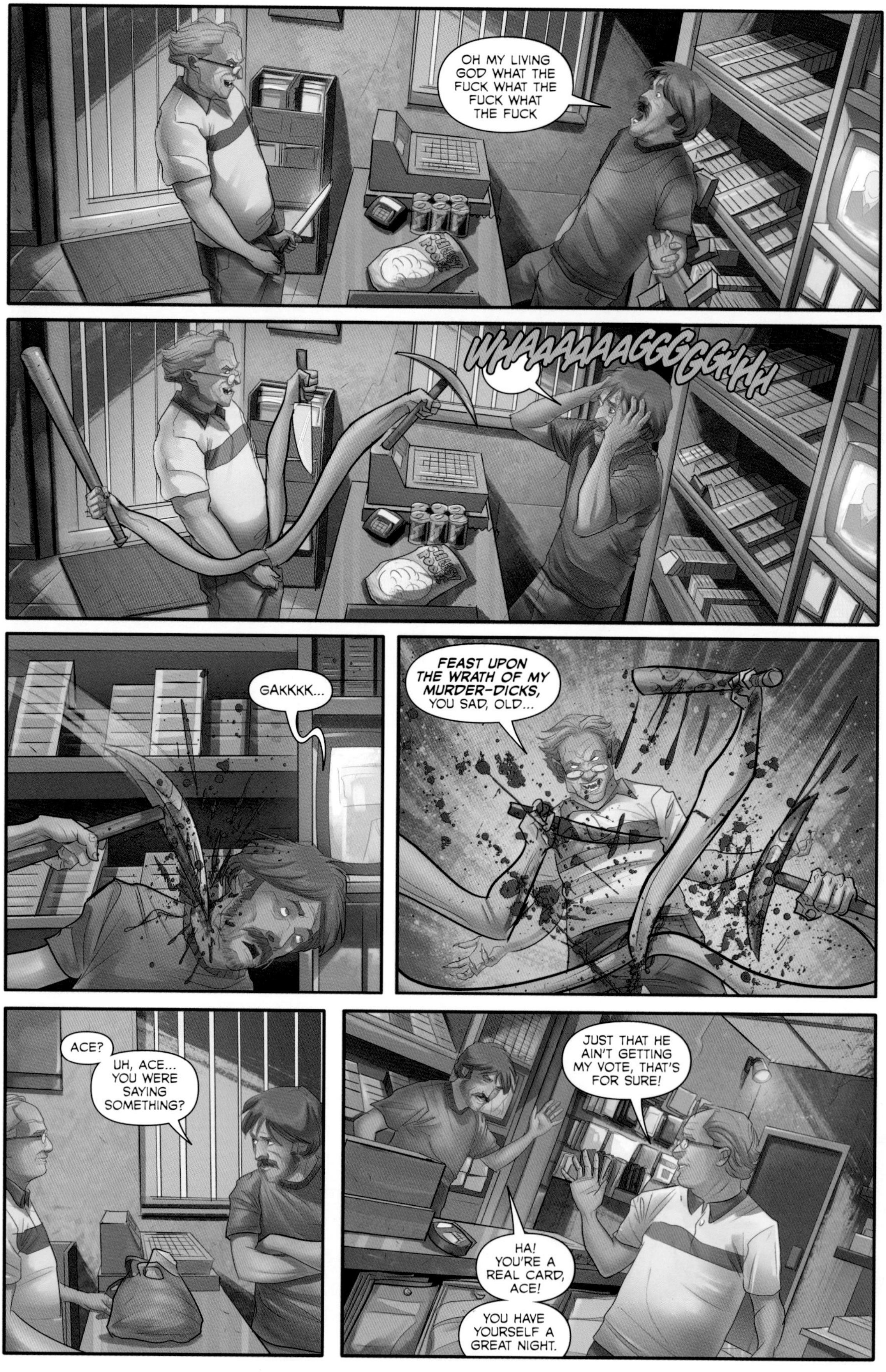
OH MY LIVING GOD WHAT THE FUCK WHAT THE FUCK WHAT THE FUCK
WHAAAAAAAGGGGGHHH
GAKKKK...
FEAST UPON THE WRATH OF MY MURDER-DICKS, YOU SAD, OLD...
ACE?
UH, ACE... YOU WERE SAYING SOMETHING?
JUST THAT HE AIN'T GETTING MY VOTE, THAT'S FOR SURE!
HA! YOU'RE A REAL CARD, ACE!
YOU HAVE YOURSELF A GREAT NIGHT.

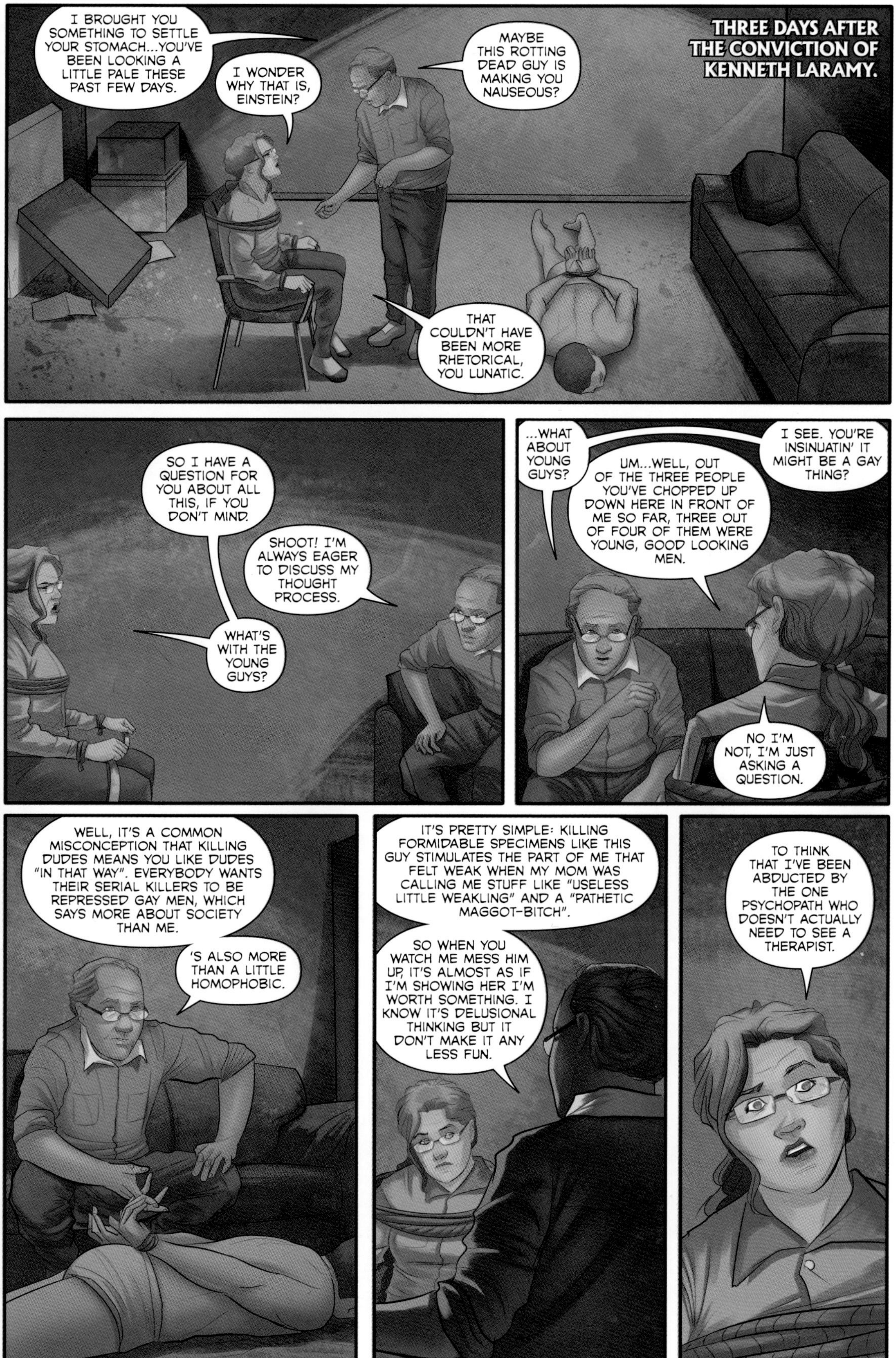
THREE DAYS AFTER THE CONVICTION OF KENNETH LARAMY.
I BROUGHT YOU SOMETHING TO SETTLE YOUR STOMACH...YOU'VE BEEN LOOKING A LITTLE PALE THESE PAST FEW DAYS.
I WONDER WHY THAT IS, EINSTEIN?
MAYBE THIS ROTTING DEAD GUY IS MAKING YOU NAUSEOUS?
THAT COULDN'T HAVE BEEN MORE RHETORICAL, YOU LUNATIC.
SO I HAVE A QUESTION FOR YOU ABOUT ALL THIS, IF YOU DON'T MIND.
SHOOT! I'M ALWAYS EAGER TO DISCUSS MY THOUGHT PROCESS.
WHAT'S WITH THE YOUNG GUYS?
...WHAT ABOUT YOUNG GUYS?
UM...WELL, OUT OF THE THREE PEOPLE YOU'VE CHOPPED UP DOWN HERE IN FRONT OF ME SO FAR, THREE OUT OF FOUR OF THEM WERE YOUNG, GOOD LOOKING MEN.
I SEE. YOU'RE INSINUATIN' IT MIGHT BE A GAY THING?
NO I'M NOT, I'M JUST ASKING A QUESTION.
WELL, IT'S A COMMON MISCONCEPTION THAT KILLING DUDES MEANS YOU LIKE DUDES "IN THAT WAY". EVERYBODY WANTS THEIR SERIAL KILLERS TO BE REPRESSED GAY MEN, WHICH SAYS MORE ABOUT SOCIETY THAN ME.
'S ALSO MORE THAN A LITTLE HOMOPHOBIC.
IT'S PRETTY SIMPLE: KILLING FORMIDABLE SPECIMENS LIKE THIS GUY STIMULATES THE PART OF ME THAT FELT WEAK WHEN MY MOM WAS CALLING ME STUFF LIKE "USELESS LITTLE WEAKLING" AND A "PATHETIC MAGGOT-BITCH".
SO WHEN YOU WATCH ME MESS HIM UP, IT'S ALMOST AS IF I'M SHOWING HER I'M WORTH SOMETHING. I KNOW IT'S DELUSIONAL THINKING BUT IT DON'T MAKE IT ANY LESS FUN.
TO THINK THAT I'VE BEEN ABDUCTED BY THE ONE PSYCHOPATH WHO DOESN'T ACTUALLY NEED TO SEE A THERAPIST.

PROFESSOR ACE TEACHES YOU

How to Properly Hunt and Murder An Innocent Victim

1.

- **IDENTIFY YOUR VICTIM**
  Your victim should have no personal connection to you, or if they do, they should at least really, really deserve to die.

2.

- **FAMILIARIZE YOURSELF WITH YOUR VICTIM'S MODES OF TRANSPORTATION AND HOME**
  Stay hidden and think of yourself as a cop staking out a dastardly criminal. Relish the irony that you're the opposite of a cop!

3.

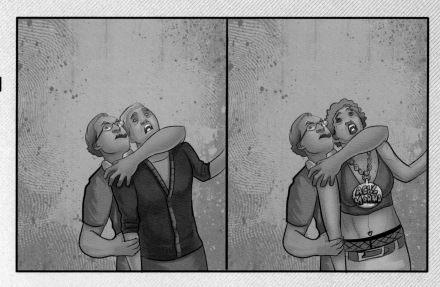

• MAKE SURE YOUR VICTIM IS ALONE AND ABDUCT THEM

All your planning is finally paying off. Remember it ain't that hard to off someone; your first is like pulling off a band-aid... and finding it gets you hard!

4.

• THE MAIN EVENT

With all the guys out there whacking people to get themselves off, you've really got to put your own stamp on it! Use an obscure household item! Find a creative new hole to fuck... or make your own!

SEE CHAPTER 2:

DISPOSING OF YOUR BODY (OR CRAFTING YOUR OWN UNIQUE ORGAN TROPHIES) FOR MORE!

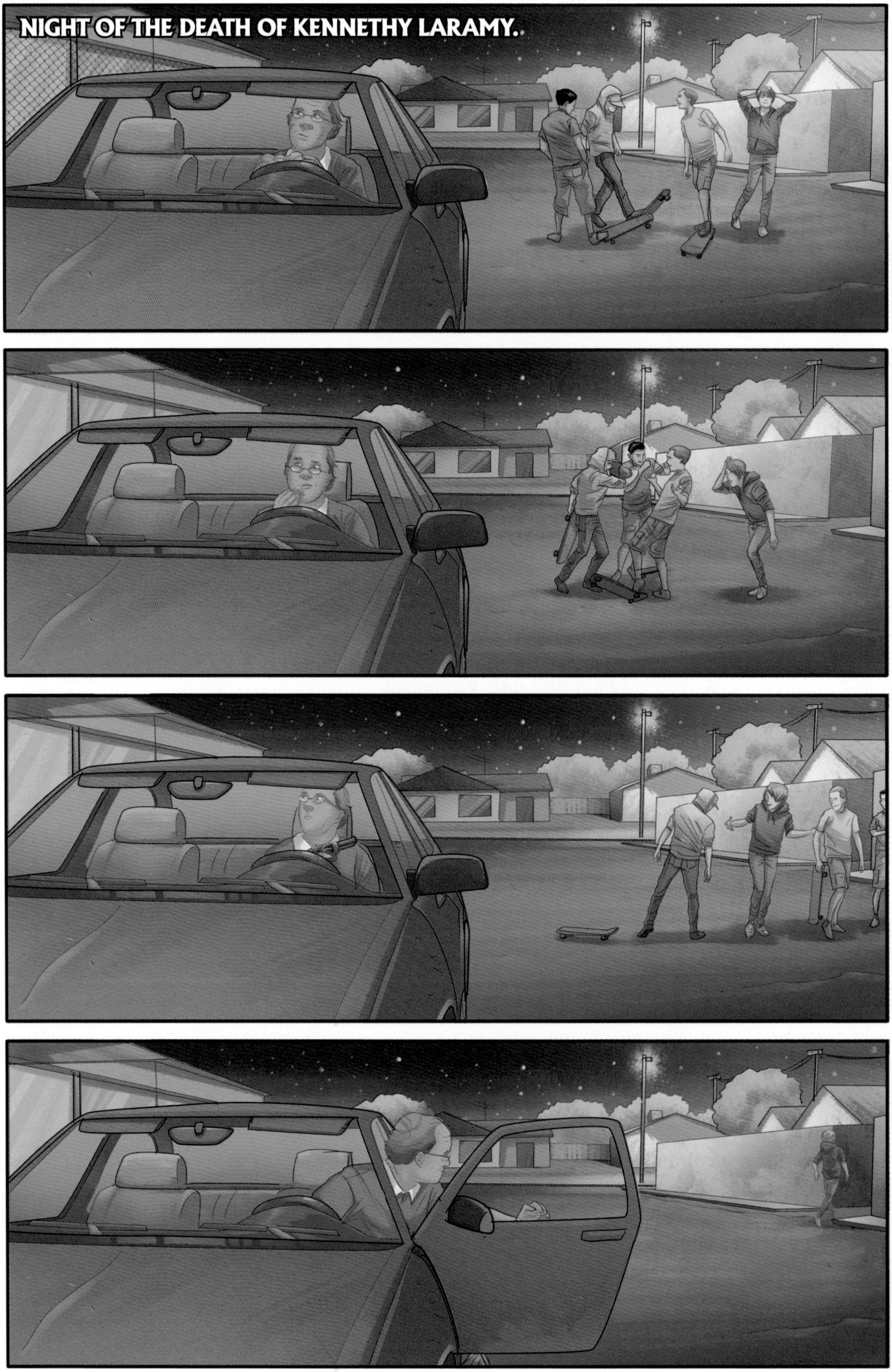
NIGHT OF THE DEATH OF KENNETHY LARAMY.

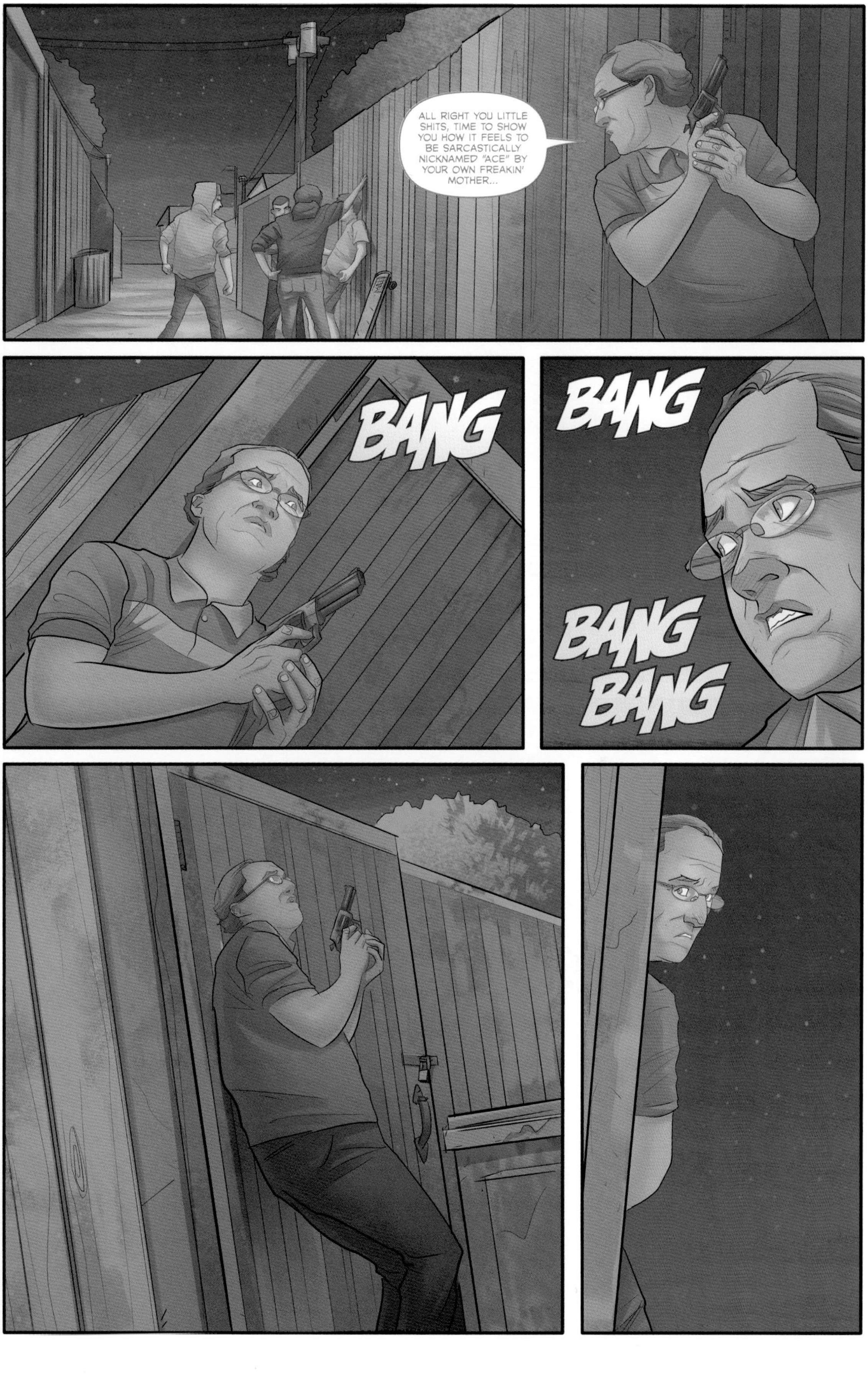
ALL RIGHT YOU LITTLE SHITS, TIME TO SHOW YOU HOW IT FEELS TO BE SARCASTICALLY NICKNAMED "ACE" BY YOUR OWN FREAKIN' MOTHER...
BANG
BANG
BANG
BANG

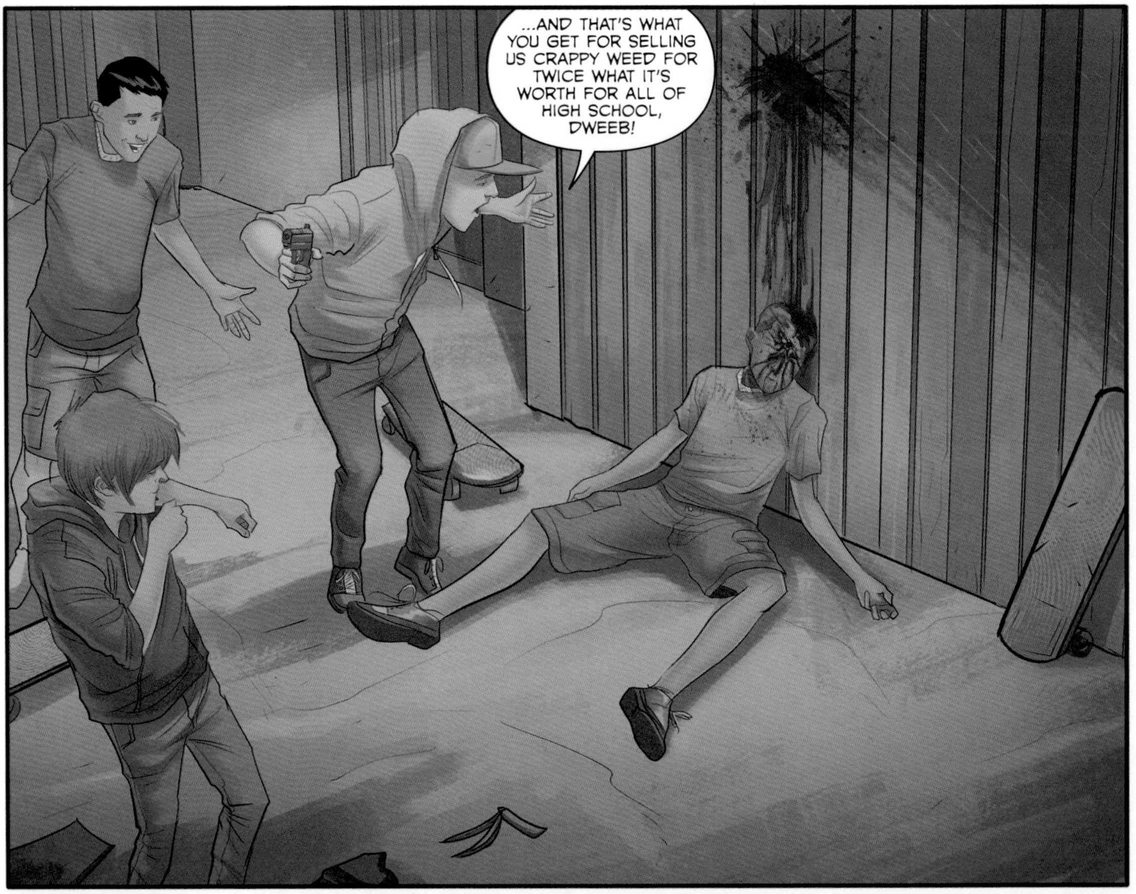
...AND THAT'S WHAT YOU GET FOR SELLING US CRAPPY WEED FOR TWICE WHAT IT'S WORTH FOR ALL OF HIGH SCHOOL, DWEEB!

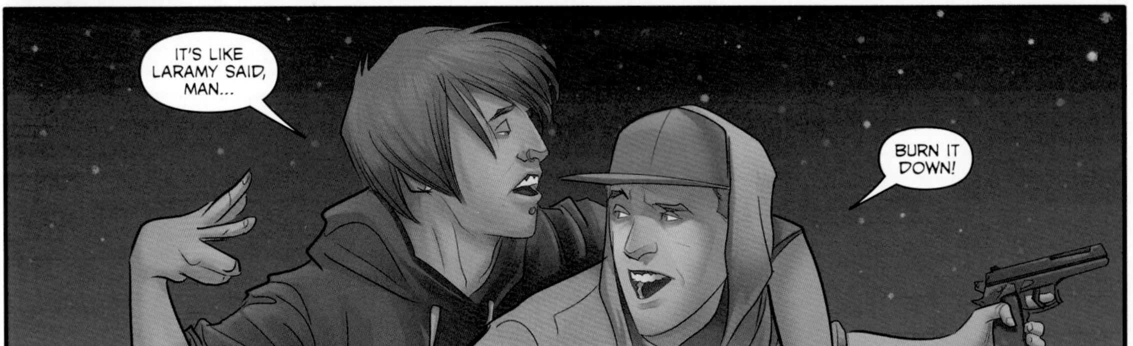
IT'S LIKE LARAMY SAID, MAN...
BURN IT DOWN!

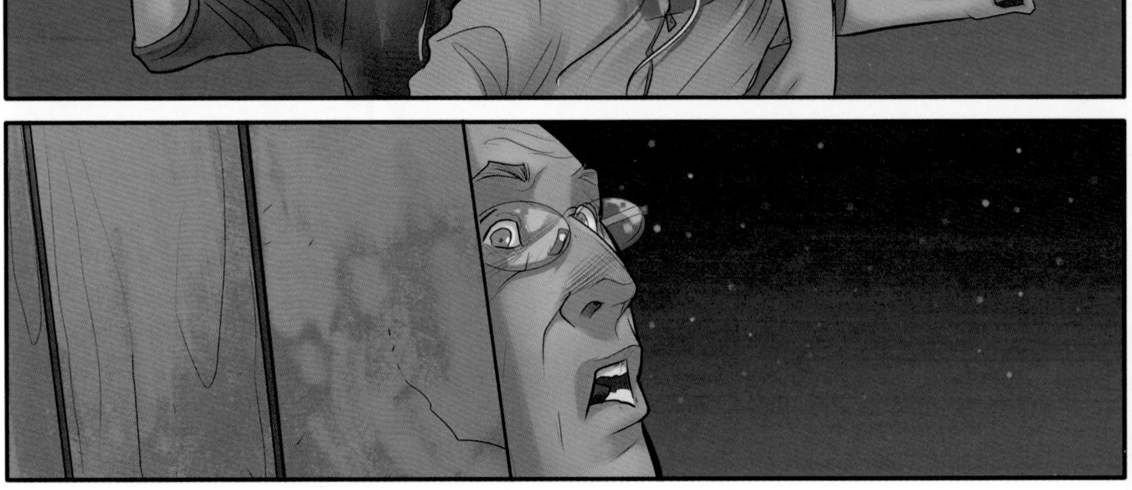

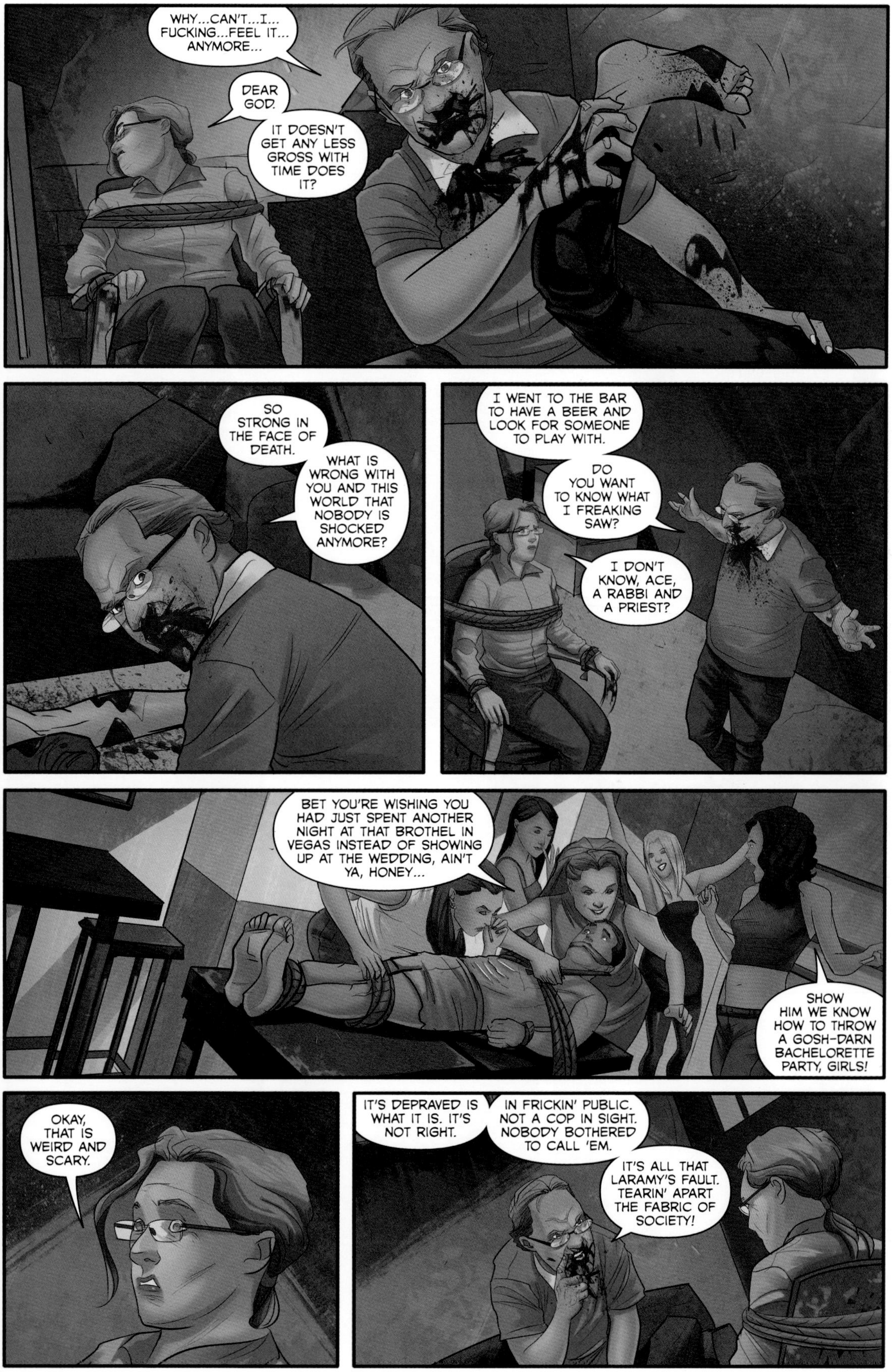

WHY...CAN'T...I... FUCKING...FEEL IT... ANYMORE...
DEAR GOD.
IT DOESN'T GET ANY LESS GROSS WITH TIME DOES IT?
SO STRONG IN THE FACE OF DEATH.
WHAT IS WRONG WITH YOU AND THIS WORLD THAT NOBODY IS SHOCKED ANYMORE?
I WENT TO THE BAR TO HAVE A BEER AND LOOK FOR SOMEONE TO PLAY WITH.
DO YOU WANT TO KNOW WHAT I FREAKING SAW?
I DON'T KNOW, ACE, A RABBI AND A PRIEST?
BET YOU'RE WISHING YOU HAD JUST SPENT ANOTHER NIGHT AT THAT BROTHEL IN VEGAS INSTEAD OF SHOWING UP AT THE WEDDING, AIN'T YA, HONEY...
SHOW HIM WE KNOW HOW TO THROW A GOSH-DARN BACHELORETTE PARTY, GIRLS!
OKAY, THAT IS WEIRD AND SCARY.
IT'S DEPRAVED IS WHAT IT IS. IT'S NOT RIGHT.
IN FRICKIN' PUBLIC. NOT A COP IN SIGHT. NOBODY BOTHERED TO CALL 'EM.
IT'S ALL THAT LARAMY'S FAULT. TEARIN' APART THE FABRIC OF SOCIETY!

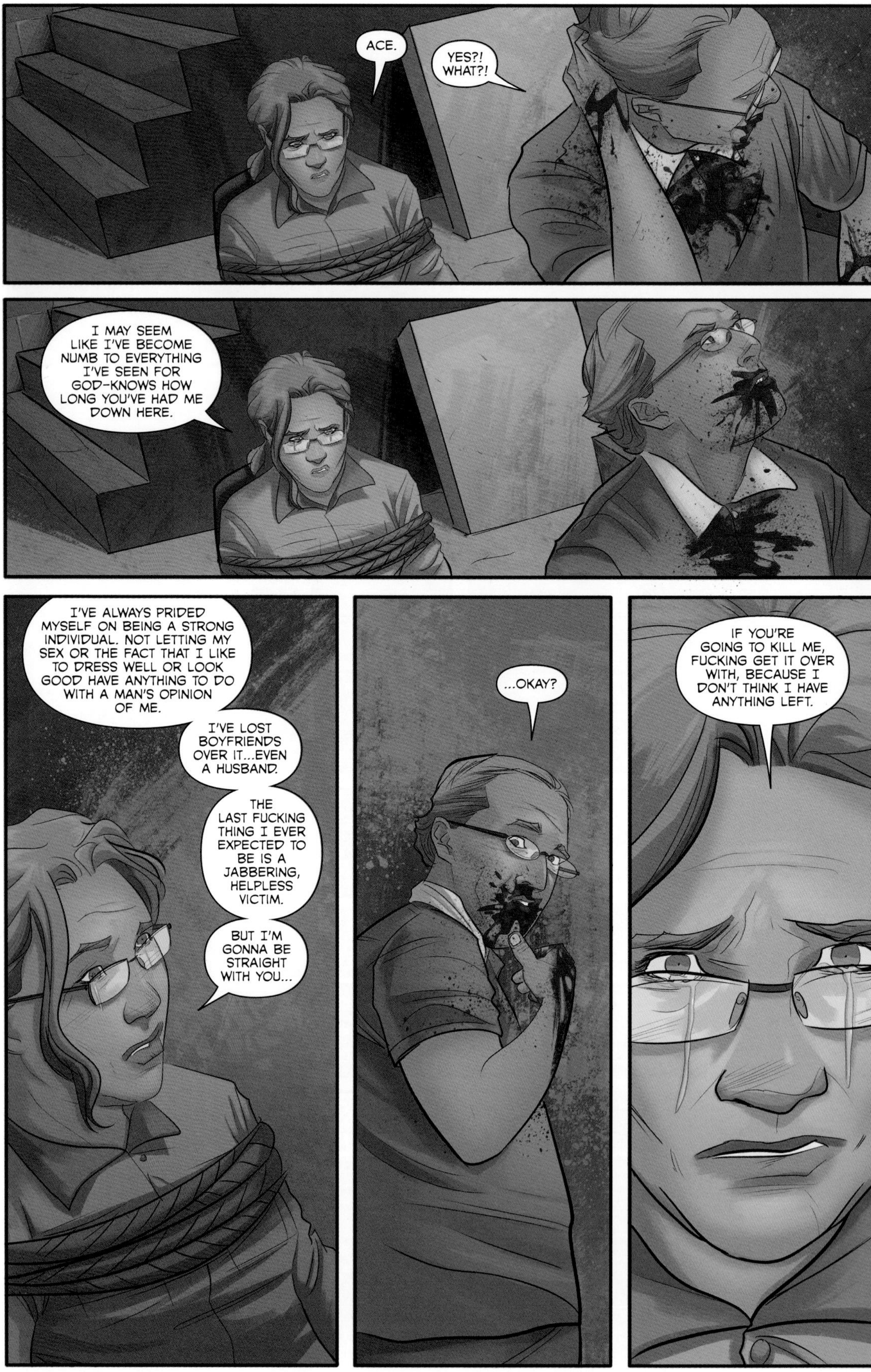
ACE.
YES?! WHAT?!
I MAY SEEM LIKE I'VE BECOME NUMB TO EVERYTHING I'VE SEEN FOR GOD-KNOWS HOW LONG YOU'VE HAD ME DOWN HERE.
I'VE ALWAYS PRIDED MYSELF ON BEING A STRONG INDIVIDUAL. NOT LETTING MY SEX OR THE FACT THAT I LIKE TO DRESS WELL OR LOOK GOOD HAVE ANYTHING TO DO WITH A MAN'S OPINION OF ME.
I'VE LOST BOYFRIENDS OVER IT...EVEN A HUSBAND.
THE LAST FUCKING THING I EVER EXPECTED TO BE IS A JABBERING, HELPLESS VICTIM.
BUT I'M GONNA BE STRAIGHT WITH YOU...
...OKAY?
IF YOU'RE GOING TO KILL ME, FUCKING GET IT OVER WITH, BECAUSE I DON'T THINK I HAVE ANYTHING LEFT.

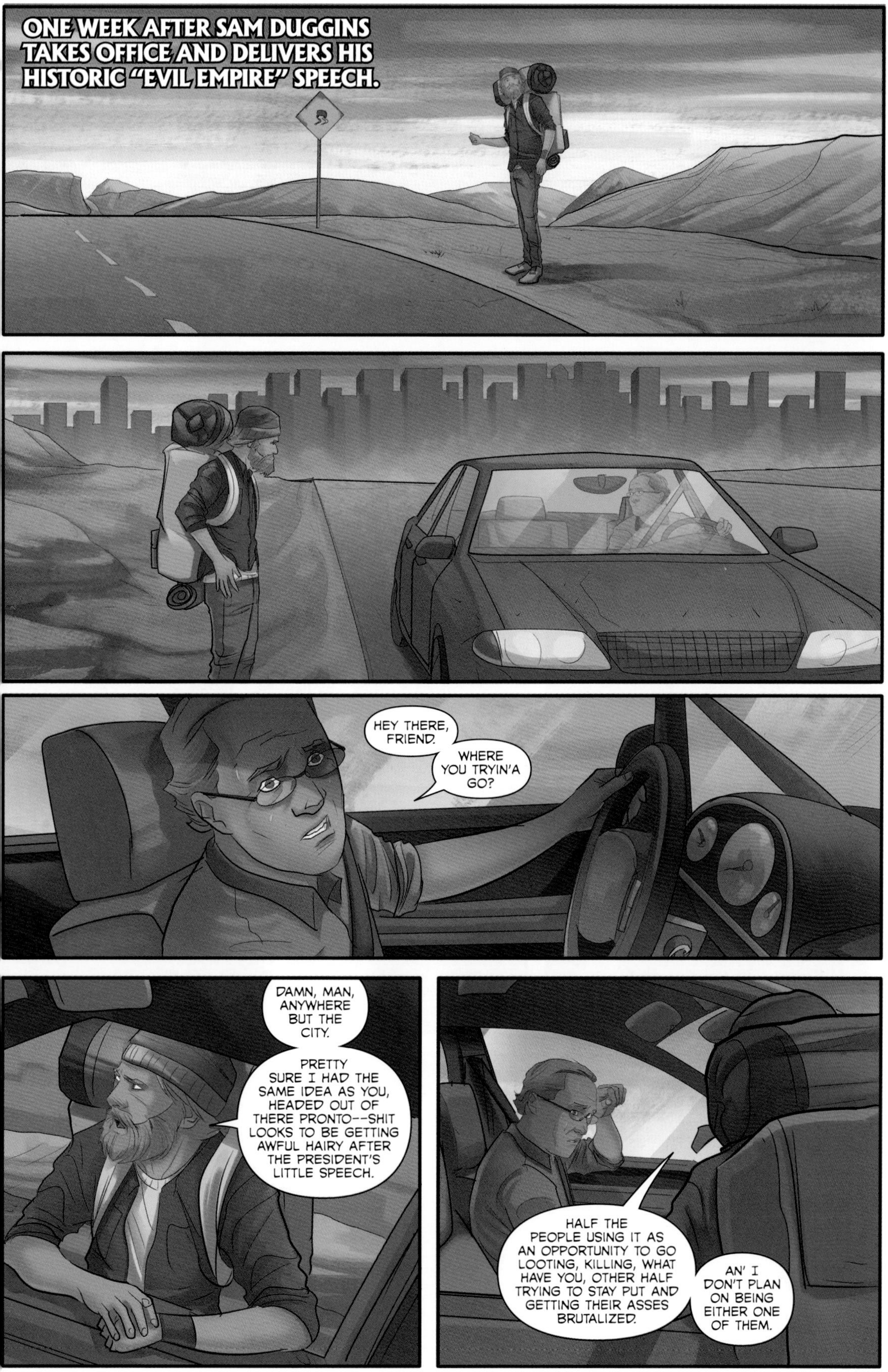
ONE WEEK AFTER SAM DUGGINS TAKES OFFICE AND DELIVERS HIS HISTORIC "EVIL EMPIRE" SPEECH.
HEY THERE, FRIEND.
WHERE YOU TRYIN'A GO?
DAMN, MAN, ANYWHERE BUT THE CITY.
PRETTY SURE I HAD THE SAME IDEA AS YOU, HEADED OUT OF THERE PRONTO--SHIT LOOKS TO BE GETTING AWFUL HAIRY AFTER THE PRESIDENT'S LITTLE SPEECH.
HALF THE PEOPLE USING IT AS AN OPPORTUNITY TO GO LOOTING, KILLING, WHAT HAVE YOU, OTHER HALF TRYING TO STAY PUT AND GETTING THEIR ASSES BRUTALIZED.
AN' I DON'T PLAN ON BEING EITHER ONE OF THEM.

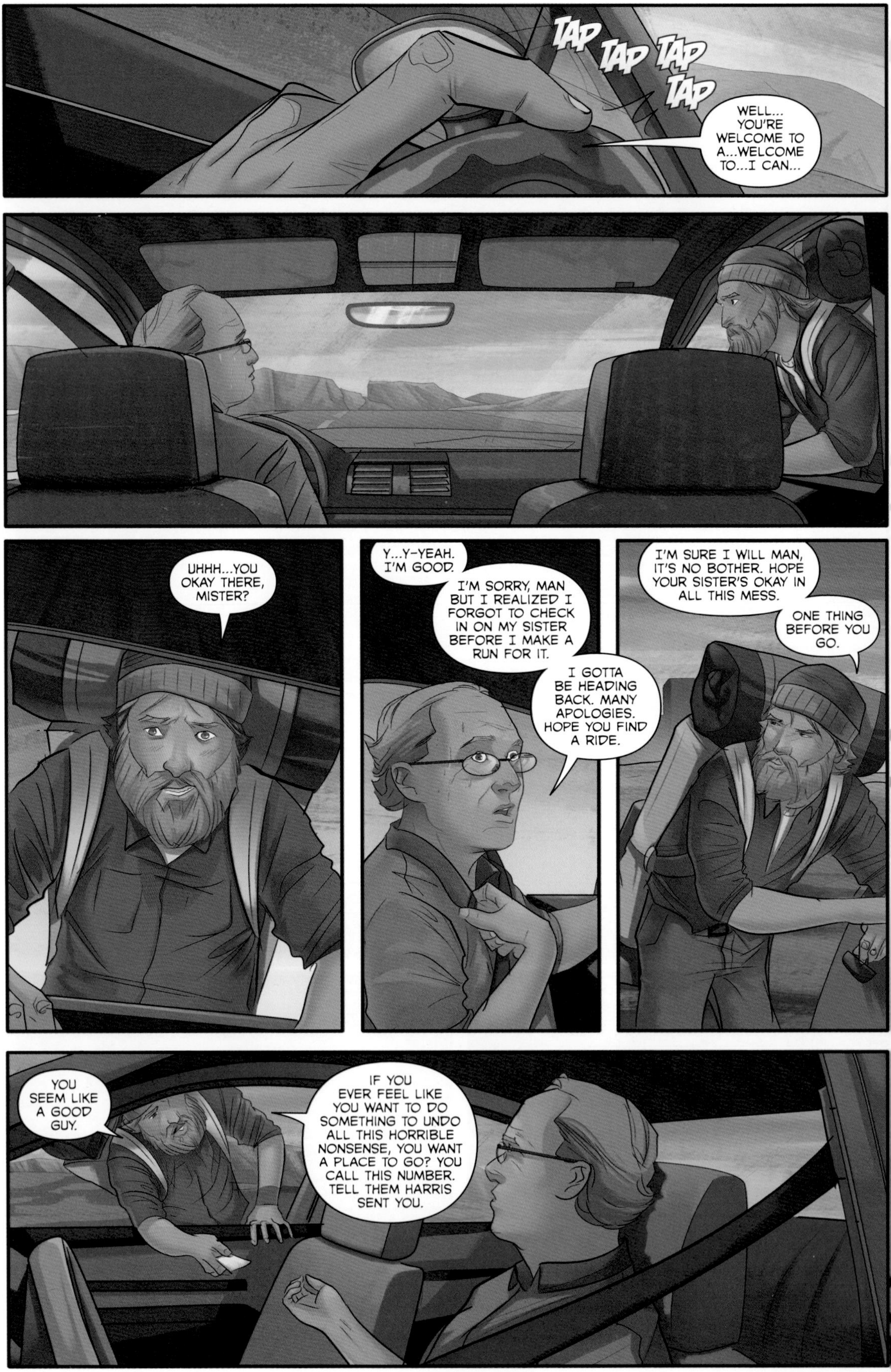
TAP TAP TAP TAP
WELL... YOU'RE WELCOME TO A...WELCOME TO...I CAN...
UHHH...YOU OKAY THERE, MISTER?
Y...Y-YEAH. I'M GOOD.
I'M SORRY, MAN BUT I REALIZED I FORGOT TO CHECK IN ON MY SISTER BEFORE I MAKE A RUN FOR IT.
I GOTTA BE HEADING BACK. MANY APOLOGIES. HOPE YOU FIND A RIDE.
I'M SURE I WILL MAN, IT'S NO BOTHER. HOPE YOUR SISTER'S OKAY IN ALL THIS MESS.
ONE THING BEFORE YOU GO.
YOU SEEM LIKE A GOOD GUY.
IF YOU EVER FEEL LIKE YOU WANT TO DO SOMETHING TO UNDO ALL THIS HORRIBLE NONSENSE, YOU WANT A PLACE TO GO? YOU CALL THIS NUMBER. TELL THEM HARRIS SENT YOU.

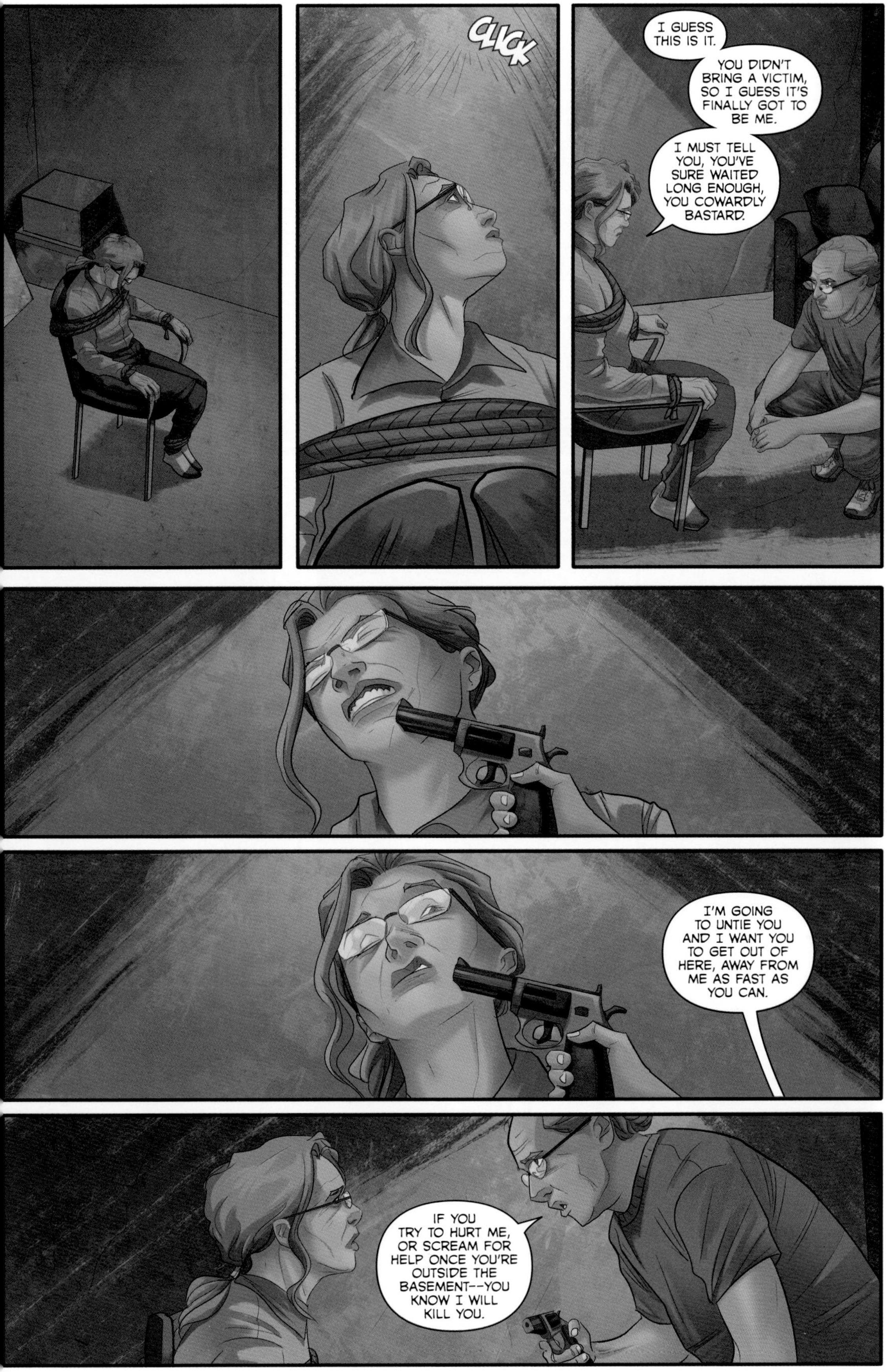
CLICK
I GUESS THIS IS IT.
YOU DIDN'T BRING A VICTIM, SO I GUESS IT'S FINALLY GOT TO BE ME.
I MUST TELL YOU, YOU'VE SURE WAITED LONG ENOUGH, YOU COWARDLY BASTARD.
I'M GOING TO UNTIE YOU AND I WANT YOU TO GET OUT OF HERE, AWAY FROM ME AS FAST AS YOU CAN.
IF YOU TRY TO HURT ME, OR SCREAM FOR HELP ONCE YOU'RE OUTSIDE THE BASEMENT--YOU KNOW I WILL KILL YOU.

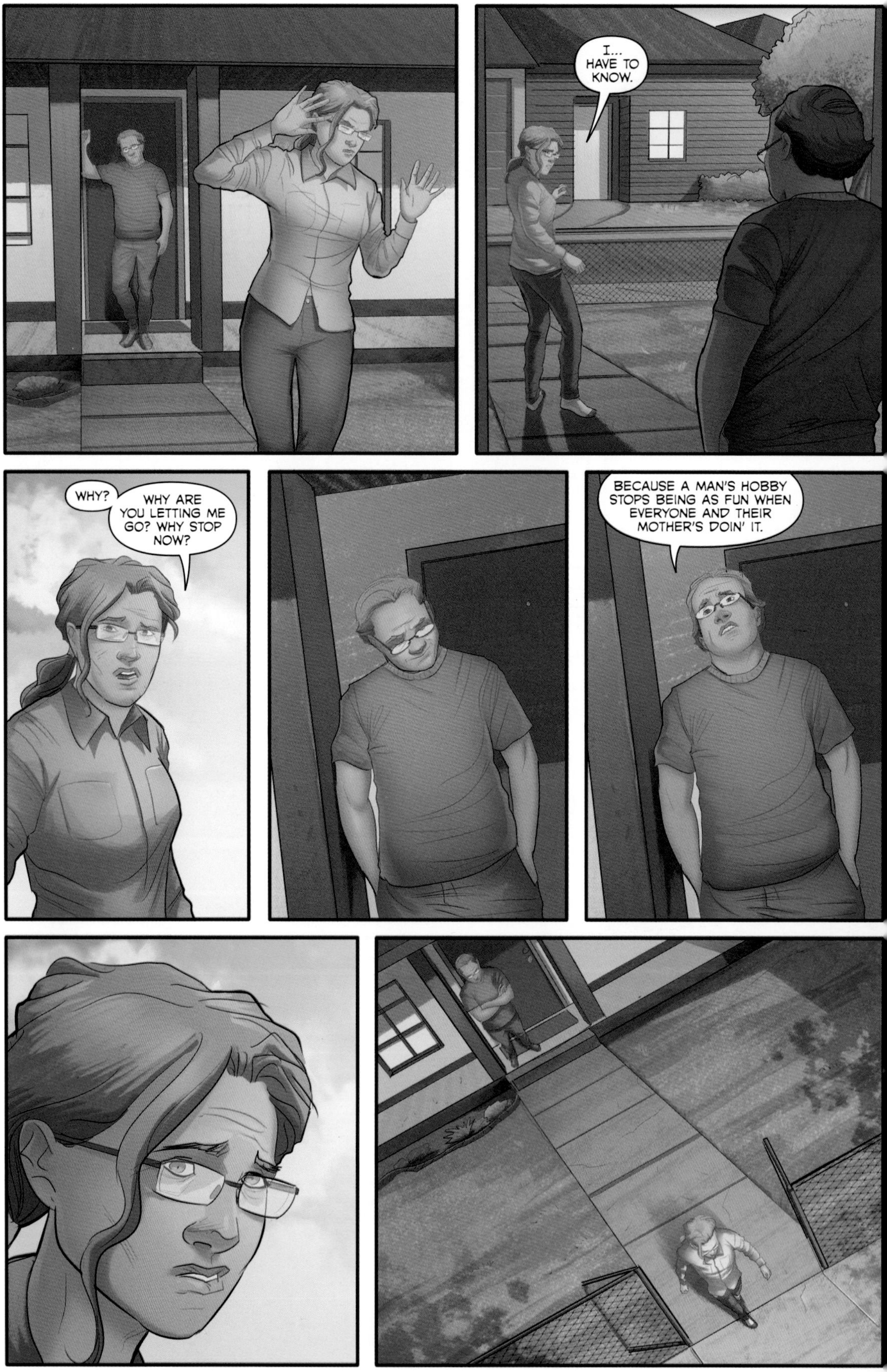
I... HAVE TO KNOW.
WHY?
WHY ARE YOU LETTING ME GO? WHY STOP NOW?
BECAUSE A MAN'S HOBBY STOPS BEING AS FUN WHEN EVERYONE AND THEIR MOTHER'S DOIN' IT.

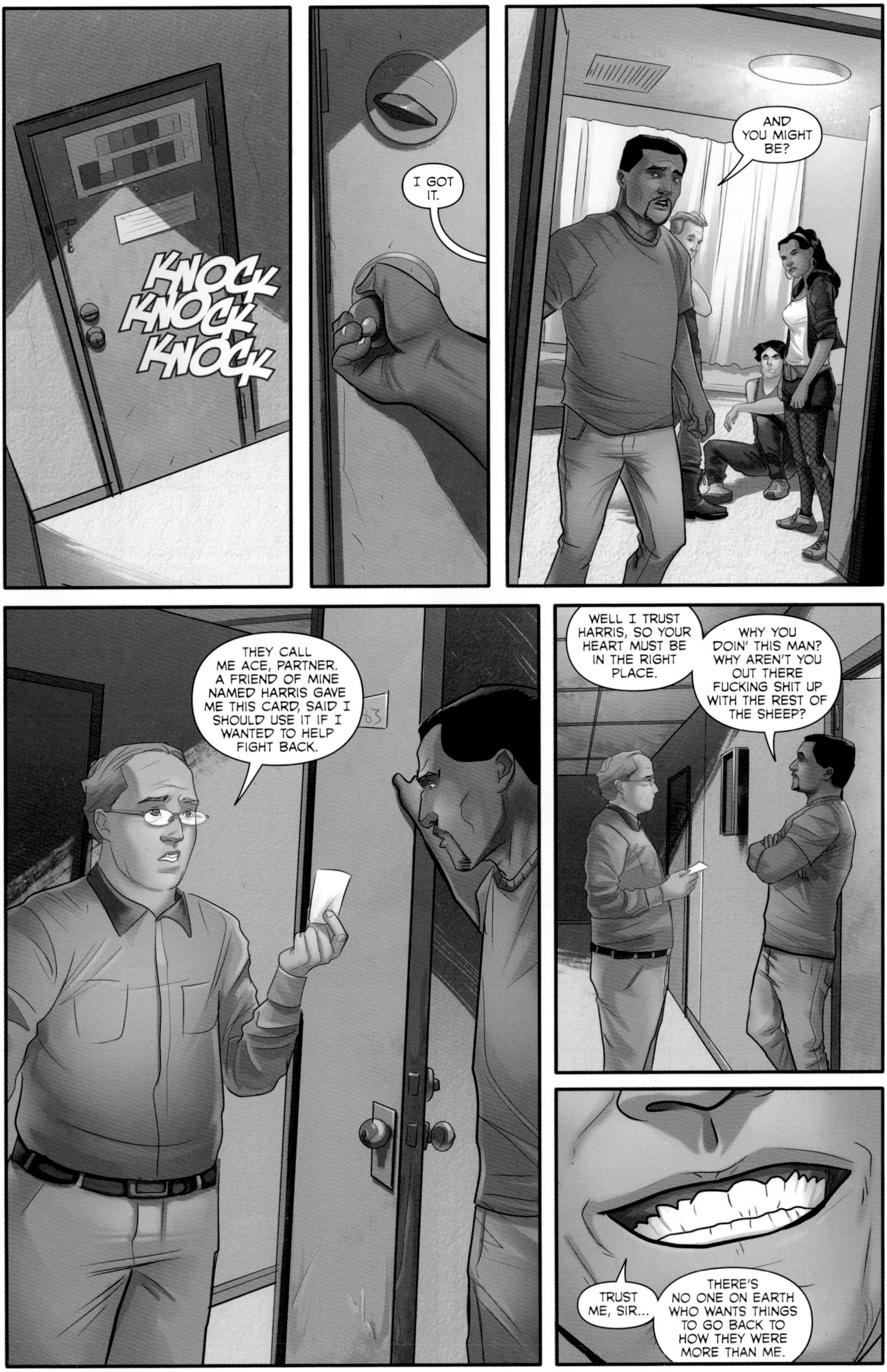

KNOCK KNOCK KNOCK
I GOT IT.
AND YOU MIGHT BE?
THEY CALL ME ACE, PARTNER. A FRIEND OF MINE NAMED HARRIS GAVE ME THIS CARD, SAID I SHOULD USE IT IF I WANTED TO HELP FIGHT BACK.
WELL I TRUST HARRIS, SO YOUR HEART MUST BE IN THE RIGHT PLACE.
WHY YOU DOIN' THIS MAN? WHY AREN'T YOU OUT THERE FUCKING SHIT UP WITH THE REST OF THE SHEEP?
TRUST ME, SIR...
THERE'S NO ONE ON EARTH WHO WANTS THINGS TO GO BACK TO HOW THEY WERE MORE THAN ME.

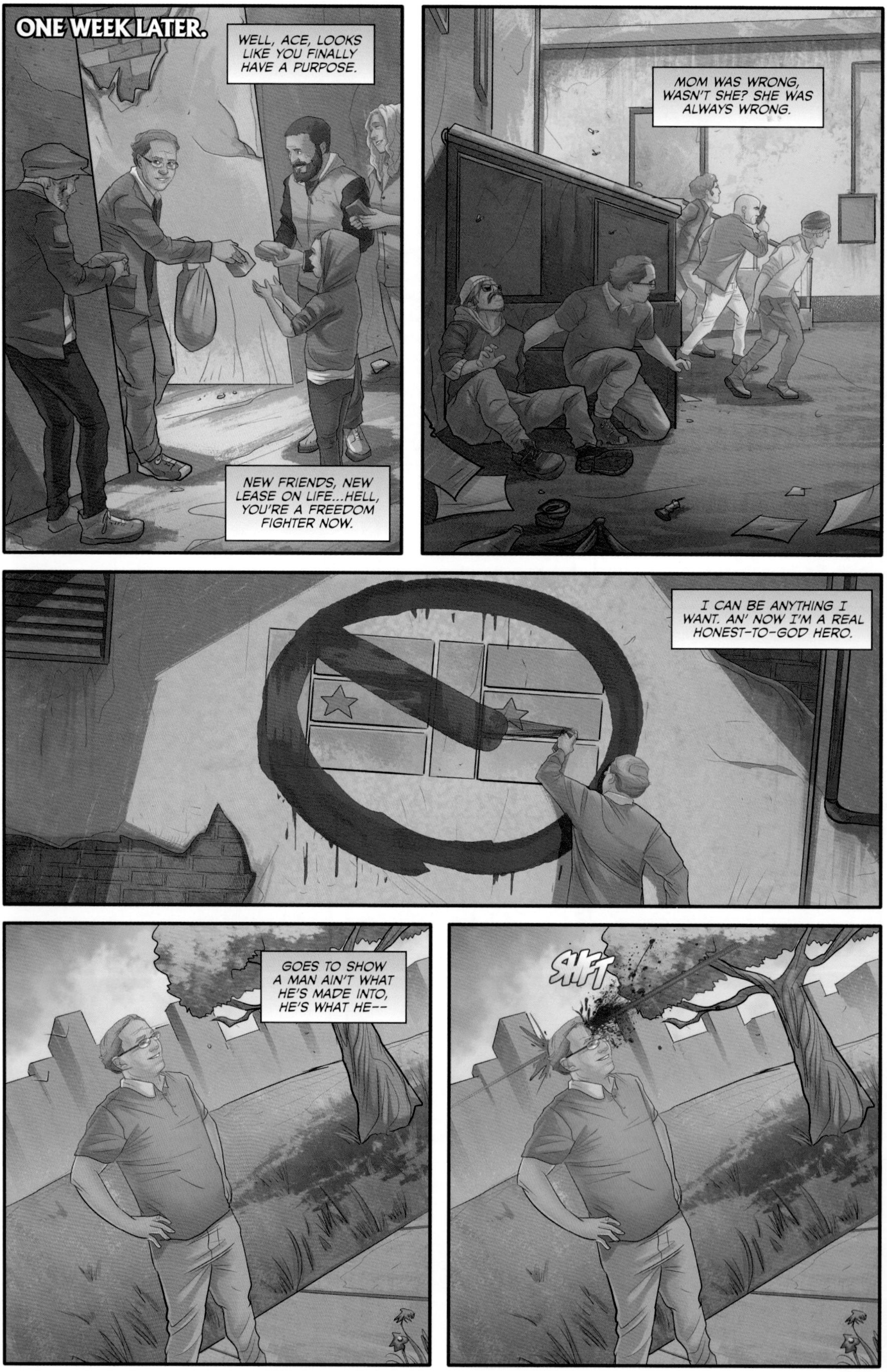
ONE WEEK LATER.
WELL, ACE, LOOKS LIKE YOU FINALLY HAVE A PURPOSE.
NEW FRIENDS, NEW LEASE ON LIFE...HELL, YOU'RE A FREEDOM FIGHTER NOW.
MOM WAS WRONG, WASN'T SHE? SHE WAS ALWAYS WRONG.
I CAN BE ANYTHING I WANT. AN' NOW I'M A REAL HONEST-TO-GOD HERO.
GOES TO SHOW A MAN AIN'T WHAT HE'S MADE INTO, HE'S WHAT HE--
SHFT

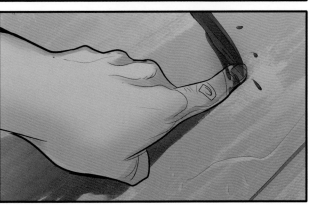

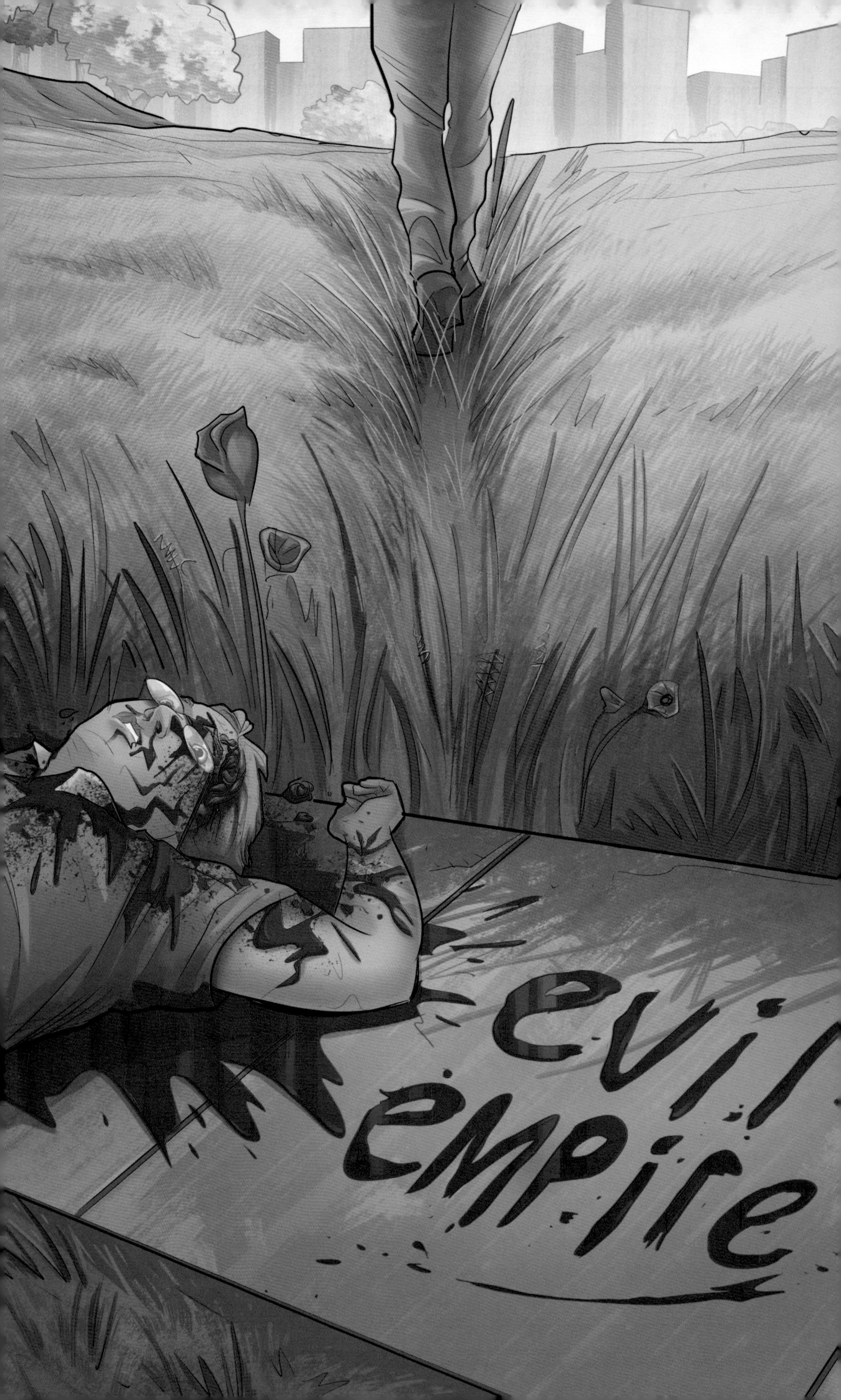
evil
empire

I'd rather have a world where people are free to do as they please, but they actually face true consequences.

rsr. 2.0

CHAPTER
SIX

fig. 2

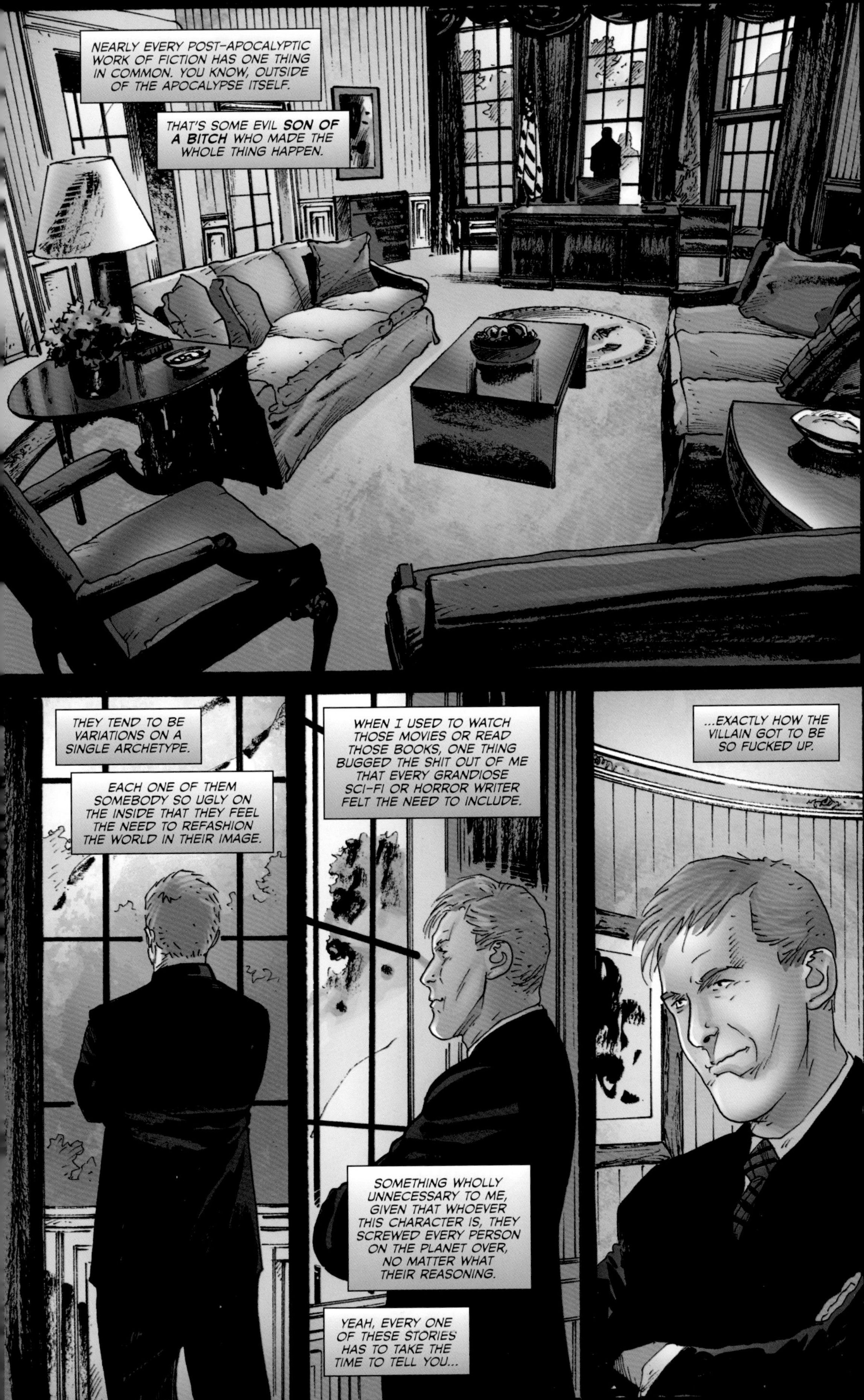

NEARLY EVERY POST-APOCALYPTIC WORK OF FICTION HAS ONE THING IN COMMON. YOU KNOW, OUTSIDE OF THE APOCALYPSE ITSELF.
THAT'S SOME EVIL **SON OF A BITCH** WHO MADE THE WHOLE THING HAPPEN.
THEY TEND TO BE VARIATIONS ON A SINGLE ARCHETYPE.
EACH ONE OF THEM SOMEBODY SO UGLY ON THE INSIDE THAT THEY FEEL THE NEED TO REFASHION THE WORLD IN THEIR IMAGE.
WHEN I USED TO WATCH THOSE MOVIES OR READ THOSE BOOKS, ONE THING BUGGED THE SHIT OUT OF ME THAT EVERY GRANDIOSE SCI-FI OR HORROR WRITER FELT THE NEED TO INCLUDE.
SOMETHING WHOLLY UNNECESSARY TO ME, GIVEN THAT WHOEVER THIS CHARACTER IS, THEY SCREWED EVERY PERSON ON THE PLANET OVER, NO MATTER WHAT THEIR REASONING.
YEAH, EVERY ONE OF THESE STORIES HAS TO TAKE THE TIME TO TELL YOU...
...EXACTLY HOW THE VILLAIN GOT TO BE SO FUCKED UP.

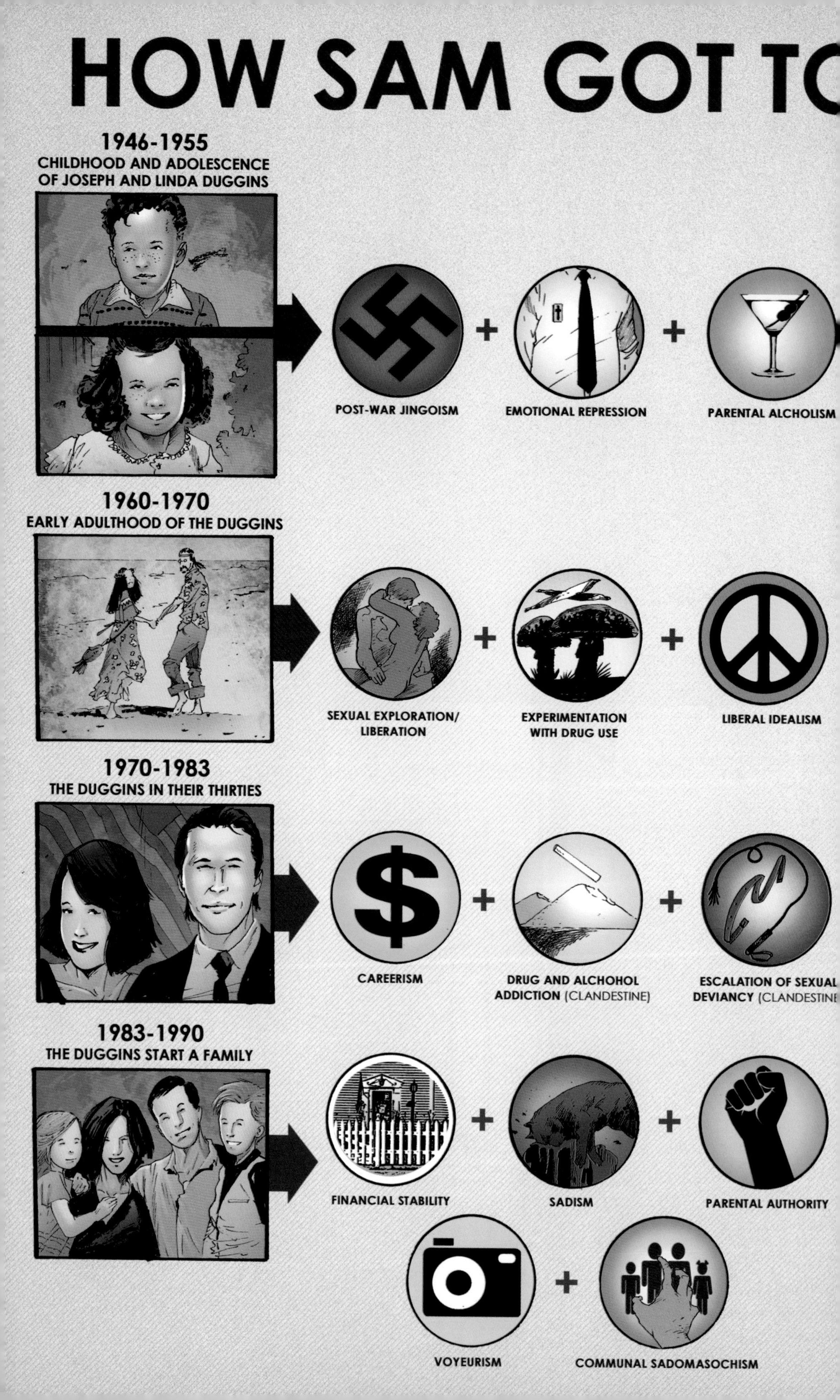
HOW SAM GOT TO
1946-1955
CHILDHOOD AND ADOLESCENCE OF JOSEPH AND LINDA DUGGINS
POST-WAR JINGOISM
+
EMOTIONAL REPRESSION
+
PARENTAL ALCHOLISM
1960-1970
EARLY ADULTHOOD OF THE DUGGINS
SEXUAL EXPLORATION/ LIBERATION
+
EXPERIMENTATION WITH DRUG USE
+
LIBERAL IDEALISM
1970-1983
THE DUGGINS IN THEIR THIRTIES
CAREERISM
+
DRUG AND ALCHOHOL ADDICTION (CLANDESTINE)
+
ESCALATION OF SEXUAL DEVIANCY (CLANDESTINE
1983-1990
THE DUGGINS START A FAMILY
FINANCIAL STABILITY
+
SADISM
+
PARENTAL AUTHORITY
VOYEURISM
+
COMMUNAL SADOMASOCHISM

BE SO FUCKED UP.

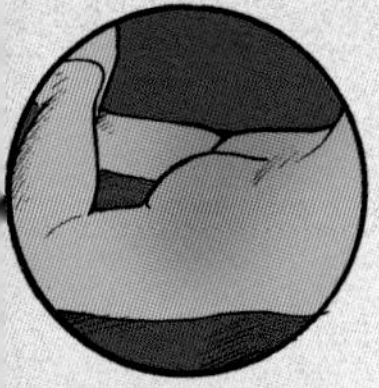

+

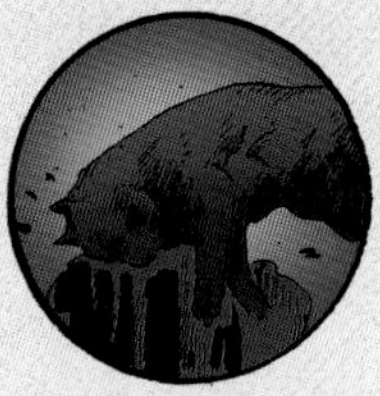

REPROACH OF
SEXUAL CURIOSITY

SADISM

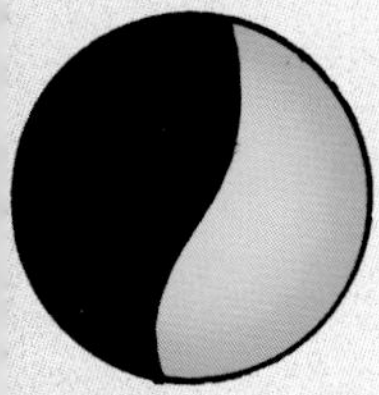

CODEPEDENCY

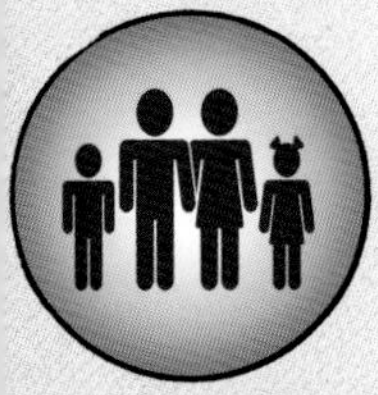

+

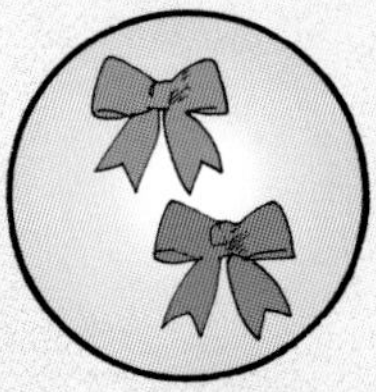

SOCIAL FAMILIAL
IDEALISM

CHILD BIRTH

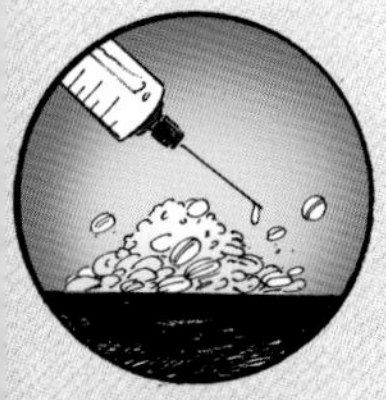

+

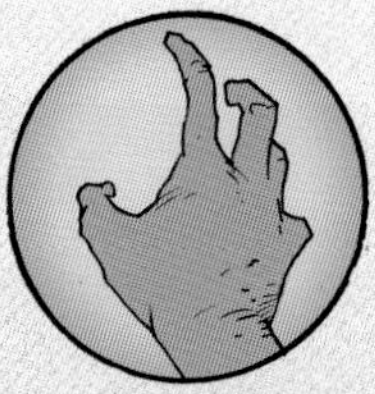

DRUG USE
(RECREATIONAL)

PEDOPHILIA
(CLANDESTINE)

=

SAM AND JULIA

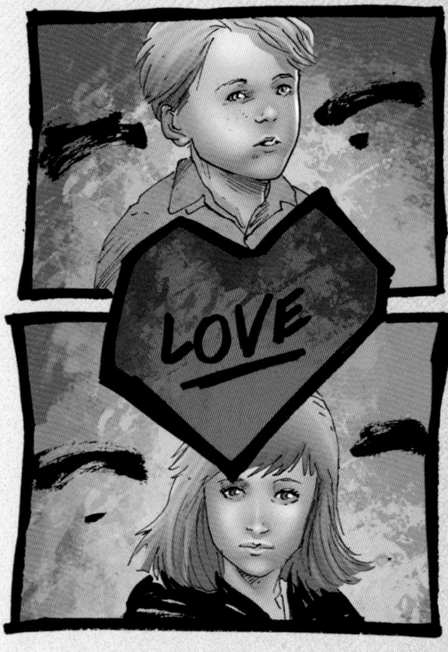
LOVE

ISOLATION (EMOTIONAL) **+**
ABUSE +
SEXUAL CONFUSION +
FRATERNAL FAMILIARITY

THE SIX MONTHS FOLLOWING THE ELECTION OF SAM DUGGINS.

CONGRESSIONAL OPPOSITION SILENCED

EVIL EMPIRE "BRAND" BUILT USING "IRONIC" FASCIST SYMBOLISM

EVIL EMPIRE PROPAGANDIZED

SPREAD OF "EE" SOCIETY OUTSIDE OF URBAN AREAS

LAWLESSNESS IMPLEMENTED CONSTITUTIONALLY

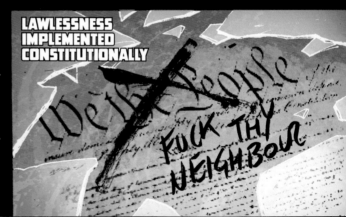

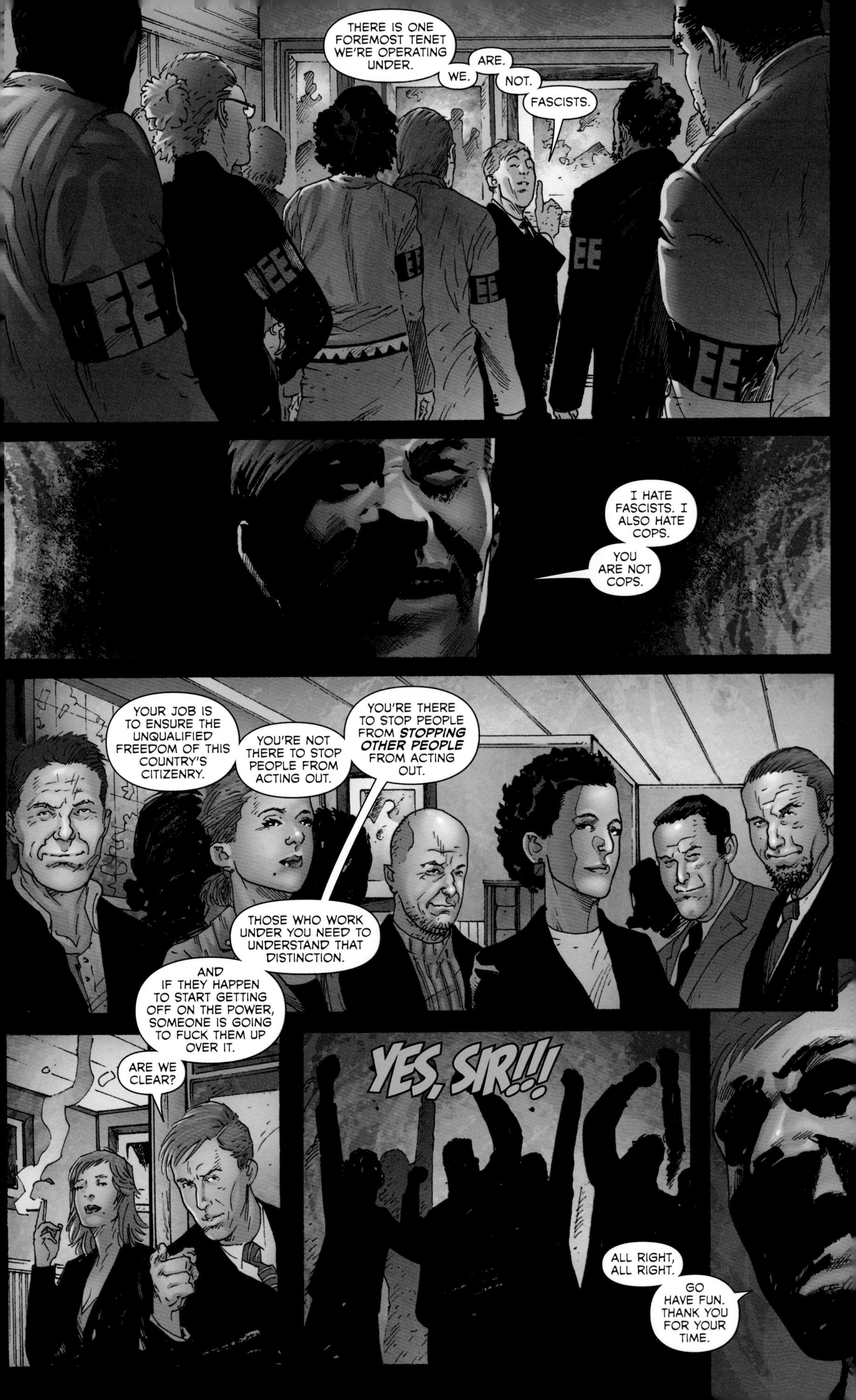
THERE IS ONE FOREMOST TENET WE'RE OPERATING UNDER.
WE.
ARE.
NOT.
FASCISTS.
I HATE FASCISTS. I ALSO HATE COPS.
YOU ARE NOT COPS.
YOUR JOB IS TO ENSURE THE UNQUALIFIED FREEDOM OF THIS COUNTRY'S CITIZENRY.
YOU'RE NOT THERE TO STOP PEOPLE FROM ACTING OUT.
YOU'RE THERE TO STOP PEOPLE FROM *STOPPING OTHER PEOPLE* FROM ACTING OUT.
THOSE WHO WORK UNDER YOU NEED TO UNDERSTAND THAT DISTINCTION.
AND IF THEY HAPPEN TO START GETTING OFF ON THE POWER, SOMEONE IS GOING TO FUCK THEM UP OVER IT.
ARE WE CLEAR?
YES, SIR!!!
ALL RIGHT, ALL RIGHT.
GO HAVE FUN. THANK YOU FOR YOUR TIME.

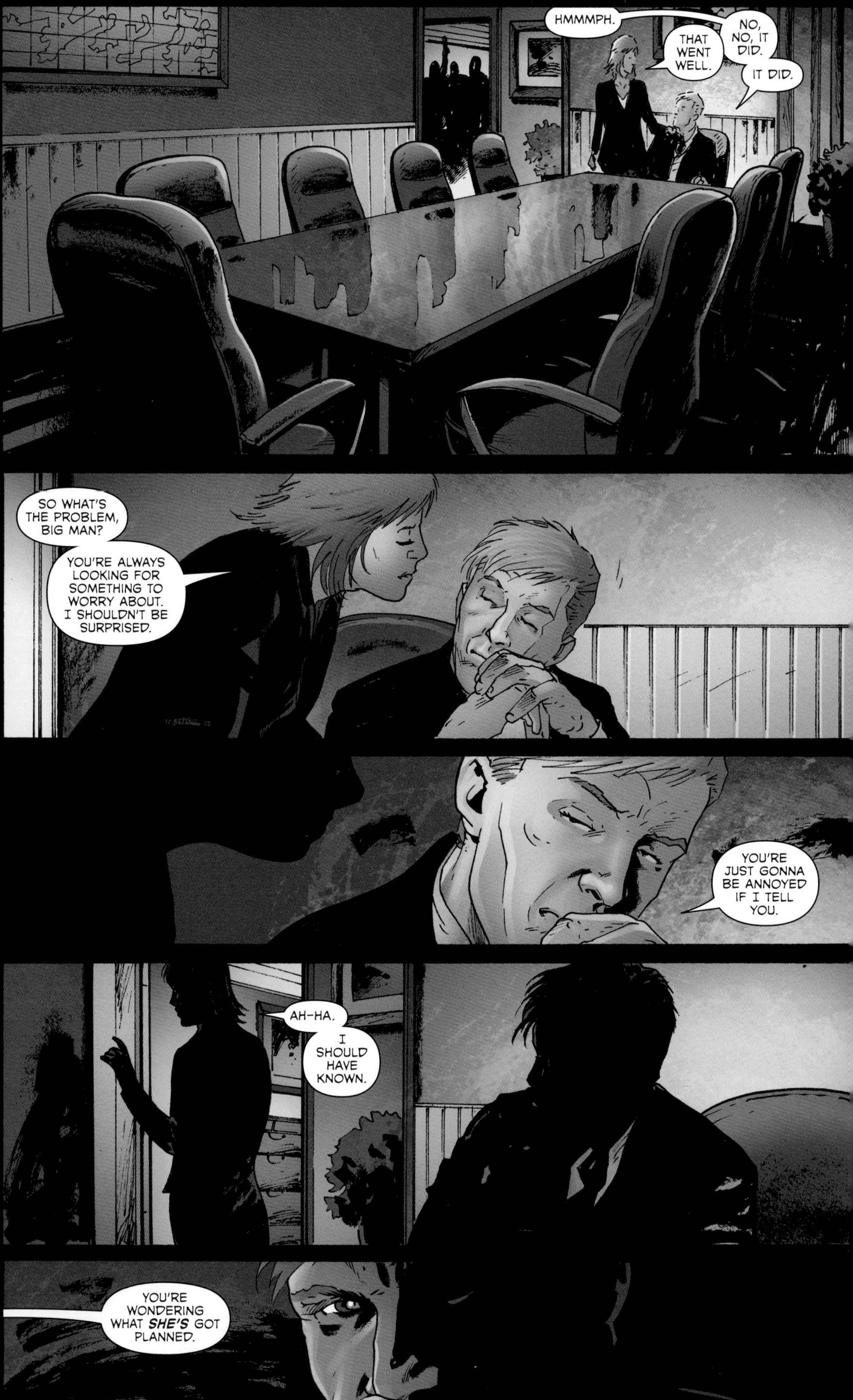
HMMMPH.
THAT WENT WELL.
NO, NO, IT DID.
IT DID.
SO WHAT'S THE PROBLEM, BIG MAN?
YOU'RE ALWAYS LOOKING FOR SOMETHING TO WORRY ABOUT. I SHOULDN'T BE SURPRISED.
YOU'RE JUST GONNA BE ANNOYED IF I TELL YOU.
AH-HA.
I SHOULD HAVE KNOWN.
YOU'RE WONDERING WHAT SHE'S GOT PLANNED.

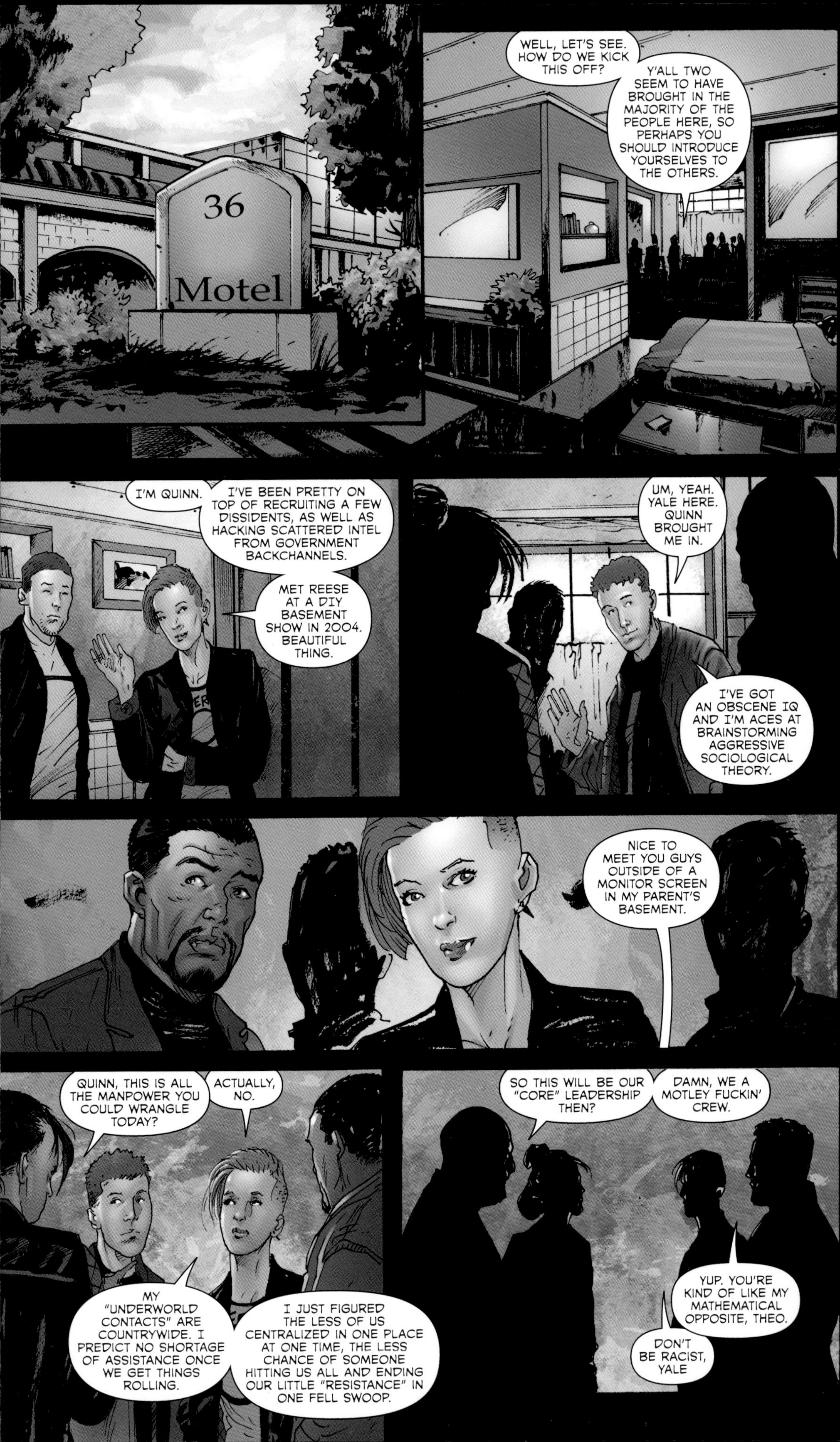
36
Motel
WELL, LET'S SEE. HOW DO WE KICK THIS OFF?
Y'ALL TWO SEEM TO HAVE BROUGHT IN THE MAJORITY OF THE PEOPLE HERE, SO PERHAPS YOU SHOULD INTRODUCE YOURSELVES TO THE OTHERS.
I'M QUINN.
I'VE BEEN PRETTY ON TOP OF RECRUITING A FEW DISSIDENTS, AS WELL AS HACKING SCATTERED INTEL FROM GOVERNMENT BACKCHANNELS.
MET REESE AT A DIY BASEMENT SHOW IN 2004. BEAUTIFUL THING.
UM, YEAH. YALE HERE. QUINN BROUGHT ME IN.
I'VE GOT AN OBSCENE IQ AND I'M ACES AT BRAINSTORMING AGGRESSIVE SOCIOLOGICAL THEORY.
NICE TO MEET YOU GUYS OUTSIDE OF A MONITOR SCREEN IN MY PARENT'S BASEMENT.
QUINN, THIS IS ALL THE MANPOWER YOU COULD WRANGLE TODAY?
ACTUALLY, NO.
MY "UNDERWORLD CONTACTS" ARE COUNTRYWIDE. I PREDICT NO SHORTAGE OF ASSISTANCE ONCE WE GET THINGS ROLLING.
I JUST FIGURED THE LESS OF US CENTRALIZED IN ONE PLACE AT ONE TIME, THE LESS CHANCE OF SOMEONE HITTING US ALL AND ENDING OUR LITTLE "RESISTANCE" IN ONE FELL SWOOP.
SO THIS WILL BE OUR "CORE" LEADERSHIP THEN?
DAMN, WE A MOTLEY FUCKIN' CREW.
YUP. YOU'RE KIND OF LIKE MY MATHEMATICAL OPPOSITE, THEO.
DON'T BE RACIST, YALE

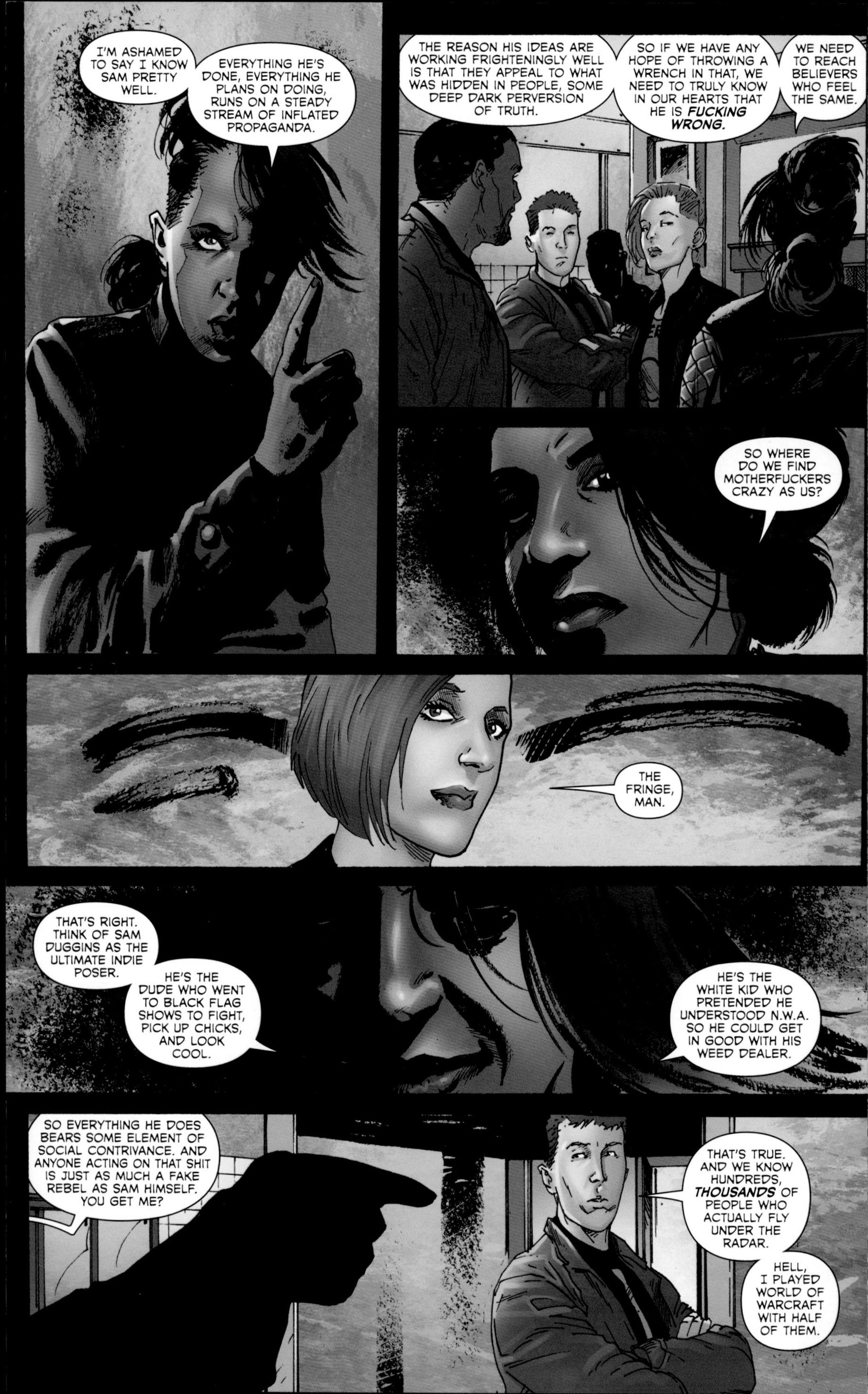

I'M ASHAMED TO SAY I KNOW SAM PRETTY WELL.
EVERYTHING HE'S DONE, EVERYTHING HE PLANS ON DOING, RUNS ON A STEADY STREAM OF INFLATED PROPAGANDA.
THE REASON HIS IDEAS ARE WORKING FRIGHTENINGLY WELL IS THAT THEY APPEAL TO WHAT WAS HIDDEN IN PEOPLE, SOME DEEP DARK PERVERSION OF TRUTH.
SO IF WE HAVE ANY HOPE OF THROWING A WRENCH IN THAT, WE NEED TO TRULY KNOW IN OUR HEARTS THAT HE IS ***FUCKING WRONG.***
WE NEED TO REACH BELIEVERS WHO FEEL THE SAME.
SO WHERE DO WE FIND MOTHERFUCKERS CRAZY AS US?
THE FRINGE, MAN.
THAT'S RIGHT. THINK OF SAM DUGGINS AS THE ULTIMATE INDIE POSER.
HE'S THE DUDE WHO WENT TO BLACK FLAG SHOWS TO FIGHT, PICK UP CHICKS, AND LOOK COOL.
HE'S THE WHITE KID WHO PRETENDED HE UNDERSTOOD N.W.A. SO HE COULD GET IN GOOD WITH HIS WEED DEALER.
SO EVERYTHING HE DOES BEARS SOME ELEMENT OF SOCIAL CONTRIVANCE. AND ANYONE ACTING ON THAT SHIT IS JUST AS MUCH A FAKE REBEL AS SAM HIMSELF. YOU GET ME?
THAT'S TRUE. AND WE KNOW HUNDREDS, ***THOUSANDS*** OF PEOPLE WHO ACTUALLY FLY UNDER THE RADAR.
HELL, I PLAYED WORLD OF WARCRAFT WITH HALF OF THEM.

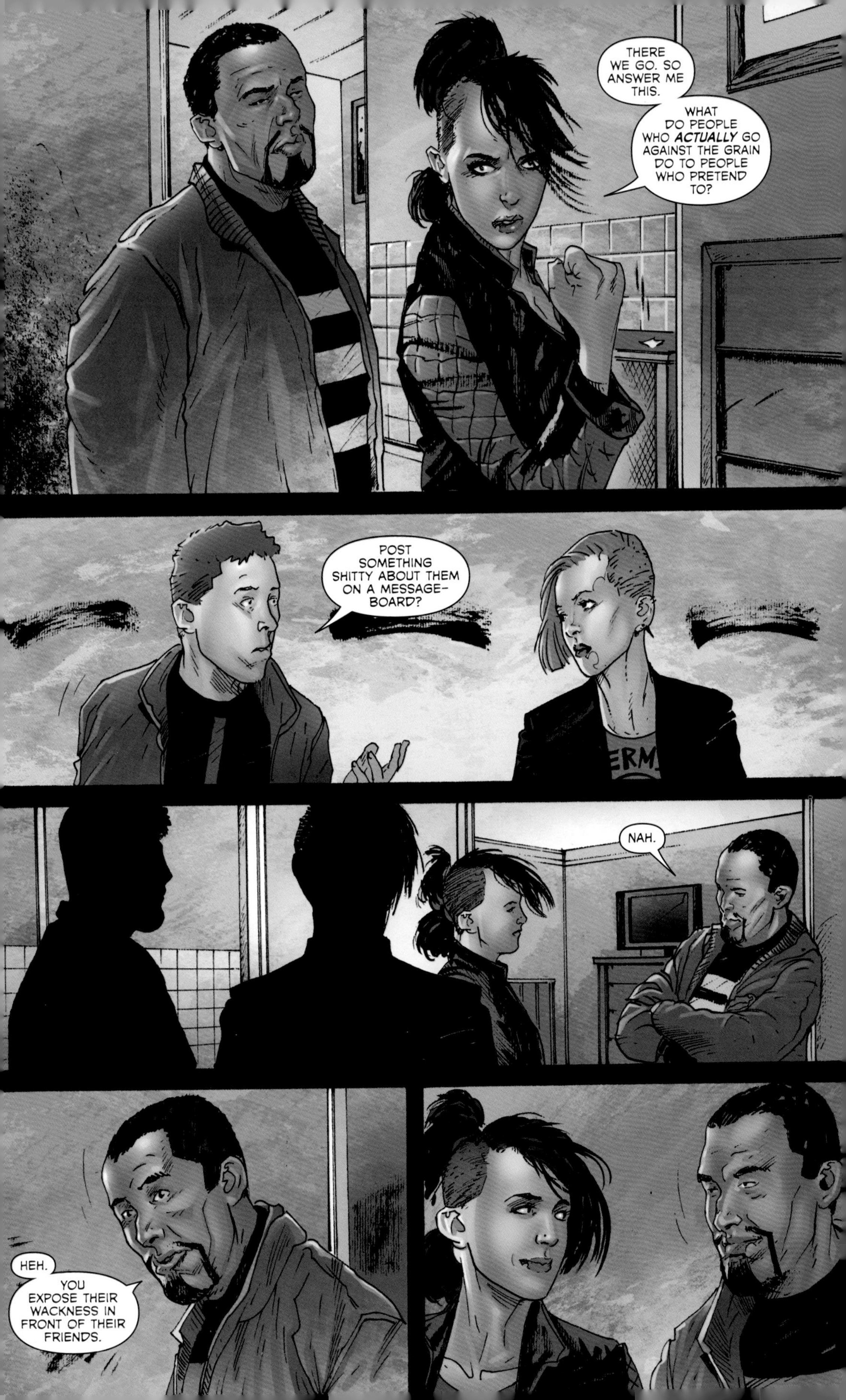
THERE WE GO. SO ANSWER ME THIS.
WHAT DO PEOPLE WHO *ACTUALLY* GO AGAINST THE GRAIN DO TO PEOPLE WHO PRETEND TO?
POST SOMETHING SHITTY ABOUT THEM ON A MESSAGE-BOARD?
NAH.
HEH.
YOU EXPOSE THEIR WACKNESS IN FRONT OF THEIR FRIENDS.

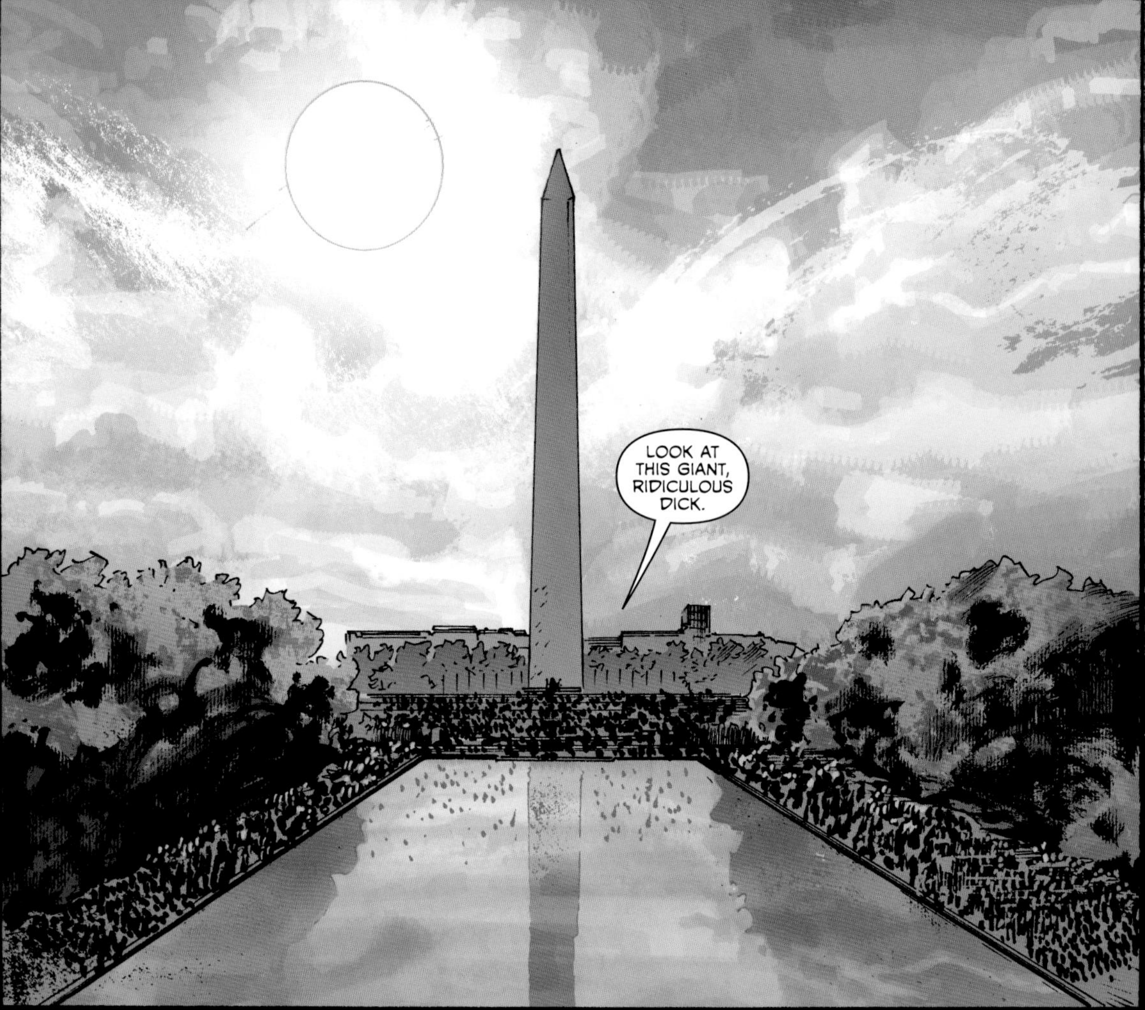
LOOK AT THIS GIANT, RIDICULOUS DICK.

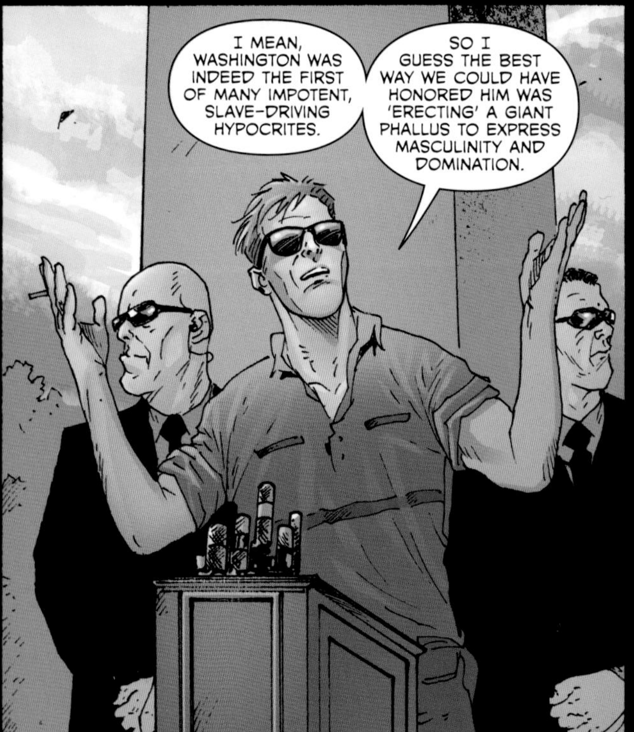
I MEAN, WASHINGTON WAS INDEED THE FIRST OF MANY IMPOTENT, SLAVE-DRIVING HYPOCRITES.
SO I GUESS THE BEST WAY WE COULD HAVE HONORED HIM WAS 'ERECTING' A GIANT PHALLUS TO EXPRESS MASCULINITY AND DOMINATION.

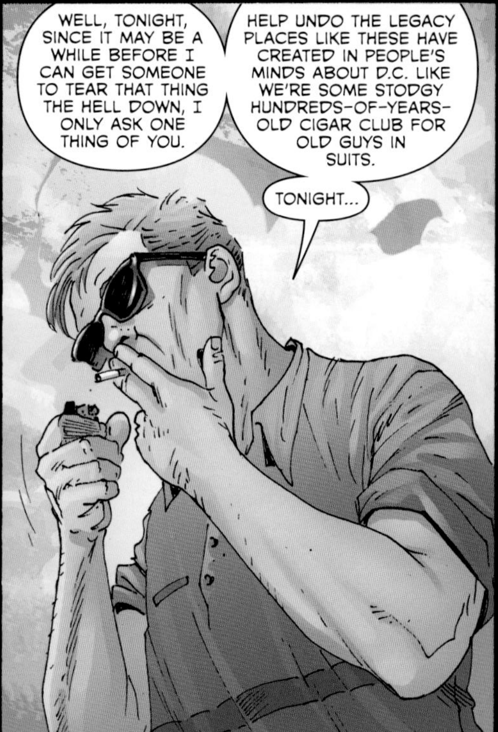
WELL, TONIGHT, SINCE IT MAY BE A WHILE BEFORE I CAN GET SOMEONE TO TEAR THAT THING THE HELL DOWN, I ONLY ASK ONE THING OF YOU.
HELP UNDO THE LEGACY PLACES LIKE THESE HAVE CREATED IN PEOPLE'S MINDS ABOUT D.C. LIKE WE'RE SOME STODGY HUNDREDS-OF-YEARS-OLD CIGAR CLUB FOR OLD GUYS IN SUITS.
TONIGHT...

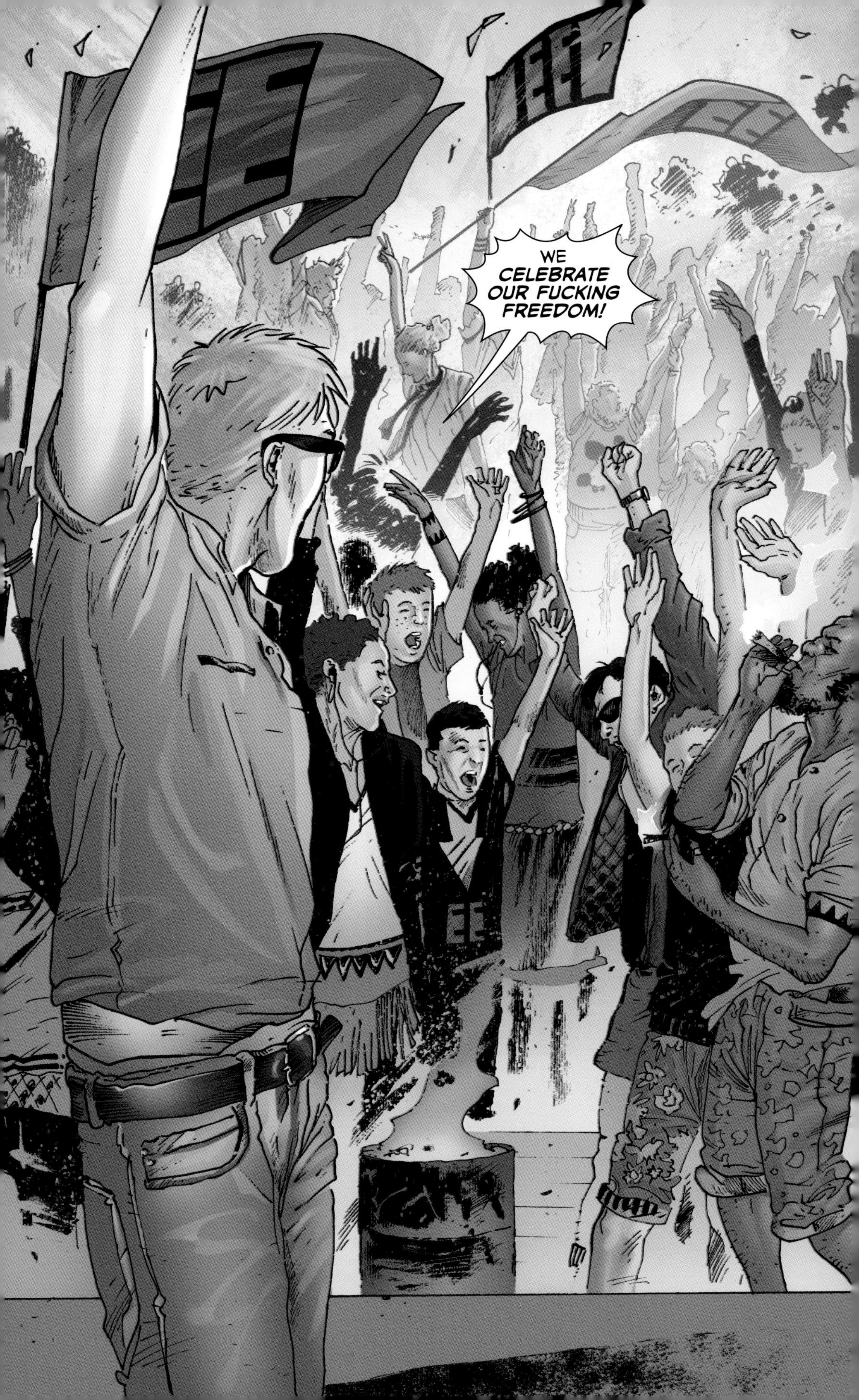
WE CELEBRATE OUR FUCKING FREEDOM!

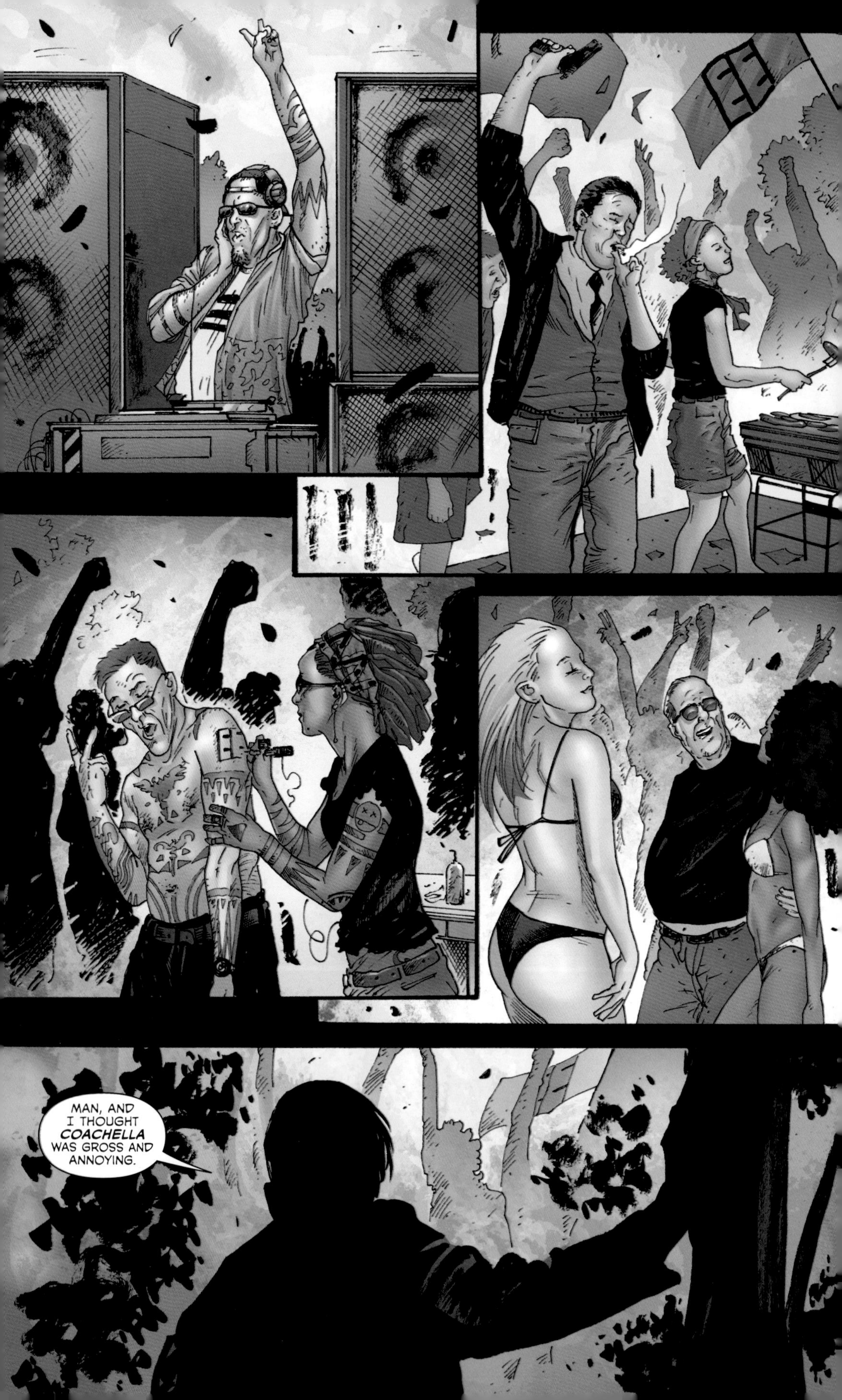
MAN, AND I THOUGHT *COACHELLA* WAS GROSS AND ANNOYING.

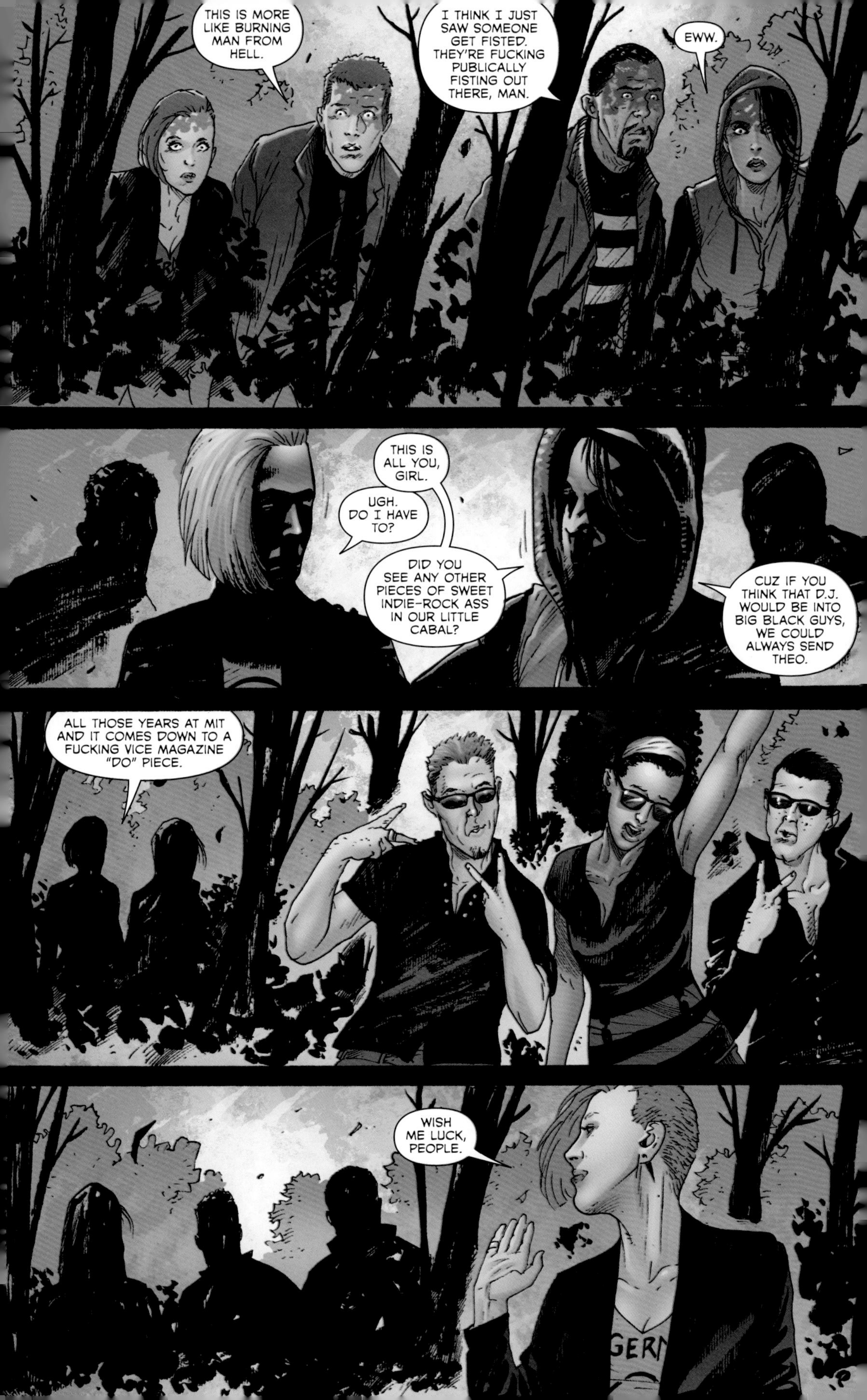
THIS IS MORE LIKE BURNING MAN FROM HELL.
I THINK I JUST SAW SOMEONE GET FISTED. THEY'RE FUCKING PUBLICALLY FISTING OUT THERE, MAN.
EWW.
THIS IS ALL YOU, GIRL.
UGH. DO I HAVE TO?
DID YOU SEE ANY OTHER PIECES OF SWEET INDIE-ROCK ASS IN OUR LITTLE CABAL?
CUZ IF YOU THINK THAT D.J. WOULD BE INTO BIG BLACK GUYS, WE COULD ALWAYS SEND THEO.
ALL THOSE YEARS AT MIT AND IT COMES DOWN TO A FUCKING VICE MAGAZINE "DO" PIECE.
WISH ME LUCK, PEOPLE.

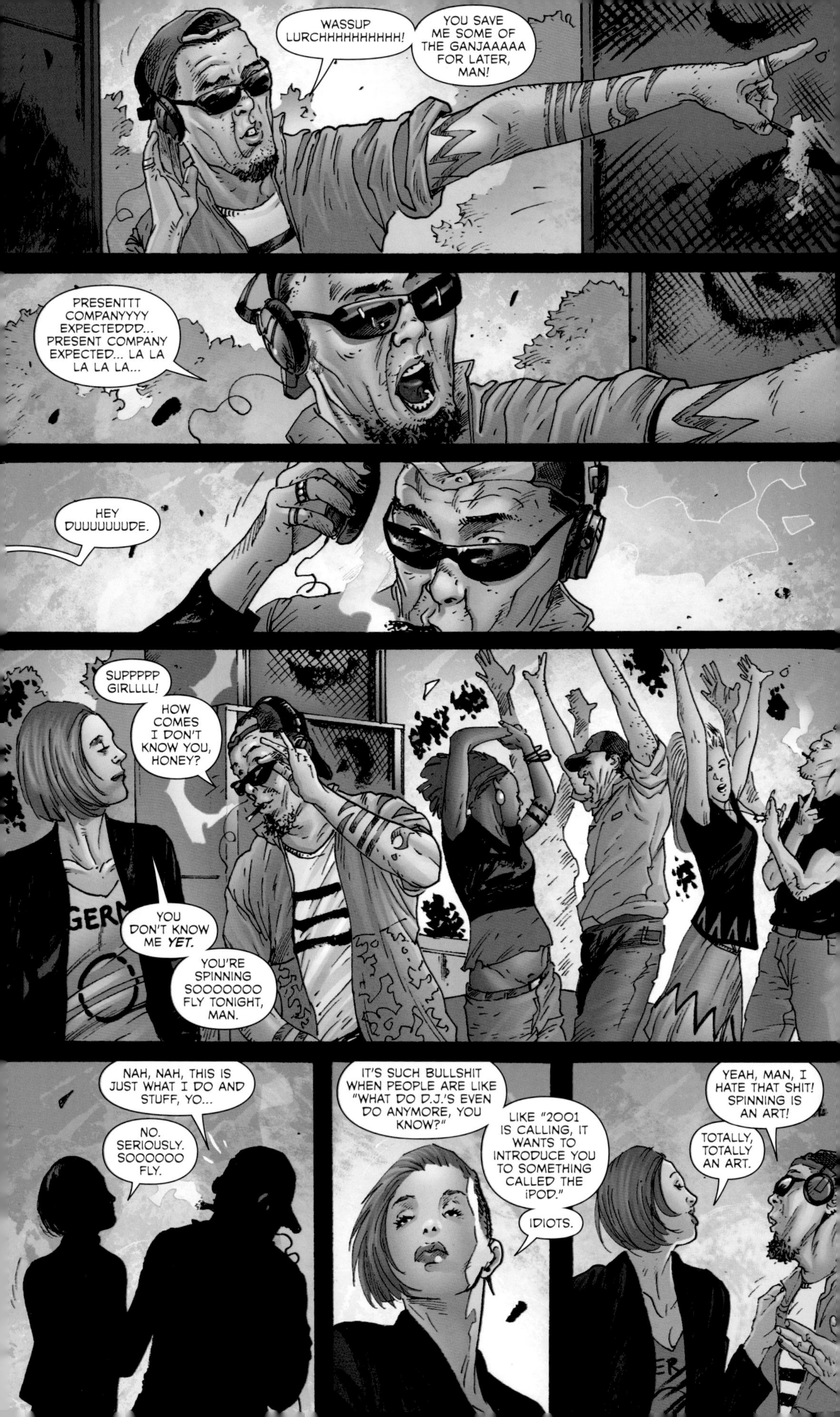
WASSUP LURCHHHHHHHHHH!
YOU SAVE ME SOME OF THE GANJAAAAA FOR LATER, MAN!
PRESENTTT COMPANYYYY EXPECTEDDD... PRESENT COMPANY EXPECTED... LA LA LA LA LA...
HEY DUUUUUUUDE.
SUPPPPP GIRLLLL!
HOW COMES I DON'T KNOW YOU, HONEY?
YOU DON'T KNOW ME *YET.*
YOU'RE SPINNING SOOOOOOO FLY TONIGHT, MAN.
NAH, NAH, THIS IS JUST WHAT I DO AND STUFF, YO...
NO. SERIOUSLY. SOOOOOO FLY.
IT'S SUCH BULLSHIT WHEN PEOPLE ARE LIKE "WHAT DO D.J.'S EVEN DO ANYMORE, YOU KNOW?"
LIKE "2001 IS CALLING, IT WANTS TO INTRODUCE YOU TO SOMETHING CALLED THE iPOD."
IDIOTS.
YEAH, MAN, I HATE THAT SHIT! SPINNING IS AN ART!
TOTALLY, TOTALLY AN ART.

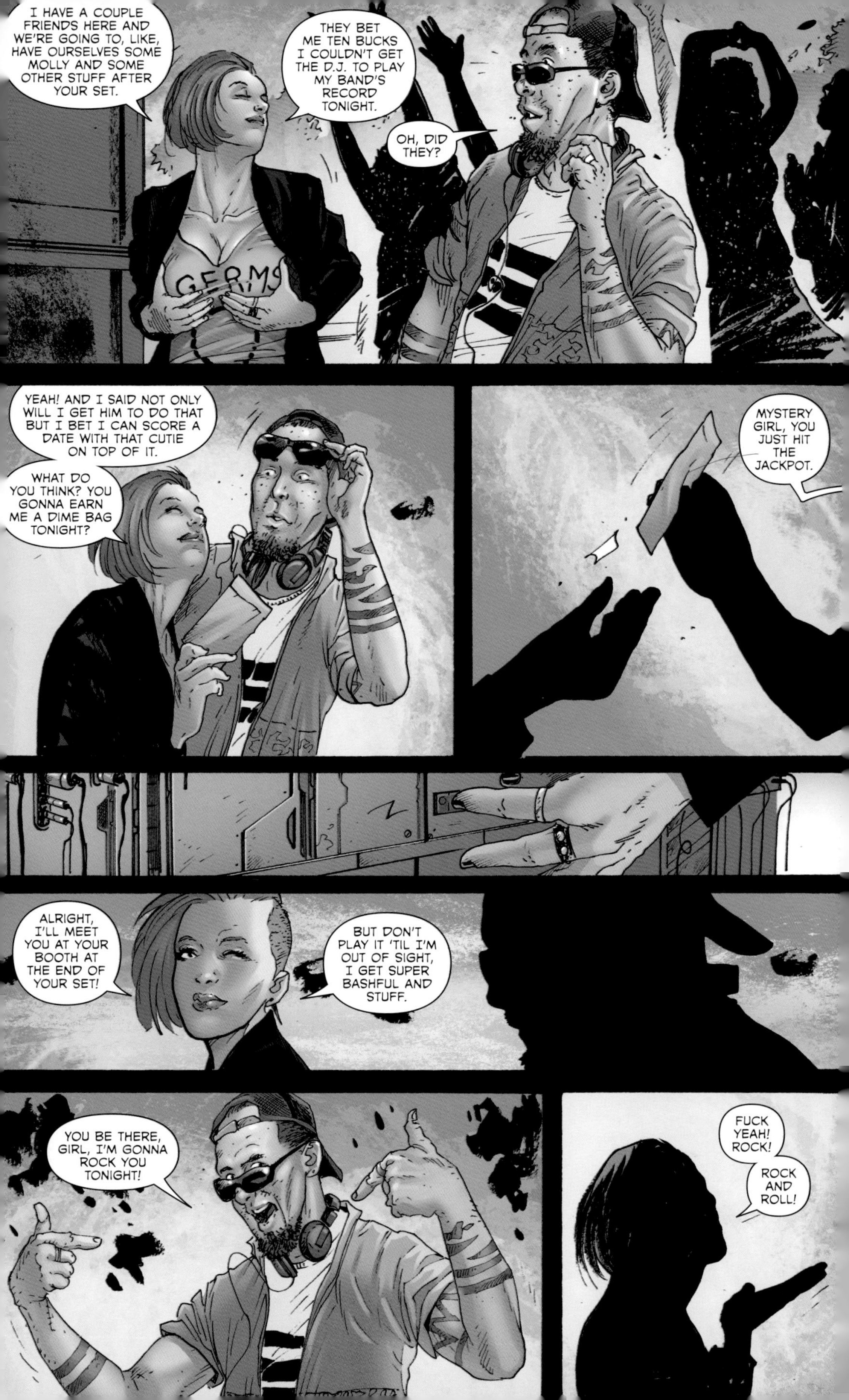
I HAVE A COUPLE FRIENDS HERE AND WE'RE GOING TO, LIKE, HAVE OURSELVES SOME MOLLY AND SOME OTHER STUFF AFTER YOUR SET.
THEY BET ME TEN BUCKS I COULDN'T GET THE D.J. TO PLAY MY BAND'S RECORD TONIGHT.
OH, DID THEY?
GERMS
YEAH! AND I SAID NOT ONLY WILL I GET HIM TO DO THAT BUT I BET I CAN SCORE A DATE WITH THAT CUTIE ON TOP OF IT.
WHAT DO YOU THINK? YOU GONNA EARN ME A DIME BAG TONIGHT?
MYSTERY GIRL, YOU JUST HIT THE JACKPOT.
ALRIGHT, I'LL MEET YOU AT YOUR BOOTH AT THE END OF YOUR SET!
BUT DON'T PLAY IT 'TIL I'M OUT OF SIGHT, I GET SUPER BASHFUL AND STUFF.
YOU BE THERE, GIRL, I'M GONNA ROCK YOU TONIGHT!
FUCK YEAH! ROCK!
ROCK AND ROLL!

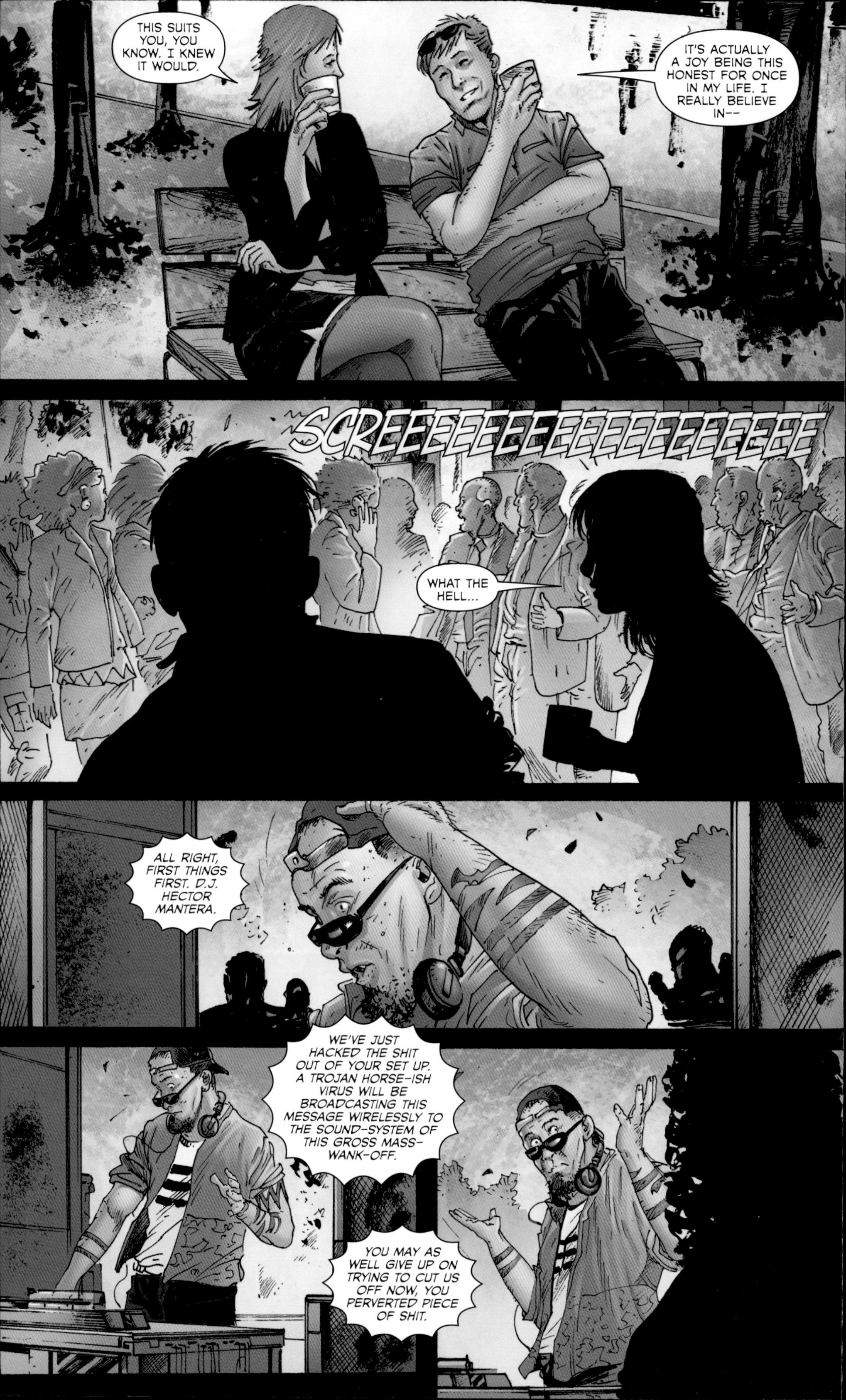
THIS SUITS YOU, YOU KNOW. I KNEW IT WOULD.
IT'S ACTUALLY A JOY BEING THIS HONEST FOR ONCE IN MY LIFE. I REALLY BELIEVE IN--
SCREEEEEEEEEEEEEEEEEEEE
WHAT THE HELL...
ALL RIGHT, FIRST THINGS FIRST. D.J. HECTOR MANTERA.
WE'VE JUST HACKED THE SHIT OUT OF YOUR SET UP. A TROJAN HORSE-ISH VIRUS WILL BE BROADCASTING THIS MESSAGE WIRELESSLY TO THE SOUND-SYSTEM OF THIS GROSS MASS-WANK-OFF.
YOU MAY AS WELL GIVE UP ON TRYING TO CUT US OFF NOW, YOU PERVERTED PIECE OF SHIT.

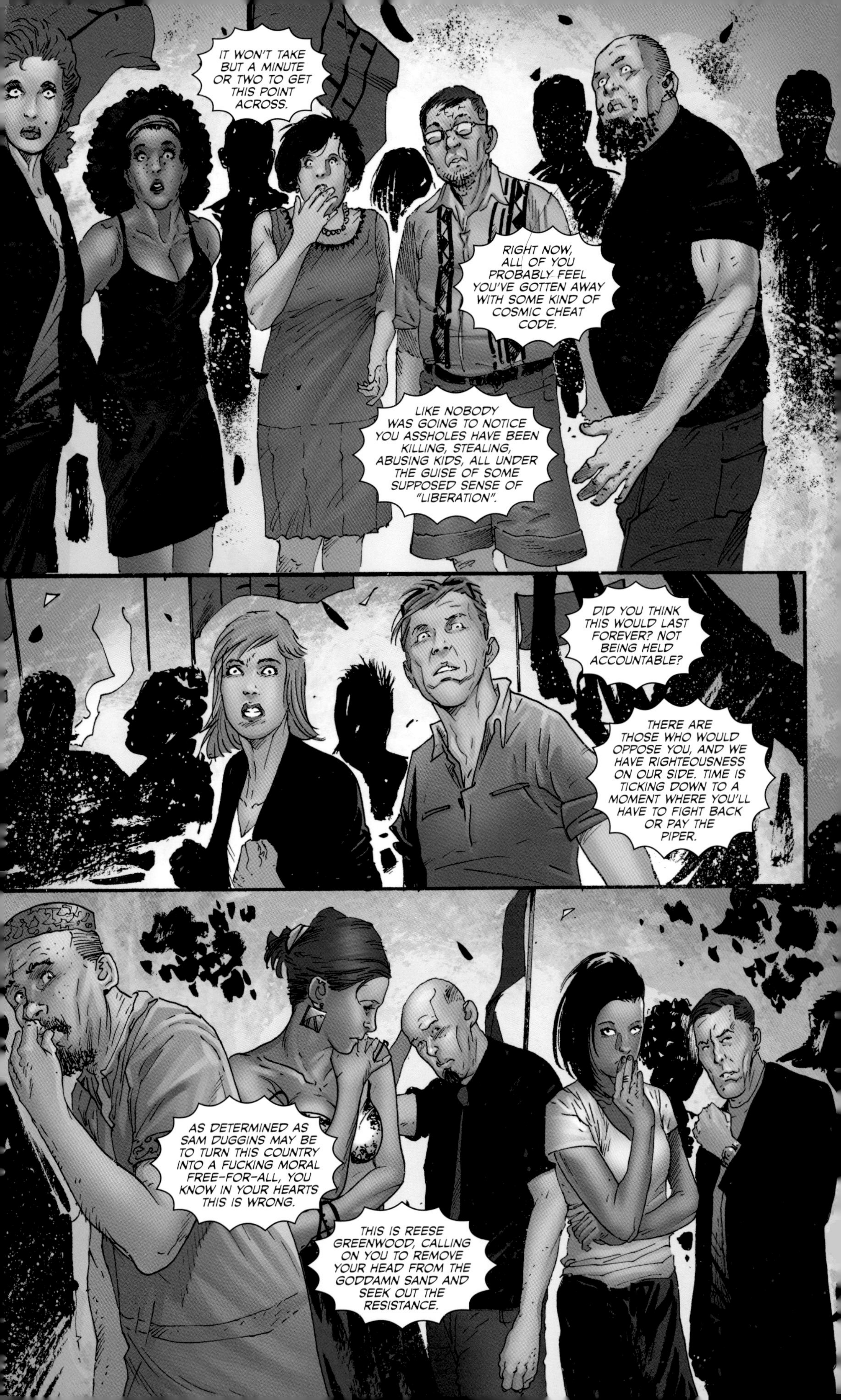
IT WON'T TAKE BUT A MINUTE OR TWO TO GET THIS POINT ACROSS.
RIGHT NOW, ALL OF YOU PROBABLY FEEL YOU'VE GOTTEN AWAY WITH SOME KIND OF COSMIC CHEAT CODE.
LIKE NOBODY WAS GOING TO NOTICE YOU ASSHOLES HAVE BEEN KILLING, STEALING, ABUSING KIDS, ALL UNDER THE GUISE OF SOME SUPPOSED SENSE OF "LIBERATION".
DID YOU THINK THIS WOULD LAST FOREVER? NOT BEING HELD ACCOUNTABLE?
THERE ARE THOSE WHO WOULD OPPOSE YOU, AND WE HAVE RIGHTEOUSNESS ON OUR SIDE. TIME IS TICKING DOWN TO A MOMENT WHERE YOU'LL HAVE TO FIGHT BACK OR PAY THE PIPER.
AS DETERMINED AS SAM DUGGINS MAY BE TO TURN THIS COUNTRY INTO A FUCKING MORAL FREE-FOR-ALL, YOU KNOW IN YOUR HEARTS THIS IS WRONG.
THIS IS REESE GREENWOOD, CALLING ON YOU TO REMOVE YOUR HEAD FROM THE GODDAMN SAND AND SEEK OUT THE RESISTANCE.

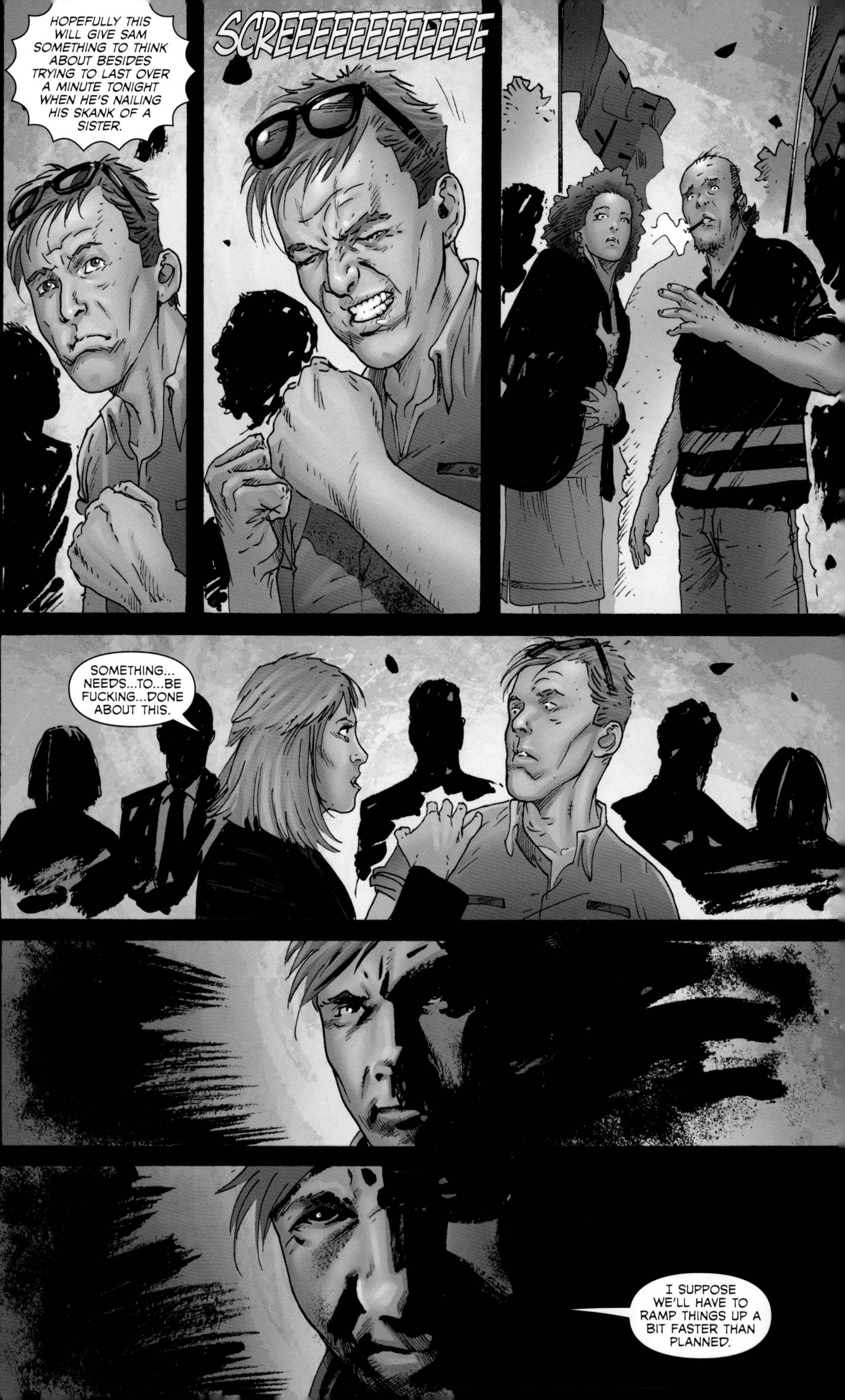
HOPEFULLY THIS WILL GIVE SAM SOMETHING TO THINK ABOUT BESIDES TRYING TO LAST OVER A MINUTE TONIGHT WHEN HE'S NAILING HIS SKANK OF A SISTER.
SCREEEEEEEEEEEEEE
SOMETHING... NEEDS...TO...BE FUCKING...DONE ABOUT THIS.
I SUPPOSE WE'LL HAVE TO RAMP THINGS UP A BIT FASTER THAN PLANNED.

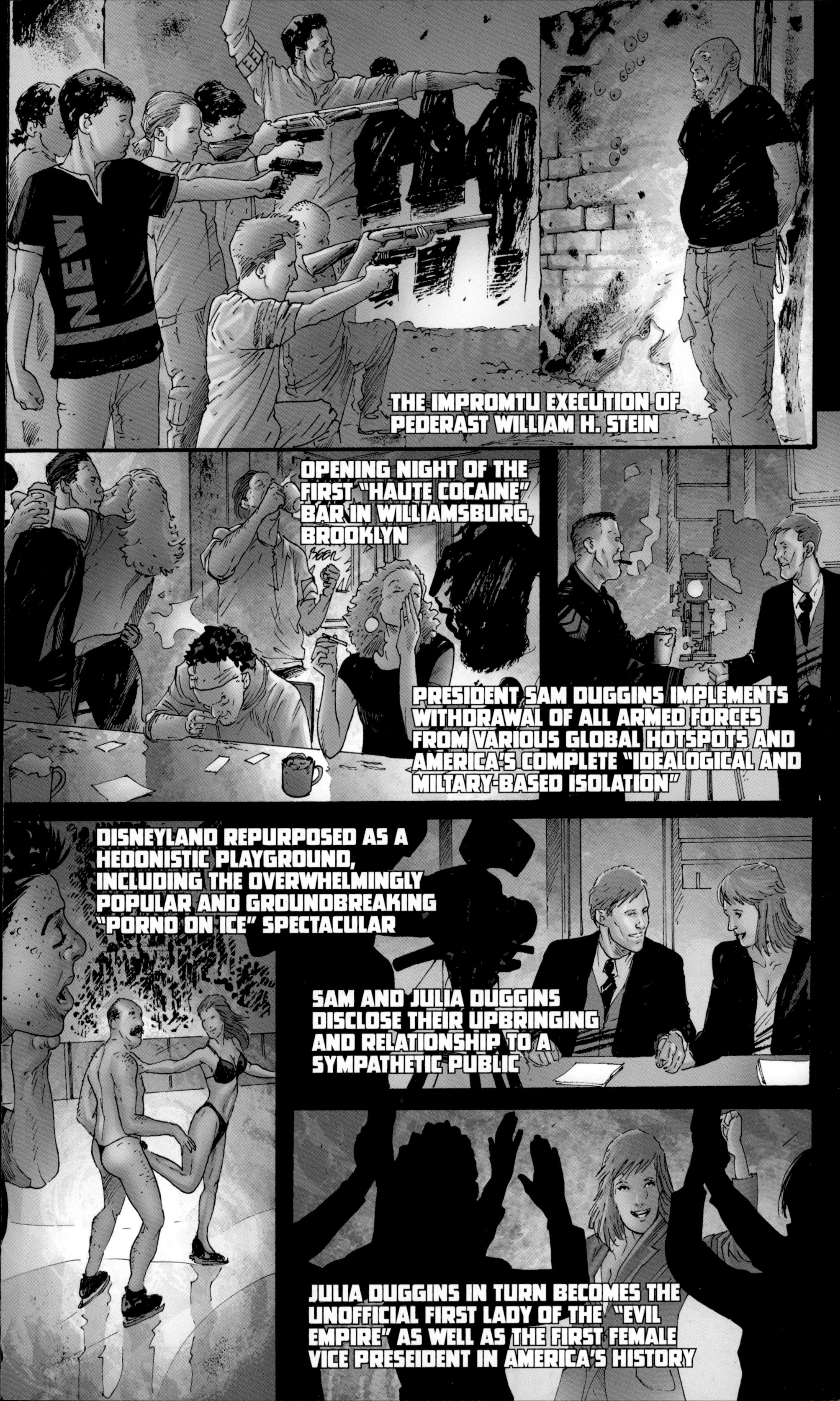
THE IMPROMTU EXECUTION OF PEDERAST WILLIAM H. STEIN
OPENING NIGHT OF THE FIRST "HAUTE COCAINE" BAR IN WILLIAMSBURG, BROOKLYN
PRESIDENT SAM DUGGINS IMPLEMENTS WITHDRAWAL OF ALL ARMED FORCES FROM VARIOUS GLOBAL HOTSPOTS AND AMERICA'S COMPLETE "IDEALOGICAL AND MILTARY-BASED ISOLATION"
DISNEYLAND REPURPOSED AS A HEDONISTIC PLAYGROUND, INCLUDING THE OVERWHELMINGLY POPULAR AND GROUNDBREAKING "PORNO ON ICE" SPECTACULAR
SAM AND JULIA DUGGINS DISCLOSE THEIR UPBRINGING AND RELATIONSHIP TO A SYMPATHETIC PUBLIC
JULIA DUGGINS IN TURN BECOMES THE UNOFFICIAL FIRST LADY OF THE "EVIL EMPIRE" AS WELL AS THE FIRST FEMALE VICE PRESEIDENT IN AMERICA'S HISTORY

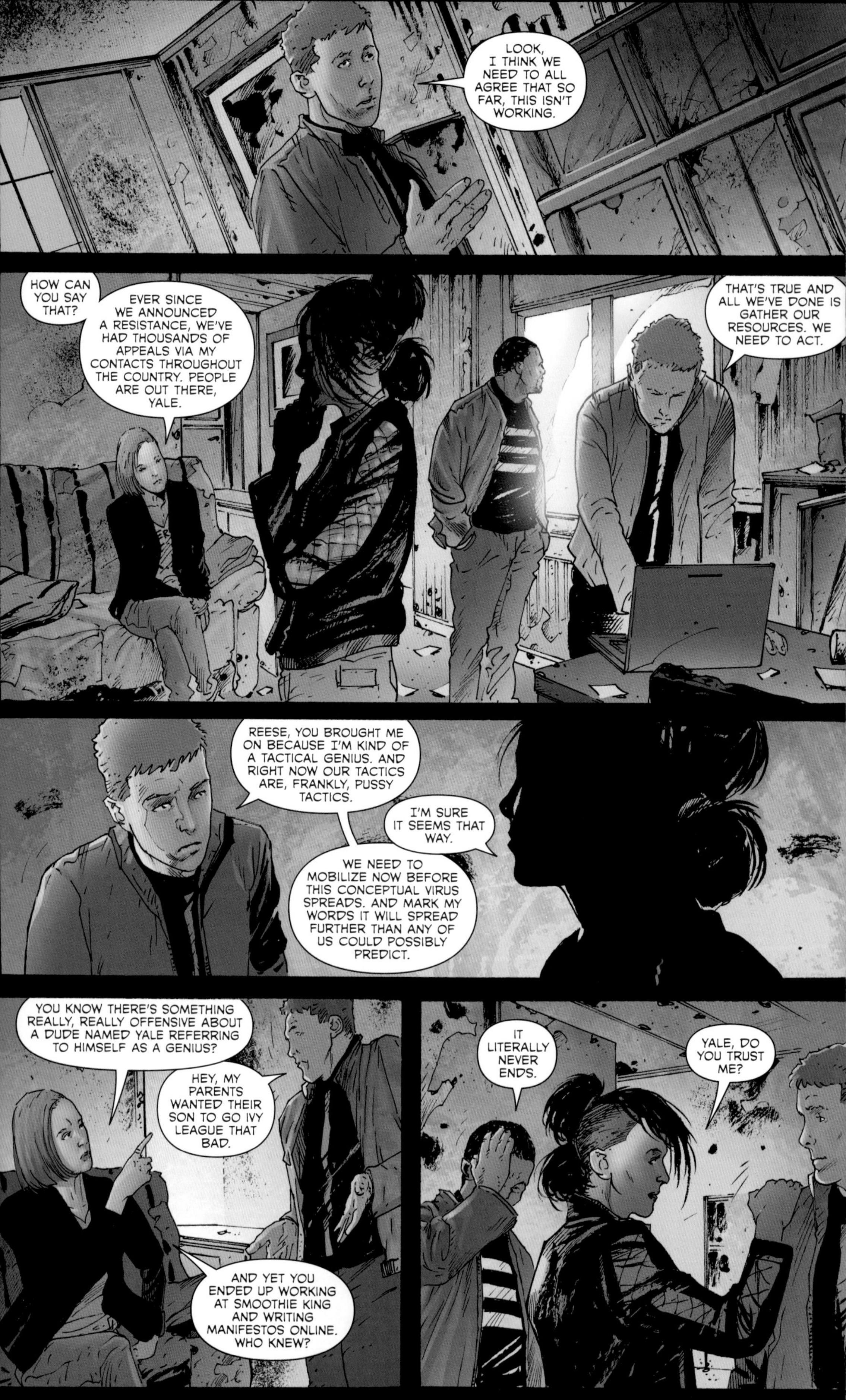
LOOK, I THINK WE NEED TO ALL AGREE THAT SO FAR, THIS ISN'T WORKING.
HOW CAN YOU SAY THAT?
EVER SINCE WE ANNOUNCED A RESISTANCE, WE'VE HAD THOUSANDS OF APPEALS VIA MY CONTACTS THROUGHOUT THE COUNTRY. PEOPLE ARE OUT THERE, YALE.
THAT'S TRUE AND ALL WE'VE DONE IS GATHER OUR RESOURCES. WE NEED TO ACT.
REESE, YOU BROUGHT ME ON BECAUSE I'M KIND OF A TACTICAL GENIUS. AND RIGHT NOW OUR TACTICS ARE, FRANKLY, PUSSY TACTICS.
I'M SURE IT SEEMS THAT WAY.
WE NEED TO MOBILIZE NOW BEFORE THIS CONCEPTUAL VIRUS SPREADS. AND MARK MY WORDS IT WILL SPREAD FURTHER THAN ANY OF US COULD POSSIBLY PREDICT.
YOU KNOW THERE'S SOMETHING REALLY, REALLY OFFENSIVE ABOUT A DUDE NAMED YALE REFERRING TO HIMSELF AS A GENIUS?
HEY, MY PARENTS WANTED THEIR SON TO GO IVY LEAGUE THAT BAD.
AND YET YOU ENDED UP WORKING AT SMOOTHIE KING AND WRITING MANIFESTOS ONLINE. WHO KNEW?
IT LITERALLY NEVER ENDS.
YALE, DO YOU TRUST ME?

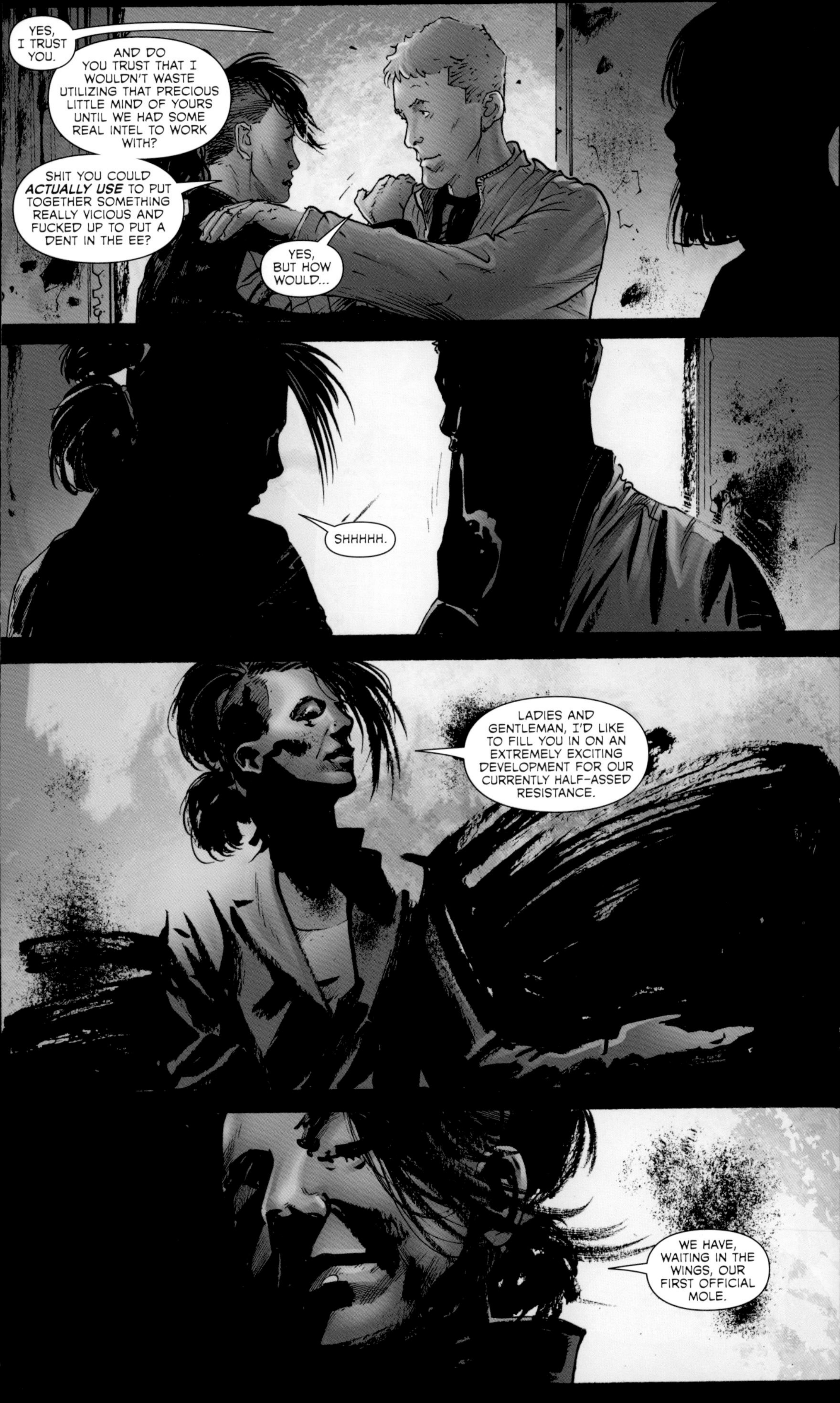
YES, I TRUST YOU.
AND DO YOU TRUST THAT I WOULDN'T WASTE UTILIZING THAT PRECIOUS LITTLE MIND OF YOURS UNTIL WE HAD SOME REAL INTEL TO WORK WITH?
SHIT YOU COULD *ACTUALLY USE* TO PUT TOGETHER SOMETHING REALLY VICIOUS AND FUCKED UP TO PUT A DENT IN THE EE?
YES, BUT HOW WOULD...
SHHHHH.
LADIES AND GENTLEMAN, I'D LIKE TO FILL YOU IN ON AN EXTREMELY EXCITING DEVELOPMENT FOR OUR CURRENTLY HALF-ASSED RESISTANCE.
WE HAVE, WAITING IN THE WINGS, OUR FIRST OFFICIAL MOLE.

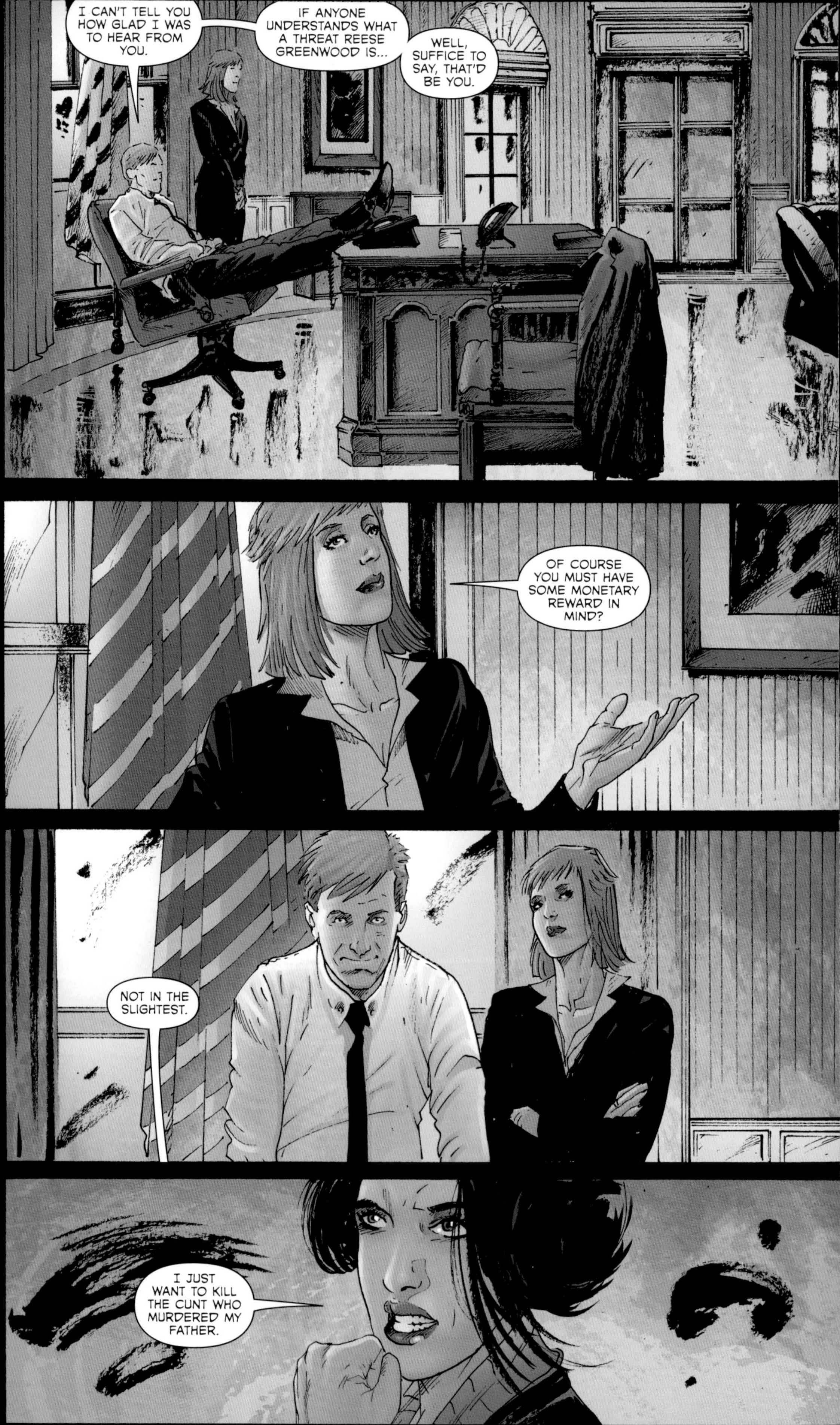
I CAN'T TELL YOU HOW GLAD I WAS TO HEAR FROM YOU.
IF ANYONE UNDERSTANDS WHAT A THREAT REESE GREENWOOD IS...
WELL, SUFFICE TO SAY, THAT'D BE YOU.
OF COURSE YOU MUST HAVE SOME MONETARY REWARD IN MIND?
NOT IN THE SLIGHTEST.
I JUST WANT TO KILL THE CUNT WHO MURDERED MY FATHER.

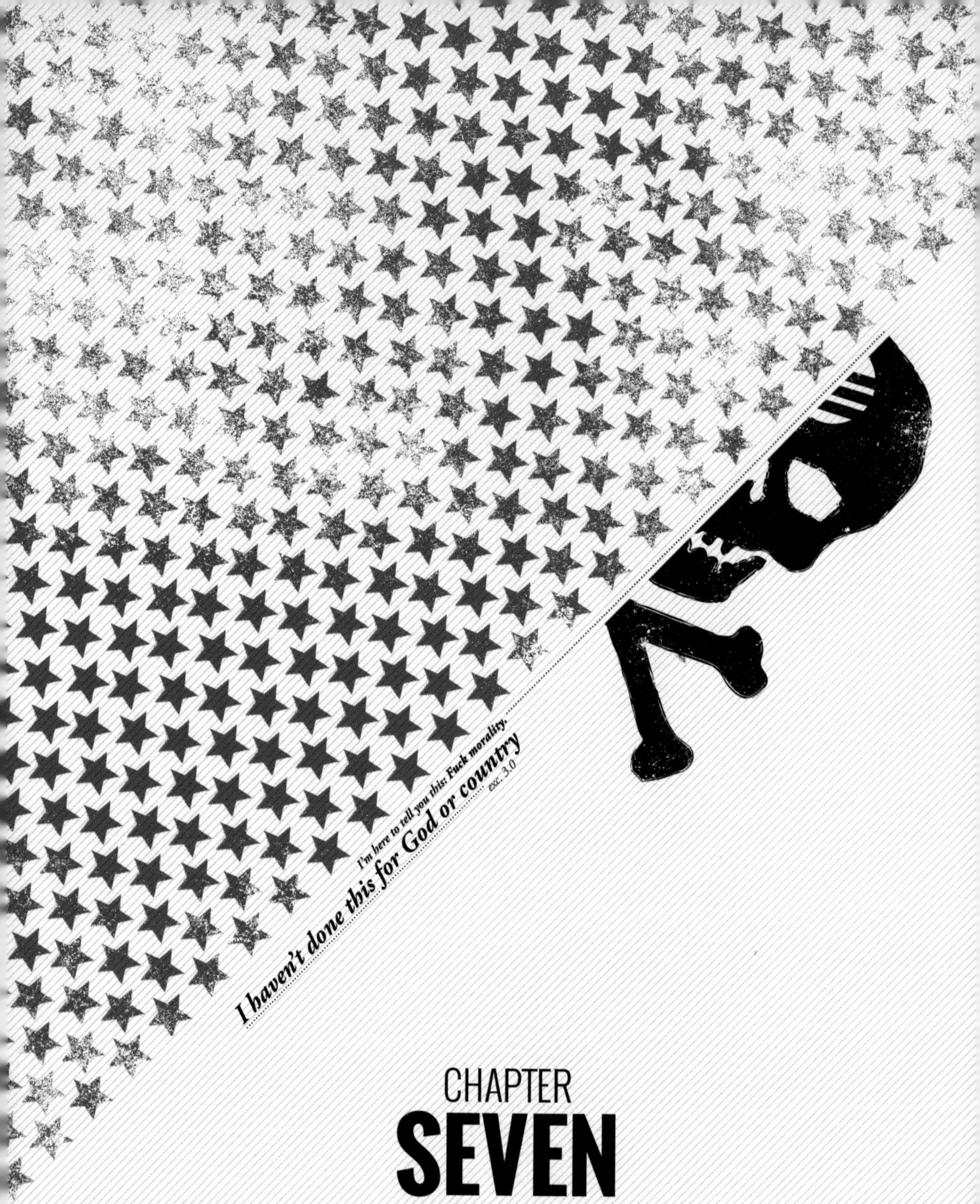
I'm here to tell you this: **Fuck morality.**
I haven't done this for God or country
exc. 3.0

CHAPTER SEVEN

fig. 3

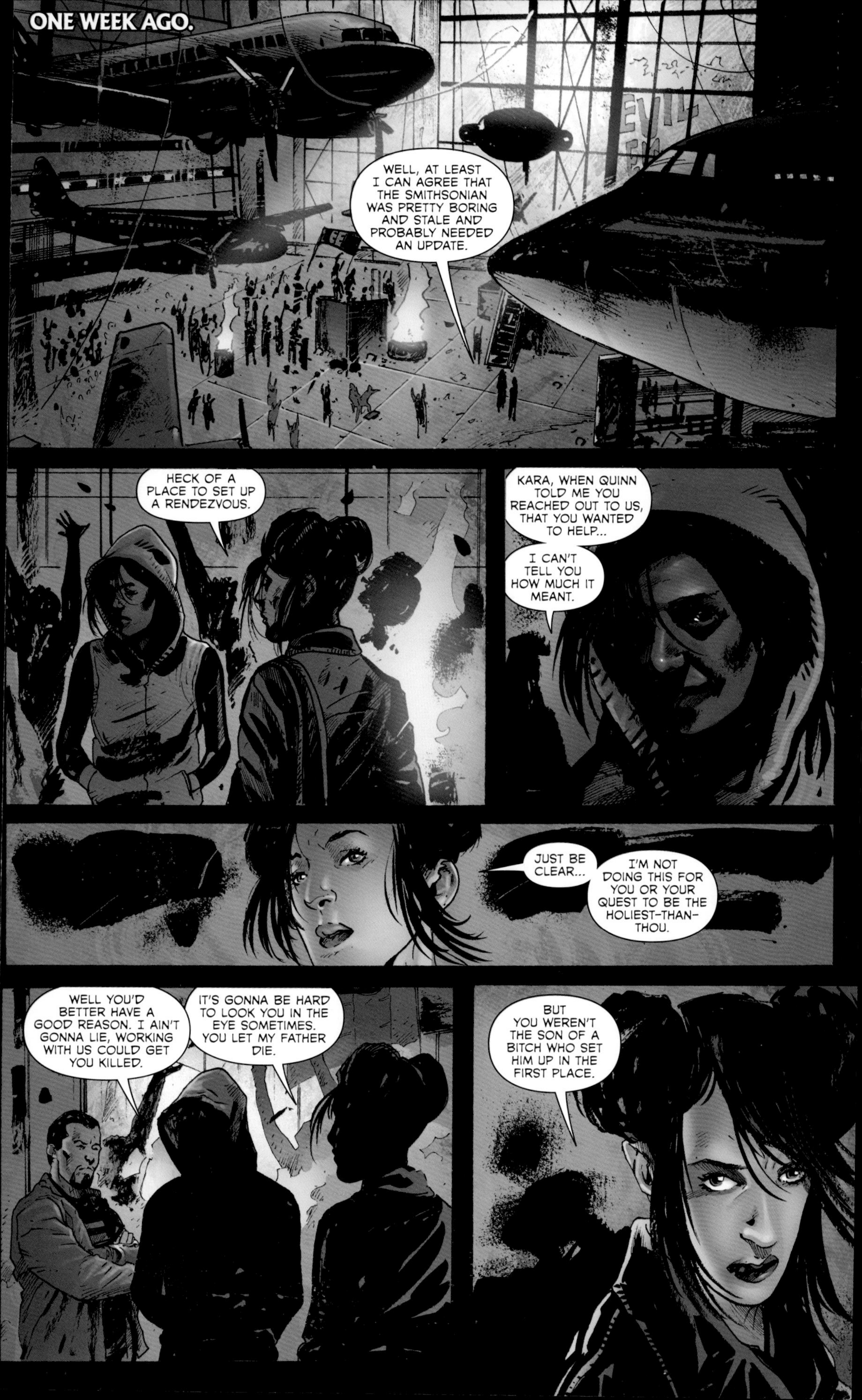
ONE WEEK AGO.
WELL, AT LEAST I CAN AGREE THAT THE SMITHSONIAN WAS PRETTY BORING AND STALE AND PROBABLY NEEDED AN UPDATE.
HECK OF A PLACE TO SET UP A RENDEZVOUS.
KARA, WHEN QUINN TOLD ME YOU REACHED OUT TO US, THAT YOU WANTED TO HELP...
I CAN'T TELL YOU HOW MUCH IT MEANT.
JUST BE CLEAR...
I'M NOT DOING THIS FOR YOU OR YOUR QUEST TO BE THE HOLIEST-THAN-THOU.
WELL YOU'D BETTER HAVE A GOOD REASON. I AIN'T GONNA LIE, WORKING WITH US COULD GET YOU KILLED.
IT'S GONNA BE HARD TO LOOK YOU IN THE EYE SOMETIMES. YOU LET MY FATHER DIE.
BUT YOU WEREN'T THE SON OF A BITCH WHO SET HIM UP IN THE FIRST PLACE.

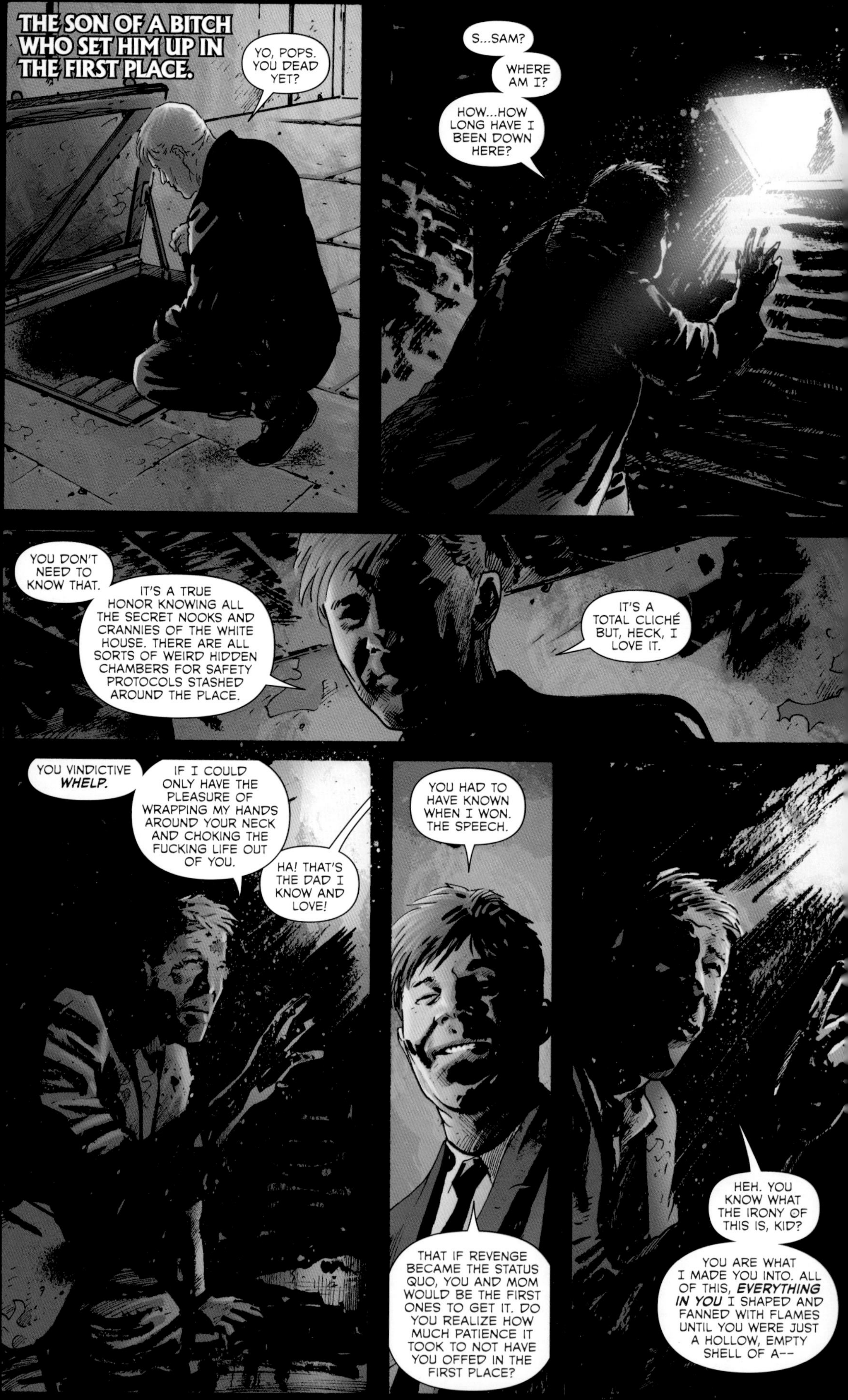
THE SON OF A BITCH WHO SET HIM UP IN THE FIRST PLACE.
YO, POPS. YOU DEAD YET?
S...SAM?
WHERE AM I?
HOW...HOW LONG HAVE I BEEN DOWN HERE?
YOU DON'T NEED TO KNOW THAT.
IT'S A TRUE HONOR KNOWING ALL THE SECRET NOOKS AND CRANNIES OF THE WHITE HOUSE. THERE ARE ALL SORTS OF WEIRD HIDDEN CHAMBERS FOR SAFETY PROTOCOLS STASHED AROUND THE PLACE.
IT'S A TOTAL CLICHÉ BUT, HECK, I LOVE IT.
YOU VINDICTIVE *WHELP.*
IF I COULD ONLY HAVE THE PLEASURE OF WRAPPING MY HANDS AROUND YOUR NECK AND CHOKING THE FUCKING LIFE OUT OF YOU.
HA! THAT'S THE DAD I KNOW AND LOVE!
YOU HAD TO HAVE KNOWN WHEN I WON. THE SPEECH.
THAT IF REVENGE BECAME THE STATUS QUO, YOU AND MOM WOULD BE THE FIRST ONES TO GET IT. DO YOU REALIZE HOW MUCH PATIENCE IT TOOK TO NOT HAVE YOU OFFED IN THE FIRST PLACE?
HEH. YOU KNOW WHAT THE IRONY OF THIS IS, KID?
YOU ARE WHAT I MADE YOU INTO. ALL OF THIS, *EVERYTHING IN YOU* I SHAPED AND FANNED WITH FLAMES UNTIL YOU WERE JUST A HOLLOW, EMPTY SHELL OF A--

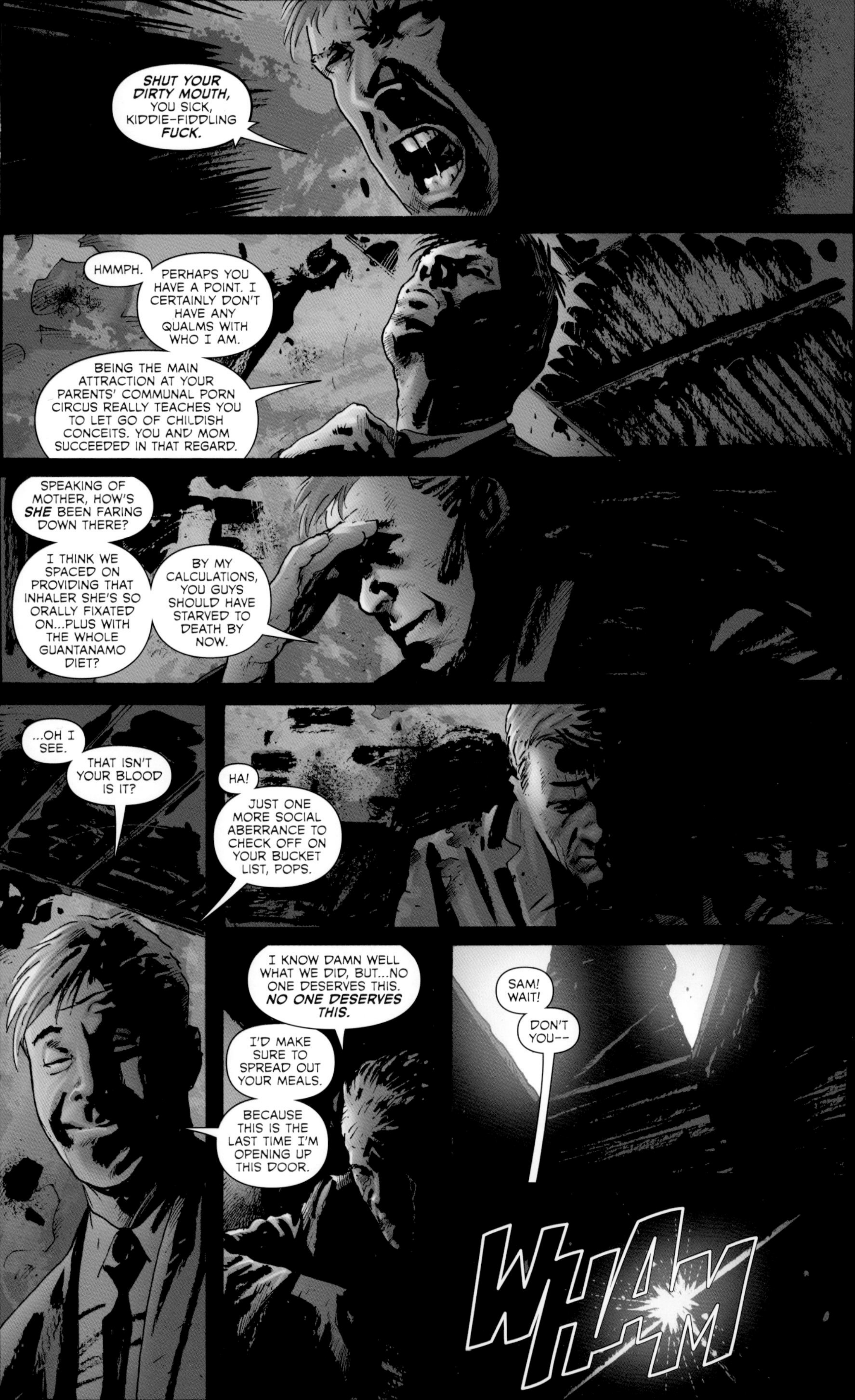
SHUT YOUR DIRTY MOUTH, YOU SICK, KIDDIE-FIDDLING FUCK.
HMMPH.
PERHAPS YOU HAVE A POINT. I CERTAINLY DON'T HAVE ANY QUALMS WITH WHO I AM.
BEING THE MAIN ATTRACTION AT YOUR PARENTS' COMMUNAL PORN CIRCUS REALLY TEACHES YOU TO LET GO OF CHILDISH CONCEITS. YOU AND MOM SUCCEEDED IN THAT REGARD.
SPEAKING OF MOTHER, HOW'S SHE BEEN FARING DOWN THERE?
I THINK WE SPACED ON PROVIDING THAT INHALER SHE'S SO ORALLY FIXATED ON...PLUS WITH THE WHOLE GUANTANAMO DIET?
BY MY CALCULATIONS, YOU GUYS SHOULD HAVE STARVED TO DEATH BY NOW.
...OH I SEE.
THAT ISN'T YOUR BLOOD IS IT?
HA!
JUST ONE MORE SOCIAL ABERRANCE TO CHECK OFF ON YOUR BUCKET LIST, POPS.
I KNOW DAMN WELL WHAT WE DID, BUT...NO ONE DESERVES THIS. NO ONE DESERVES THIS.
I'D MAKE SURE TO SPREAD OUT YOUR MEALS.
BECAUSE THIS IS THE LAST TIME I'M OPENING UP THIS DOOR.
SAM! WAIT!
DON'T YOU--
WHAM

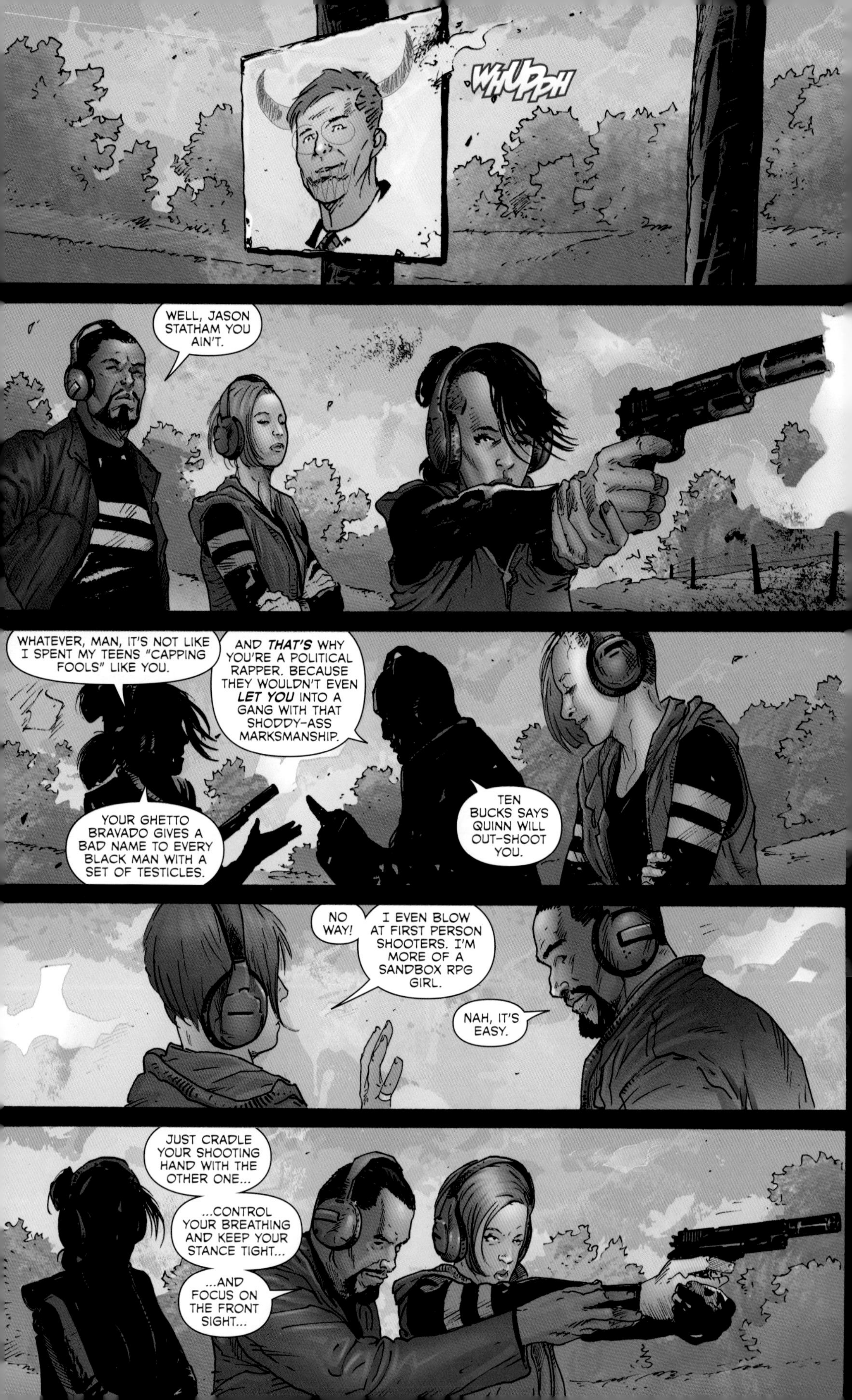
WHUPPH
WELL, JASON STATHAM YOU AIN'T.
WHATEVER, MAN, IT'S NOT LIKE I SPENT MY TEENS "CAPPING FOOLS" LIKE YOU.
AND THAT'S WHY YOU'RE A POLITICAL RAPPER. BECAUSE THEY WOULDN'T EVEN LET YOU INTO A GANG WITH THAT SHODDY-ASS MARKSMANSHIP.
YOUR GHETTO BRAVADO GIVES A BAD NAME TO EVERY BLACK MAN WITH A SET OF TESTICLES.
TEN BUCKS SAYS QUINN WILL OUT-SHOOT YOU.
NO WAY!
I EVEN BLOW AT FIRST PERSON SHOOTERS. I'M MORE OF A SANDBOX RPG GIRL.
NAH, IT'S EASY.
JUST CRADLE YOUR SHOOTING HAND WITH THE OTHER ONE...
...CONTROL YOUR BREATHING AND KEEP YOUR STANCE TIGHT...
...AND FOCUS ON THE FRONT SIGHT...

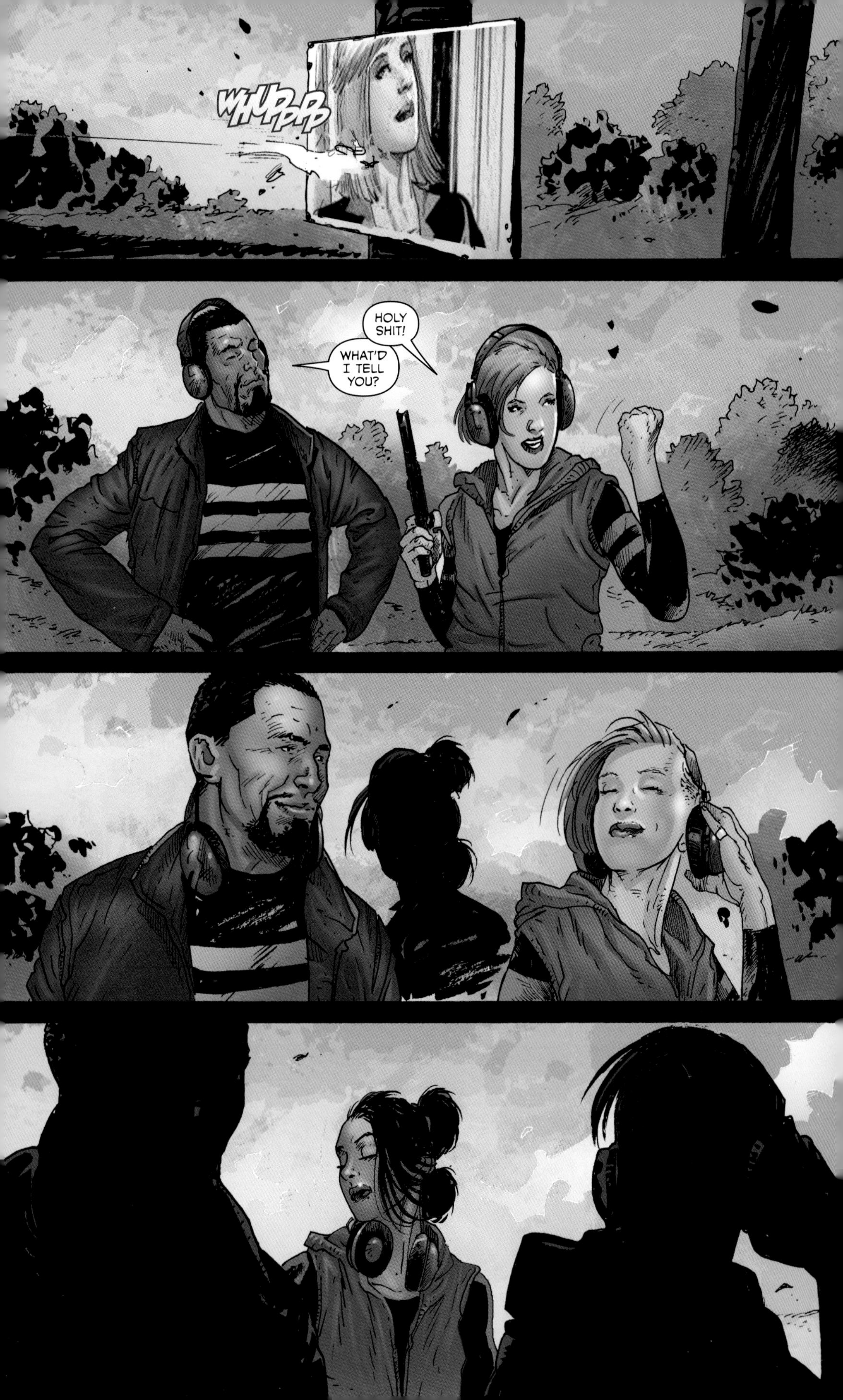
WHUDDDP
HOLY SHIT!
WHAT'D I TELL YOU?

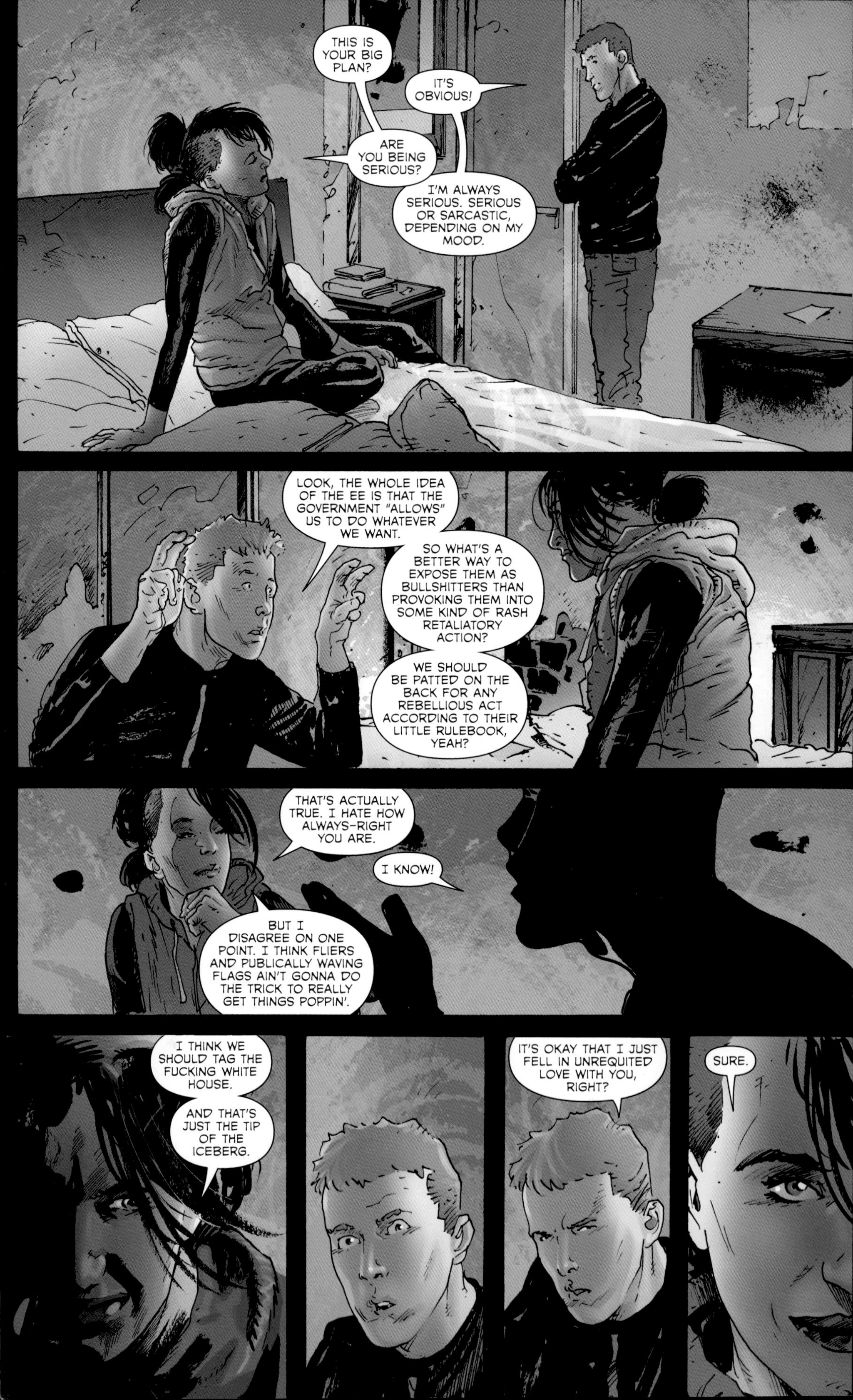

THIS IS YOUR BIG PLAN?
IT'S OBVIOUS!
ARE YOU BEING SERIOUS?
I'M ALWAYS SERIOUS. SERIOUS OR SARCASTIC, DEPENDING ON MY MOOD.
LOOK, THE WHOLE IDEA OF THE EE IS THAT THE GOVERNMENT "ALLOWS" US TO DO WHATEVER WE WANT.
SO WHAT'S A BETTER WAY TO EXPOSE THEM AS BULLSHITTERS THAN PROVOKING THEM INTO SOME KIND OF RASH RETALIATORY ACTION?
WE SHOULD BE PATTED ON THE BACK FOR ANY REBELLIOUS ACT ACCORDING TO THEIR LITTLE RULEBOOK, YEAH?
THAT'S ACTUALLY TRUE. I HATE HOW ALWAYS-RIGHT YOU ARE.
I KNOW!
BUT I DISAGREE ON ONE POINT. I THINK FLIERS AND PUBLICALLY WAVING FLAGS AIN'T GONNA DO THE TRICK TO REALLY GET THINGS POPPIN'.
I THINK WE SHOULD TAG THE FUCKING WHITE HOUSE.
AND THAT'S JUST THE TIP OF THE ICEBERG.
IT'S OKAY THAT I JUST FELL IN UNREQUITED LOVE WITH YOU, RIGHT?
SURE.

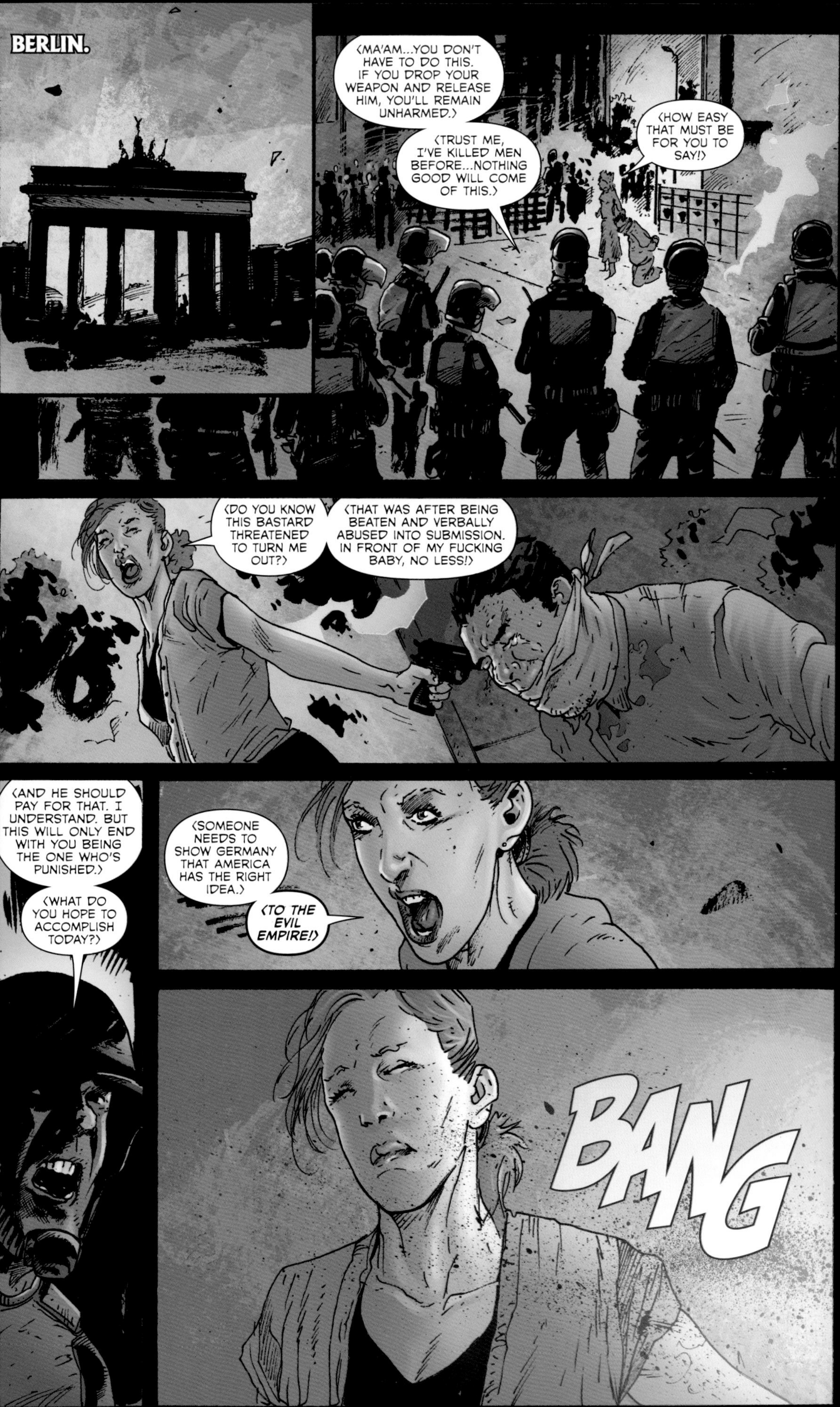

BERLIN.
‹MA'AM...YOU DON'T HAVE TO DO THIS. IF YOU DROP YOUR WEAPON AND RELEASE HIM, YOU'LL REMAIN UNHARMED.›
‹TRUST ME, I'VE KILLED MEN BEFORE...NOTHING GOOD WILL COME OF THIS.›
‹HOW EASY THAT MUST BE FOR YOU TO SAY!›
‹DO YOU KNOW THIS BASTARD THREATENED TO TURN ME OUT?›
‹THAT WAS AFTER BEING BEATEN AND VERBALLY ABUSED INTO SUBMISSION. IN FRONT OF MY FUCKING BABY, NO LESS!›
‹AND HE SHOULD PAY FOR THAT. I UNDERSTAND. BUT THIS WILL ONLY END WITH YOU BEING THE ONE WHO'S PUNISHED.›
‹WHAT DO YOU HOPE TO ACCOMPLISH TODAY?›
‹SOMEONE NEEDS TO SHOW GERMANY THAT AMERICA HAS THE RIGHT IDEA.›
‹TO THE EVIL EMPIRE!›
BANG

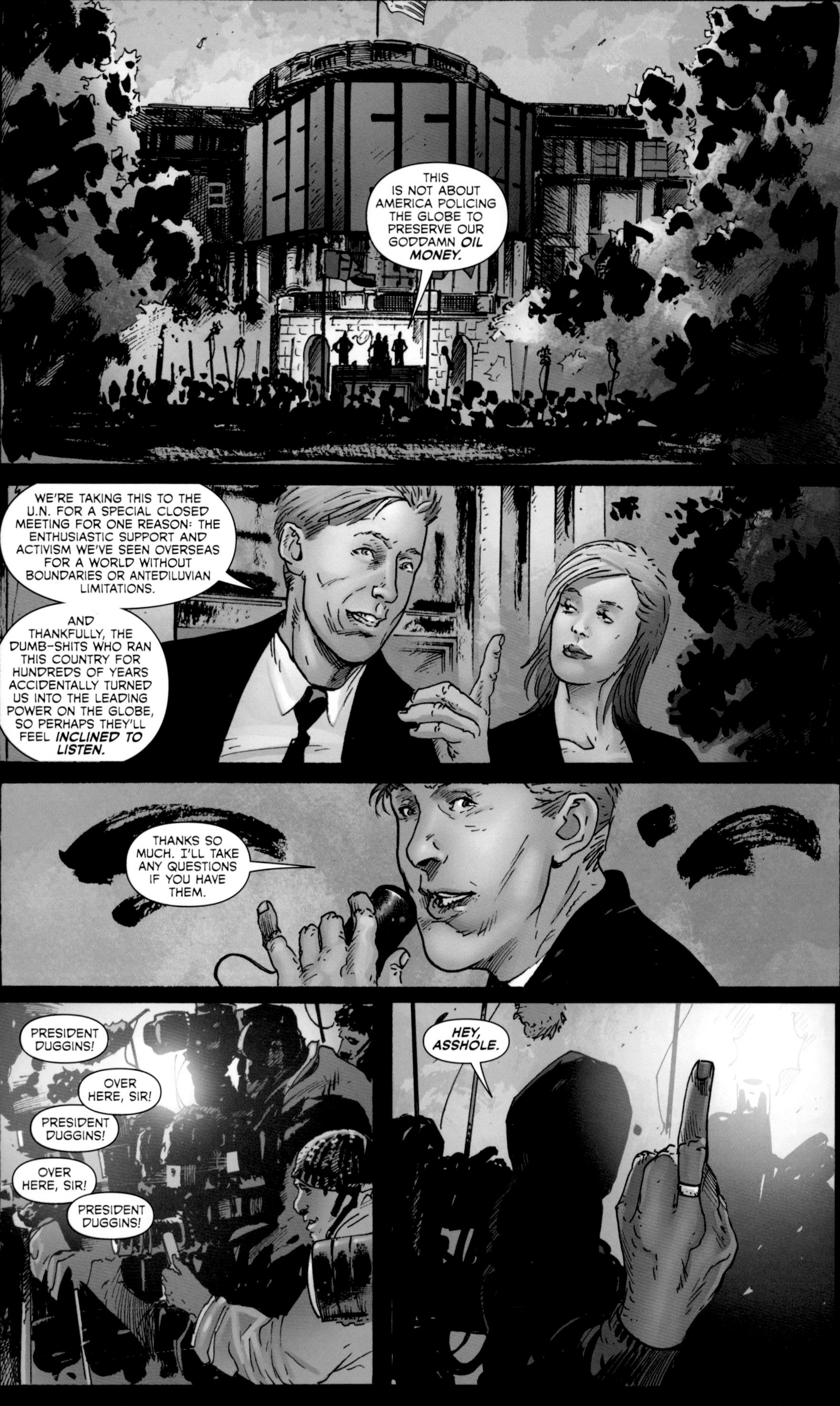
THIS IS NOT ABOUT AMERICA POLICING THE GLOBE TO PRESERVE OUR GODDAMN *OIL MONEY.*
WE'RE TAKING THIS TO THE U.N. FOR A SPECIAL CLOSED MEETING FOR ONE REASON: THE ENTHUSIASTIC SUPPORT AND ACTIVISM WE'VE SEEN OVERSEAS FOR A WORLD WITHOUT BOUNDARIES OR ANTEDILUVIAN LIMITATIONS.
AND THANKFULLY, THE DUMB-SHITS WHO RAN THIS COUNTRY FOR HUNDREDS OF YEARS ACCIDENTALLY TURNED US INTO THE LEADING POWER ON THE GLOBE, SO PERHAPS THEY'LL FEEL *INCLINED TO LISTEN.*
THANKS SO MUCH. I'LL TAKE ANY QUESTIONS IF YOU HAVE THEM.
PRESIDENT DUGGINS!
OVER HERE, SIR!
PRESIDENT DUGGINS!
OVER HERE, SIR!
PRESIDENT DUGGINS!
HEY, ASSHOLE.

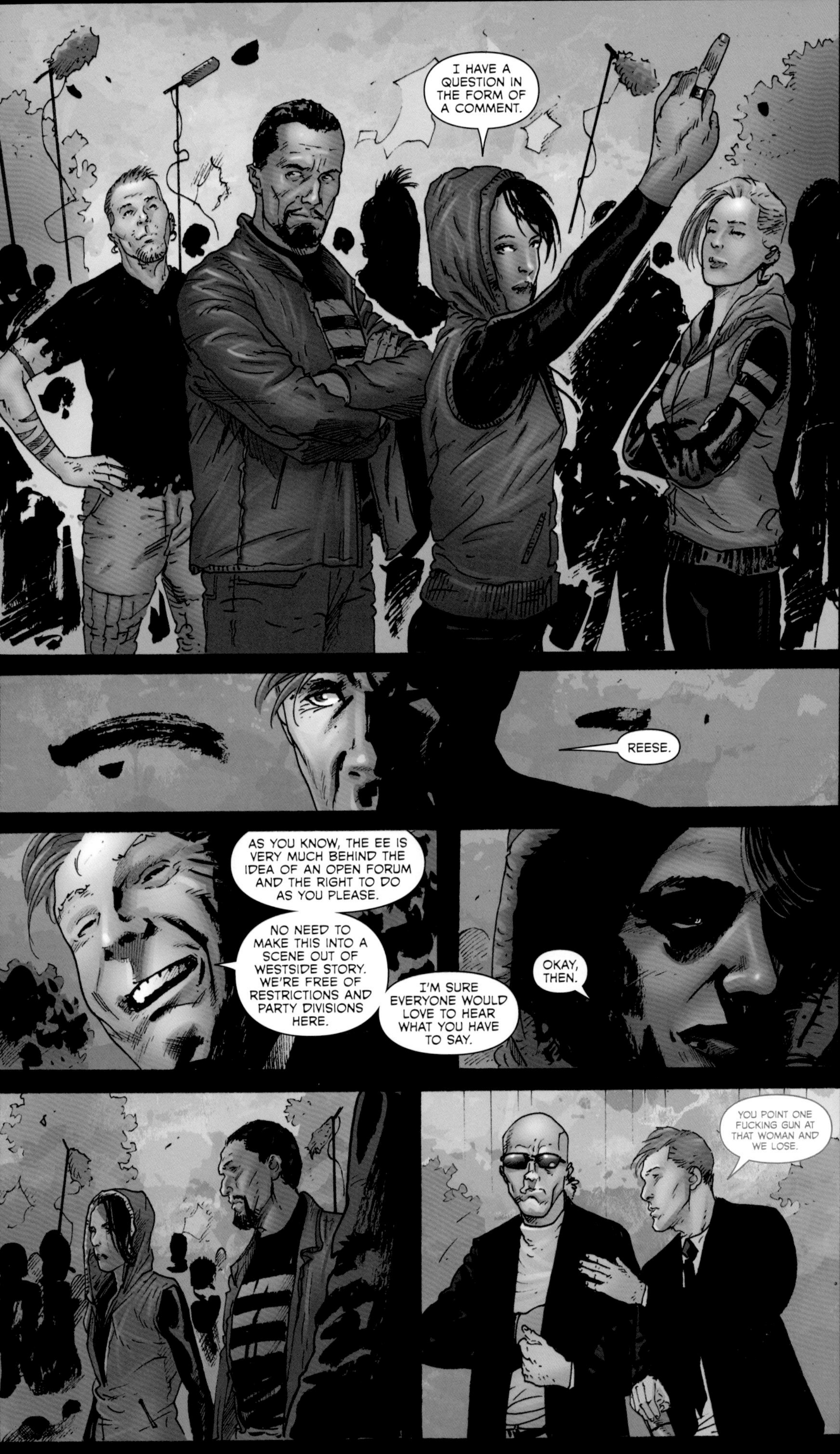
I HAVE A QUESTION IN THE FORM OF A COMMENT.
REESE.
AS YOU KNOW, THE EE IS VERY MUCH BEHIND THE IDEA OF AN OPEN FORUM AND THE RIGHT TO DO AS YOU PLEASE.
NO NEED TO MAKE THIS INTO A SCENE OUT OF WESTSIDE STORY. WE'RE FREE OF RESTRICTIONS AND PARTY DIVISIONS HERE.
I'M SURE EVERYONE WOULD LOVE TO HEAR WHAT YOU HAVE TO SAY.
OKAY, THEN.
YOU POINT ONE FUCKING GUN AT THAT WOMAN AND WE LOSE.

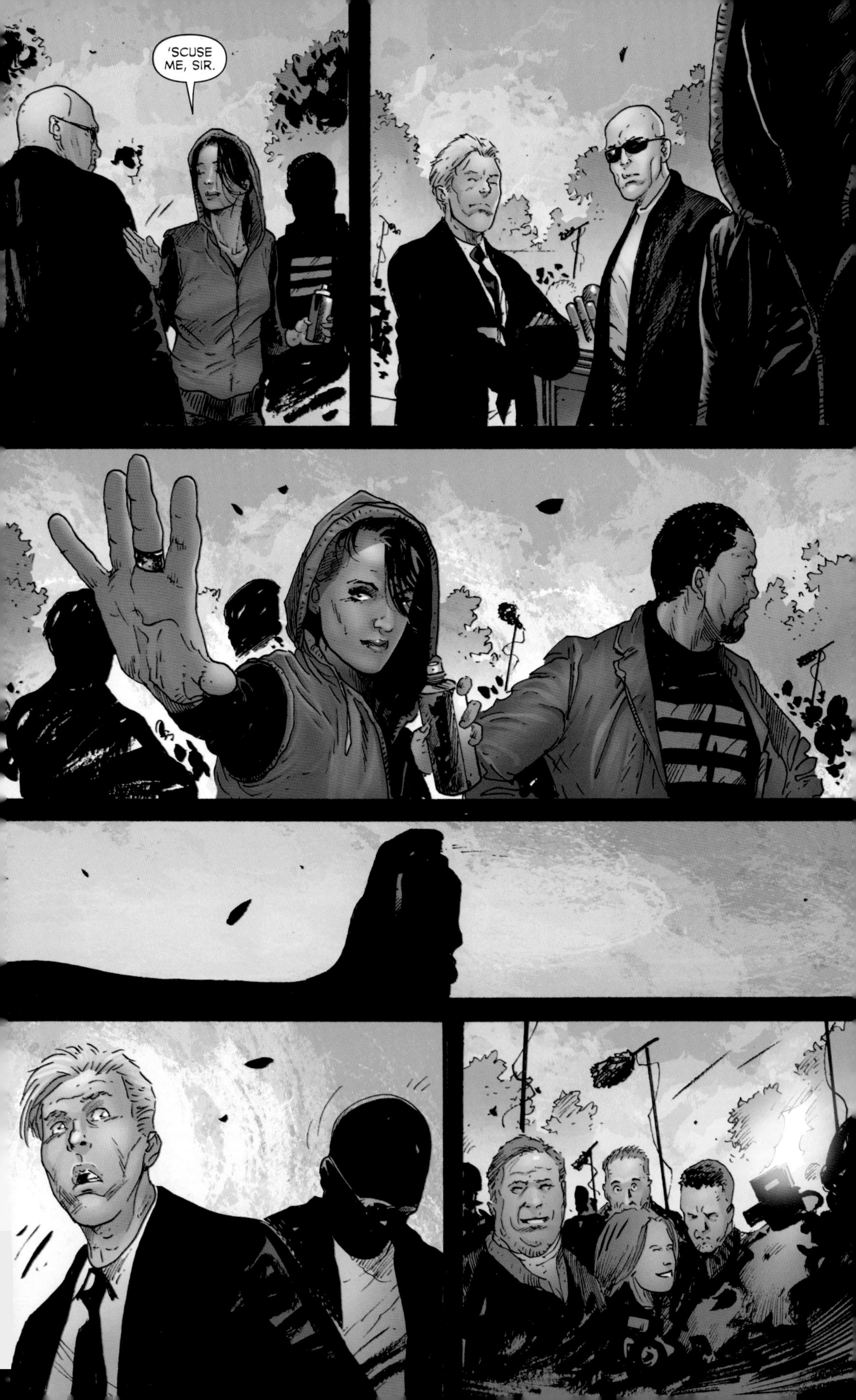
'SCUSE ME, SIR.

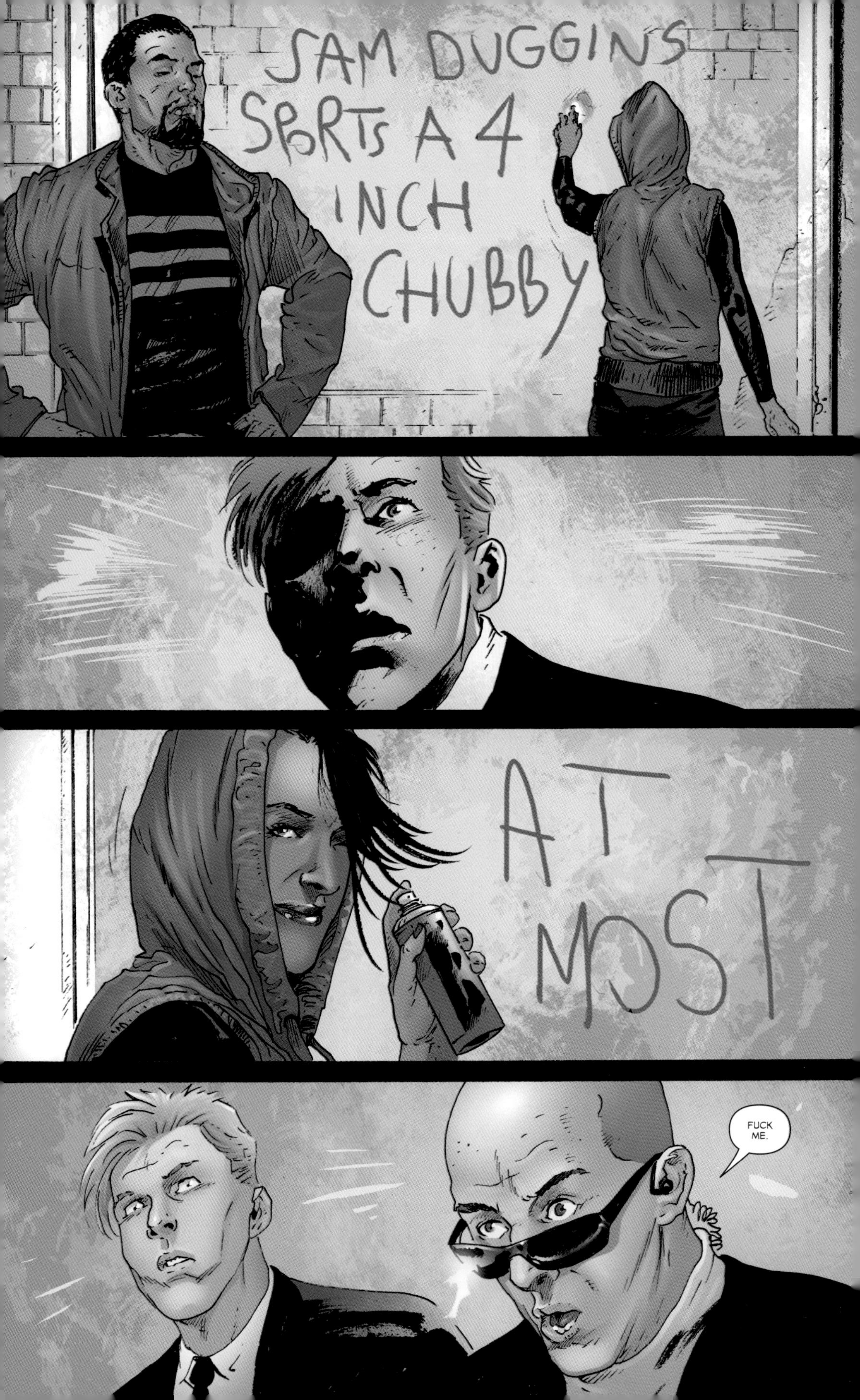
SAM DUGGINS SPORTS A 4 INCH CHUBBY
AT MOST
FUCK ME.

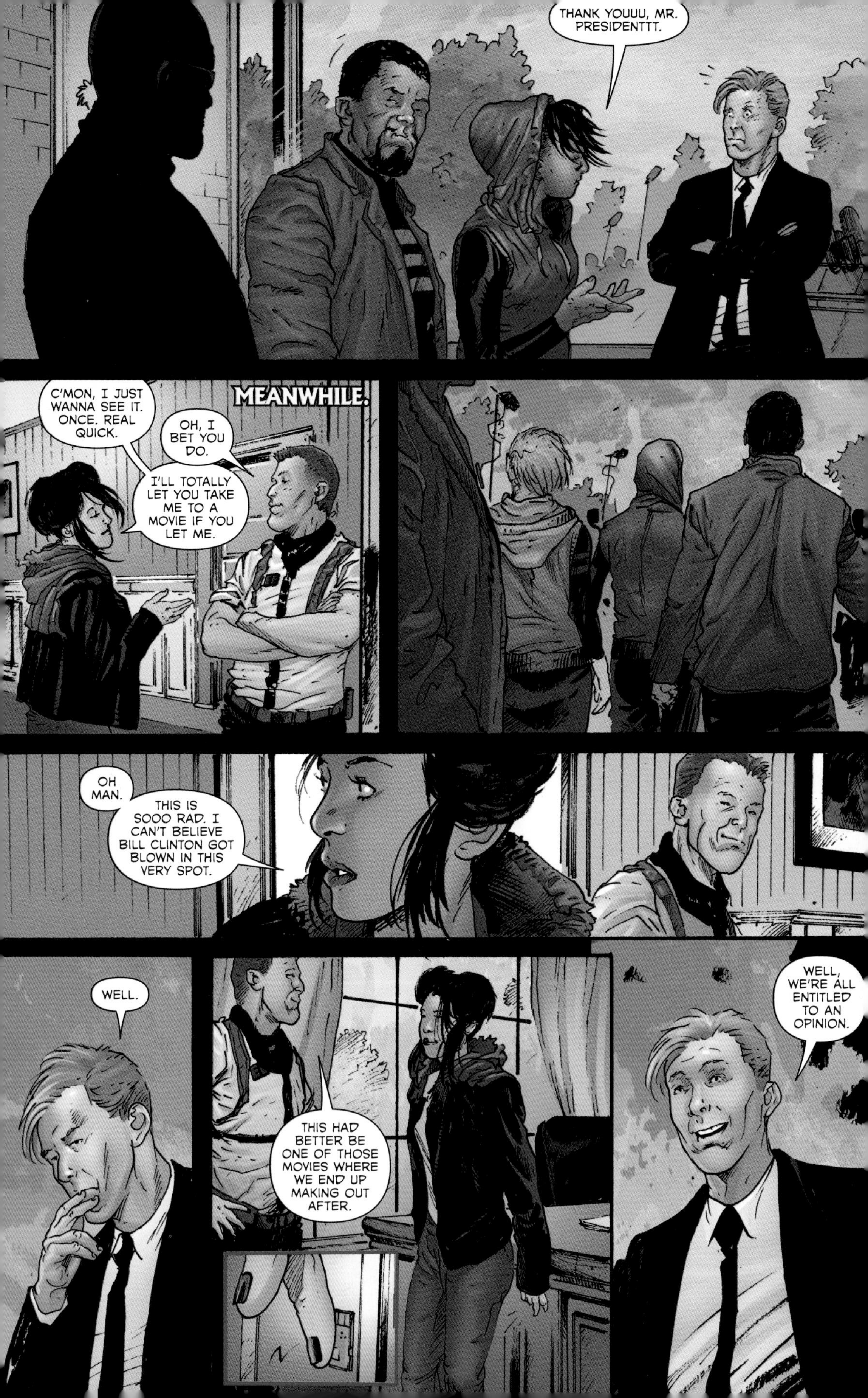
THANK YOUUU, MR. PRESIDENTTT.
MEANWHILE.
C'MON, I JUST WANNA SEE IT. ONCE. REAL QUICK.
OH, I BET YOU DO.
I'LL TOTALLY LET YOU TAKE ME TO A MOVIE IF YOU LET ME.
OH MAN.
THIS IS SOOO RAD. I CAN'T BELIEVE BILL CLINTON GOT BLOWN IN THIS VERY SPOT.
WELL.
THIS HAD BETTER BE ONE OF THOSE MOVIES WHERE WE END UP MAKING OUT AFTER.
WELL, WE'RE ALL ENTITLED TO AN OPINION.

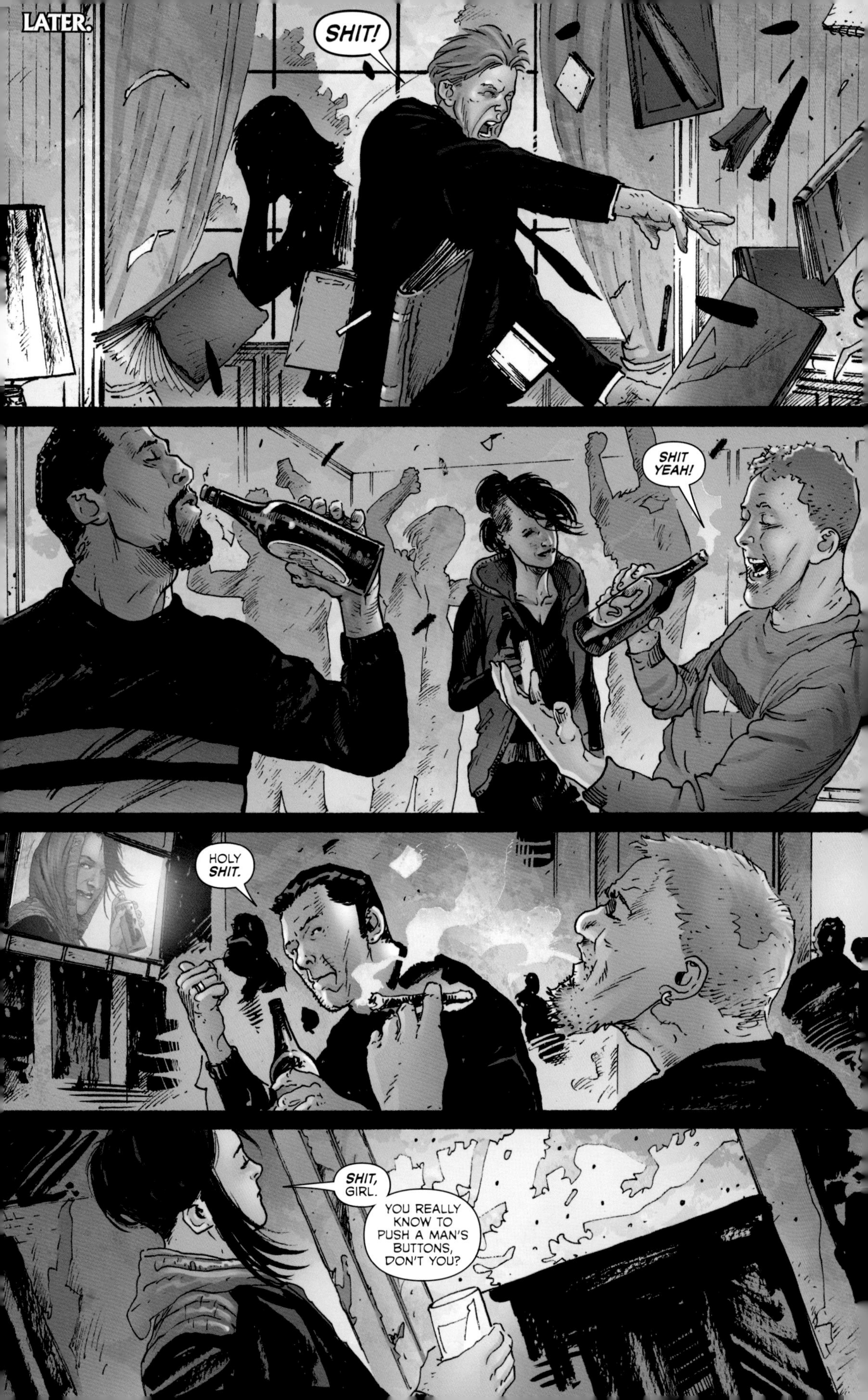
LATER.
SHIT!
SHIT YEAH!
HOLY SHIT.
SHIT, GIRL.
YOU REALLY KNOW TO PUSH A MAN'S BUTTONS, DON'T YOU?

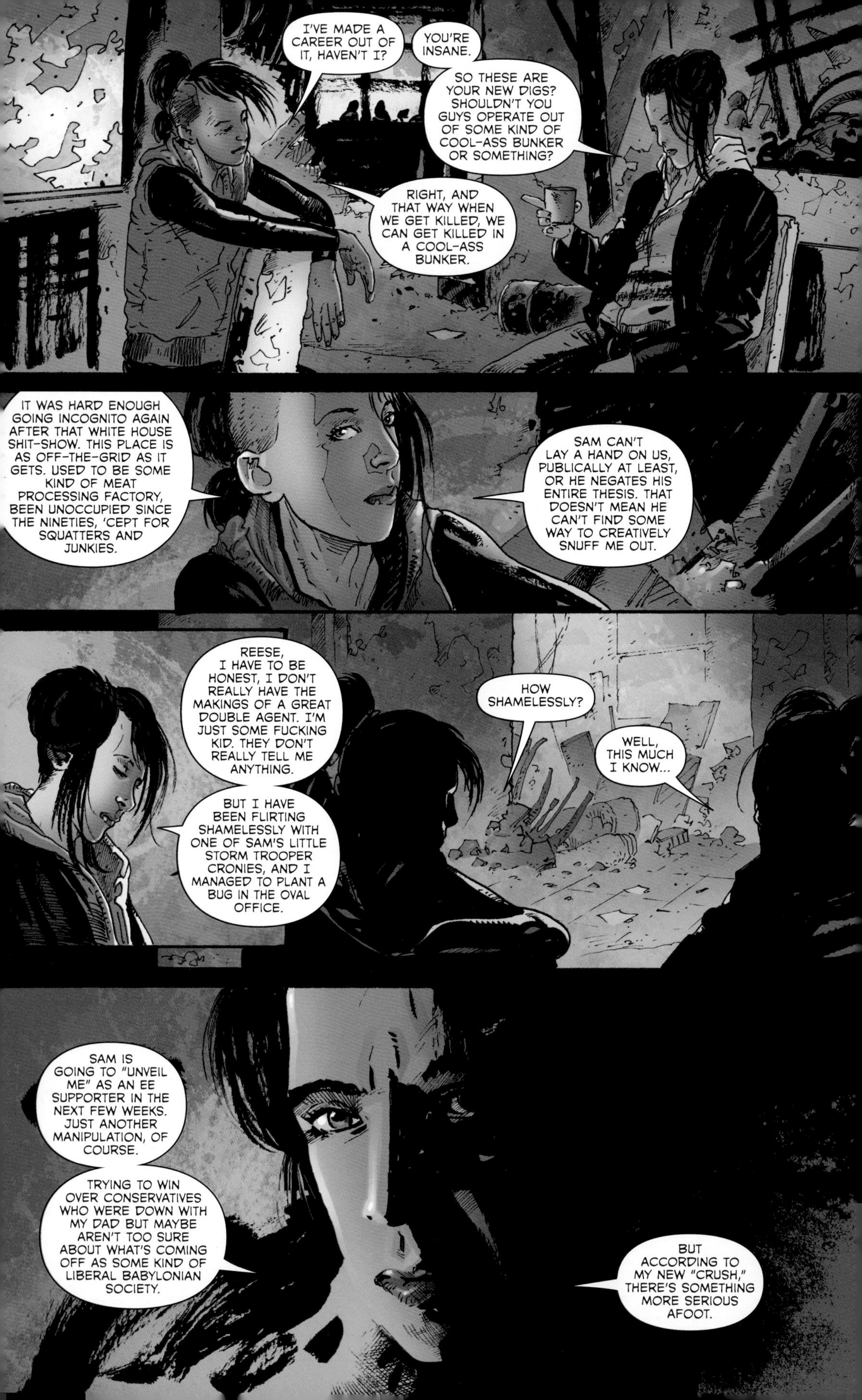
I'VE MADE A CAREER OUT OF IT, HAVEN'T I?
YOU'RE INSANE.
SO THESE ARE YOUR NEW DIGS? SHOULDN'T YOU GUYS OPERATE OUT OF SOME KIND OF COOL-ASS BUNKER OR SOMETHING?
RIGHT, AND THAT WAY WHEN WE GET KILLED, WE CAN GET KILLED IN A COOL-ASS BUNKER.
IT WAS HARD ENOUGH GOING INCOGNITO AGAIN AFTER THAT WHITE HOUSE SHIT-SHOW. THIS PLACE IS AS OFF-THE-GRID AS IT GETS. USED TO BE SOME KIND OF MEAT PROCESSING FACTORY, BEEN UNOCCUPIED SINCE THE NINETIES, 'CEPT FOR SQUATTERS AND JUNKIES.
SAM CAN'T LAY A HAND ON US, PUBLICALLY AT LEAST, OR HE NEGATES HIS ENTIRE THESIS. THAT DOESN'T MEAN HE CAN'T FIND SOME WAY TO CREATIVELY SNUFF ME OUT.
REESE, I HAVE TO BE HONEST, I DON'T REALLY HAVE THE MAKINGS OF A GREAT DOUBLE AGENT. I'M JUST SOME FUCKING KID. THEY DON'T REALLY TELL ME ANYTHING.
BUT I HAVE BEEN FLIRTING SHAMELESSLY WITH ONE OF SAM'S LITTLE STORM TROOPER CRONIES, AND I MANAGED TO PLANT A BUG IN THE OVAL OFFICE.
HOW SHAMELESSLY?
WELL, THIS MUCH I KNOW...
SAM IS GOING TO "UNVEIL ME" AS AN EE SUPPORTER IN THE NEXT FEW WEEKS. JUST ANOTHER MANIPULATION, OF COURSE.
TRYING TO WIN OVER CONSERVATIVES WHO WERE DOWN WITH MY DAD BUT MAYBE AREN'T TOO SURE ABOUT WHAT'S COMING OFF AS SOME KIND OF LIBERAL BABYLONIAN SOCIETY.
BUT ACCORDING TO MY NEW "CRUSH," THERE'S SOMETHING MORE SERIOUS AFOOT.

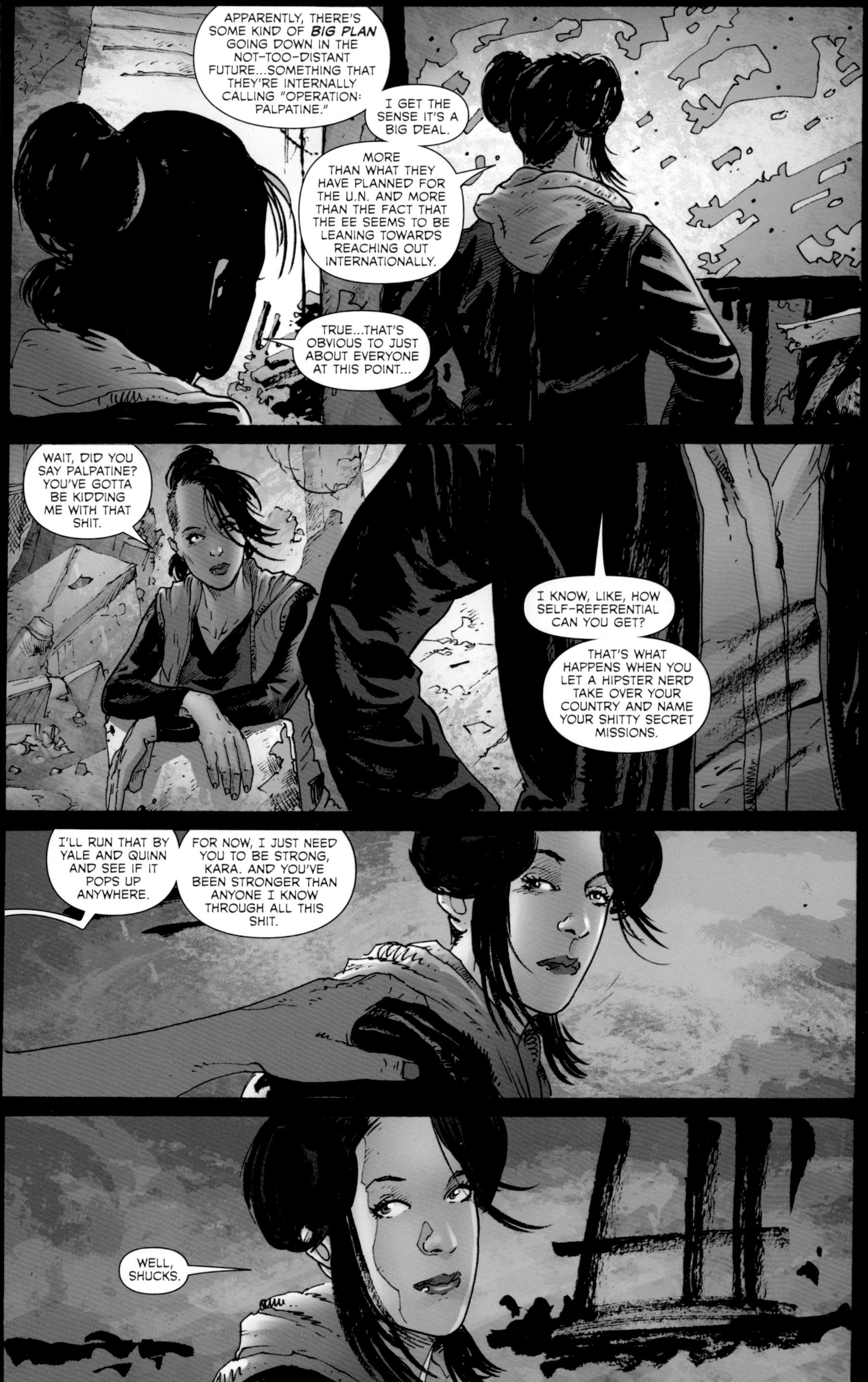
APPARENTLY, THERE'S SOME KIND OF BIG PLAN GOING DOWN IN THE NOT-TOO-DISTANT FUTURE...SOMETHING THAT THEY'RE INTERNALLY CALLING "OPERATION: PALPATINE."
I GET THE SENSE IT'S A BIG DEAL.
MORE THAN WHAT THEY HAVE PLANNED FOR THE U.N. AND MORE THAN THE FACT THAT THE EE SEEMS TO BE LEANING TOWARDS REACHING OUT INTERNATIONALLY.
TRUE...THAT'S OBVIOUS TO JUST ABOUT EVERYONE AT THIS POINT...
WAIT, DID YOU SAY PALPATINE? YOU'VE GOTTA BE KIDDING ME WITH THAT SHIT.
I KNOW, LIKE, HOW SELF-REFERENTIAL CAN YOU GET?
THAT'S WHAT HAPPENS WHEN YOU LET A HIPSTER NERD TAKE OVER YOUR COUNTRY AND NAME YOUR SHITTY SECRET MISSIONS.
I'LL RUN THAT BY YALE AND QUINN AND SEE IF IT POPS UP ANYWHERE.
FOR NOW, I JUST NEED YOU TO BE STRONG, KARA. AND YOU'VE BEEN STRONGER THAN ANYONE I KNOW THROUGH ALL THIS SHIT.
WELL, SHUCKS.

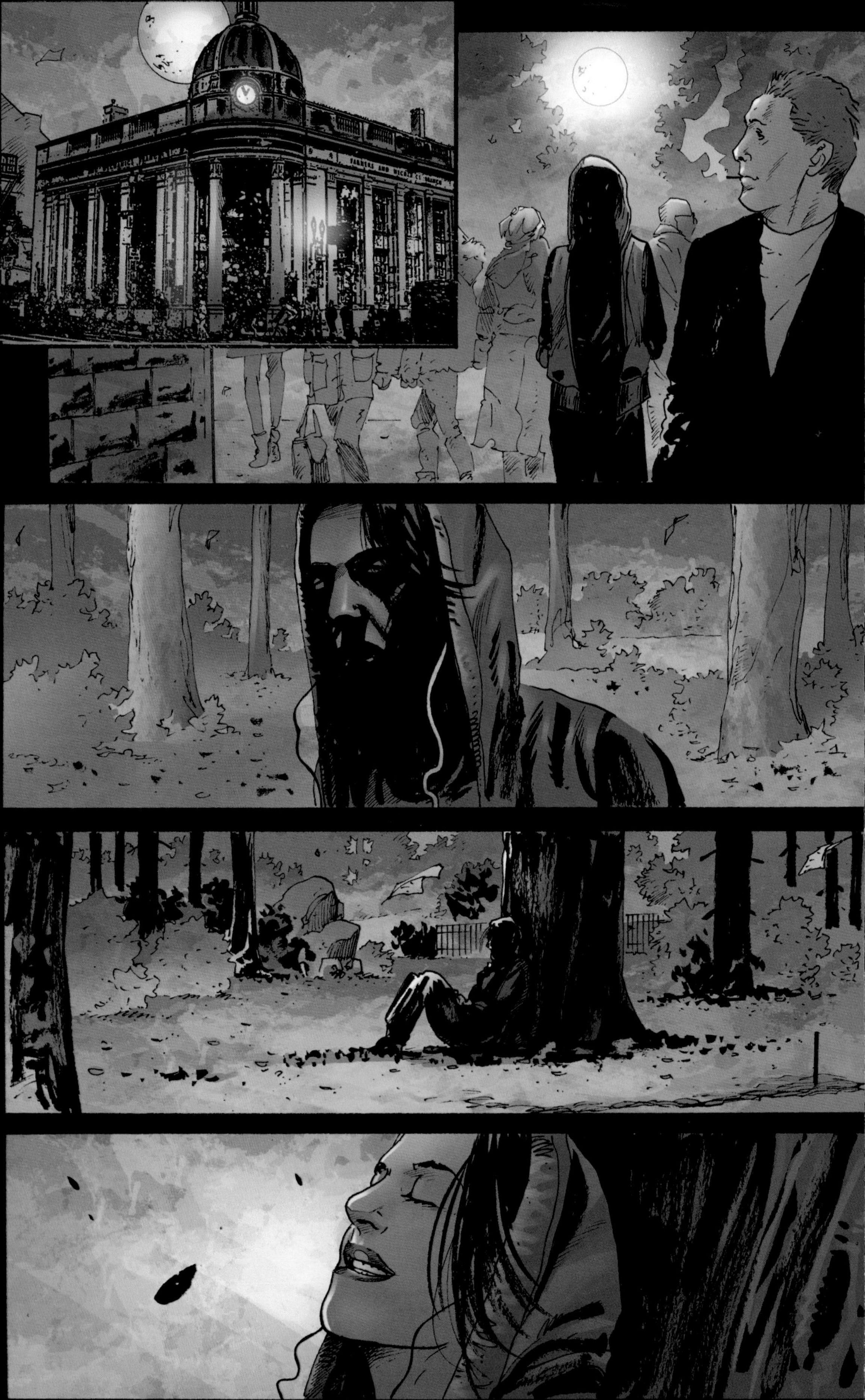

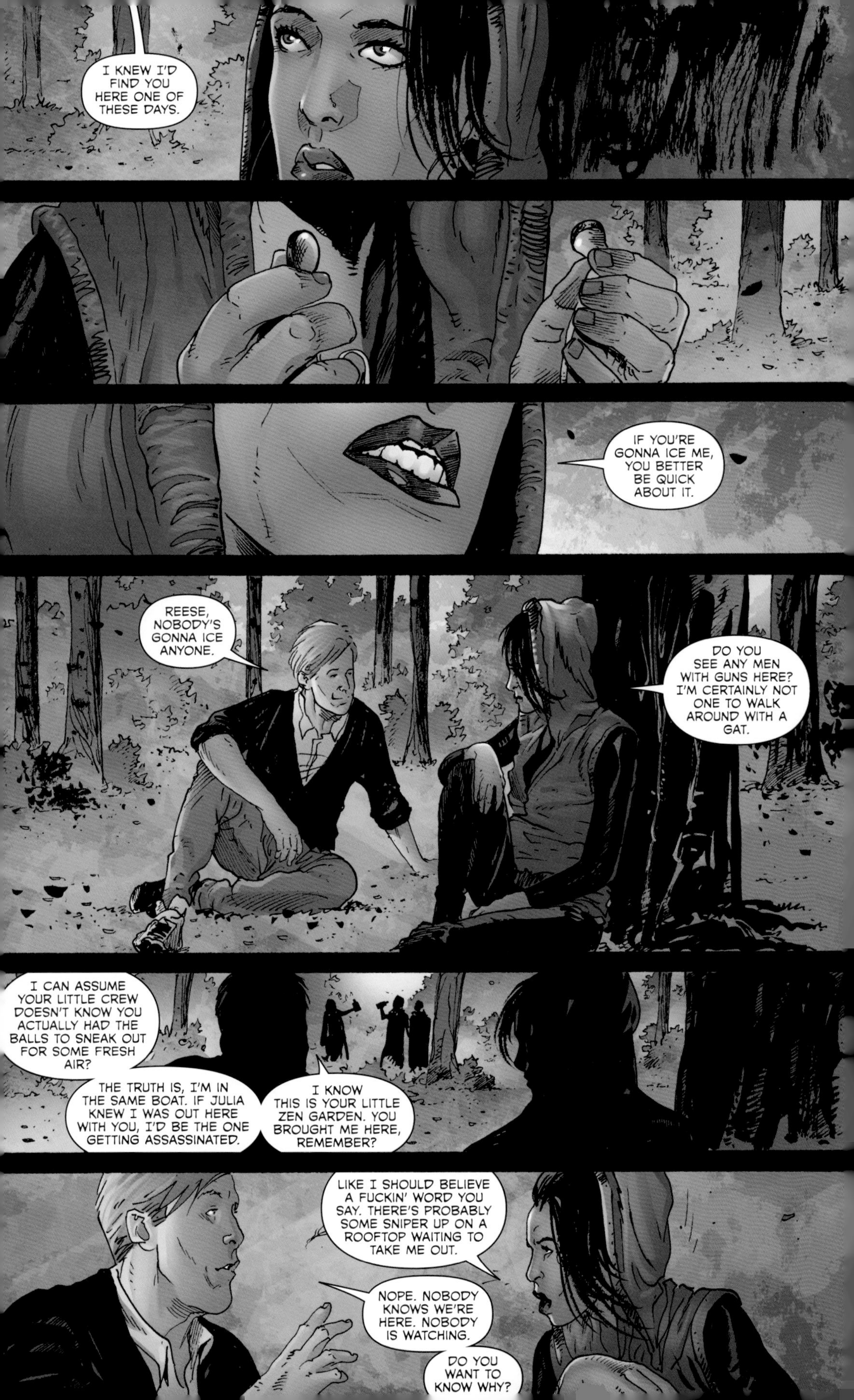
I KNEW I'D FIND YOU HERE ONE OF THESE DAYS.
IF YOU'RE GONNA ICE ME, YOU BETTER BE QUICK ABOUT IT.
REESE, NOBODY'S GONNA ICE ANYONE.
DO YOU SEE ANY MEN WITH GUNS HERE? I'M CERTAINLY NOT ONE TO WALK AROUND WITH A GAT.
I CAN ASSUME YOUR LITTLE CREW DOESN'T KNOW YOU ACTUALLY HAD THE BALLS TO SNEAK OUT FOR SOME FRESH AIR?
THE TRUTH IS, I'M IN THE SAME BOAT. IF JULIA KNEW I WAS OUT HERE WITH YOU, I'D BE THE ONE GETTING ASSASSINATED.
I KNOW THIS IS YOUR LITTLE ZEN GARDEN. YOU BROUGHT ME HERE, REMEMBER?
LIKE I SHOULD BELIEVE A FUCKIN' WORD YOU SAY. THERE'S PROBABLY SOME SNIPER UP ON A ROOFTOP WAITING TO TAKE ME OUT.
NOPE. NOBODY KNOWS WE'RE HERE. NOBODY IS WATCHING.
DO YOU WANT TO KNOW WHY?

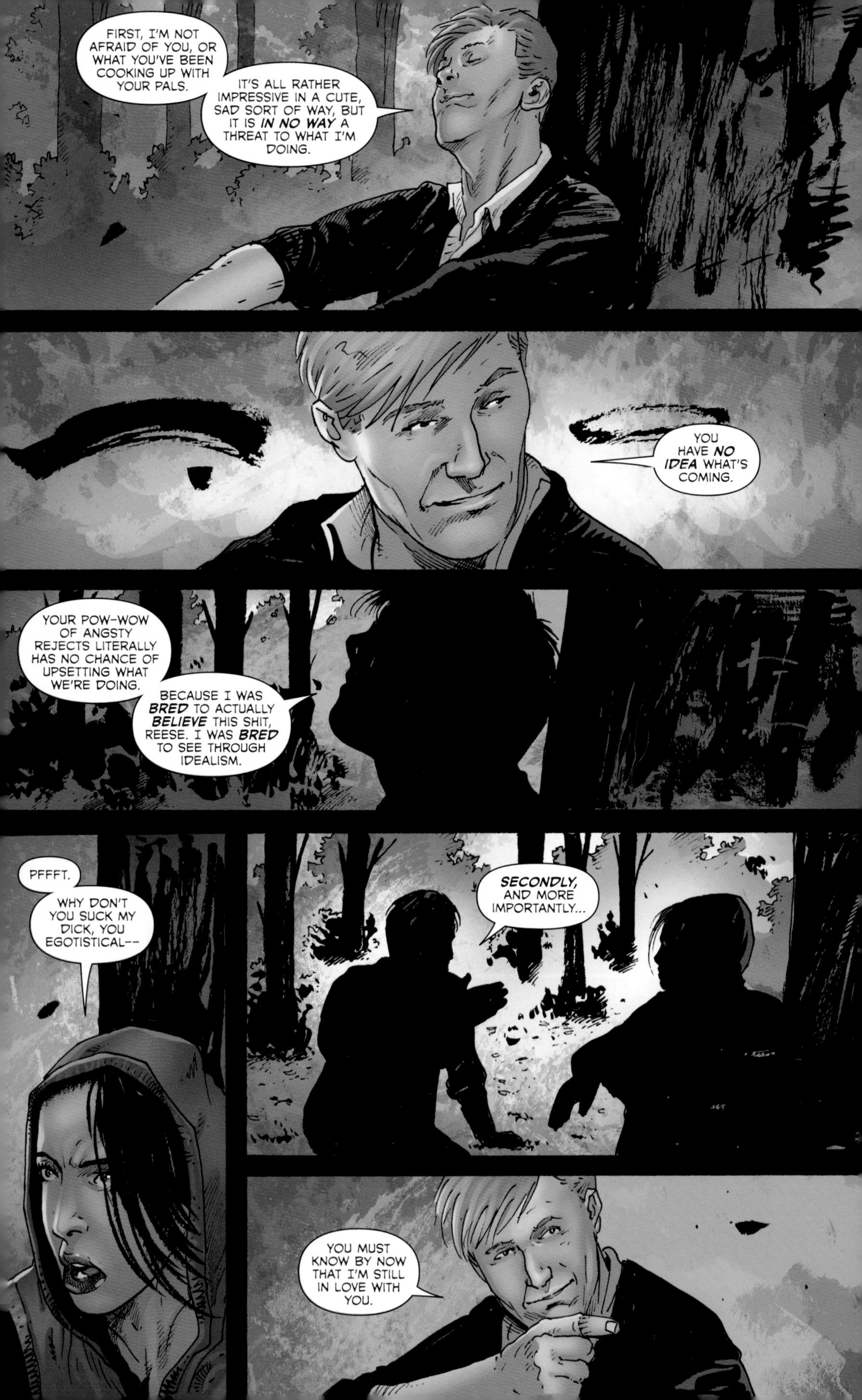
FIRST, I'M NOT AFRAID OF YOU, OR WHAT YOU'VE BEEN COOKING UP WITH YOUR PALS.
IT'S ALL RATHER IMPRESSIVE IN A CUTE, SAD SORT OF WAY, BUT IT IS *IN NO WAY* A THREAT TO WHAT I'M DOING.
YOU HAVE *NO IDEA* WHAT'S COMING.
YOUR POW-WOW OF ANGSTY REJECTS LITERALLY HAS NO CHANCE OF UPSETTING WHAT WE'RE DOING.
BECAUSE I WAS *BRED* TO ACTUALLY *BELIEVE* THIS SHIT, REESE. I WAS *BRED* TO SEE THROUGH IDEALISM.
PFFFT.
WHY DON'T YOU SUCK MY DICK, YOU EGOTISTICAL--
SECONDLY, AND MORE IMPORTANTLY...
YOU MUST KNOW BY NOW THAT I'M STILL IN LOVE WITH YOU.

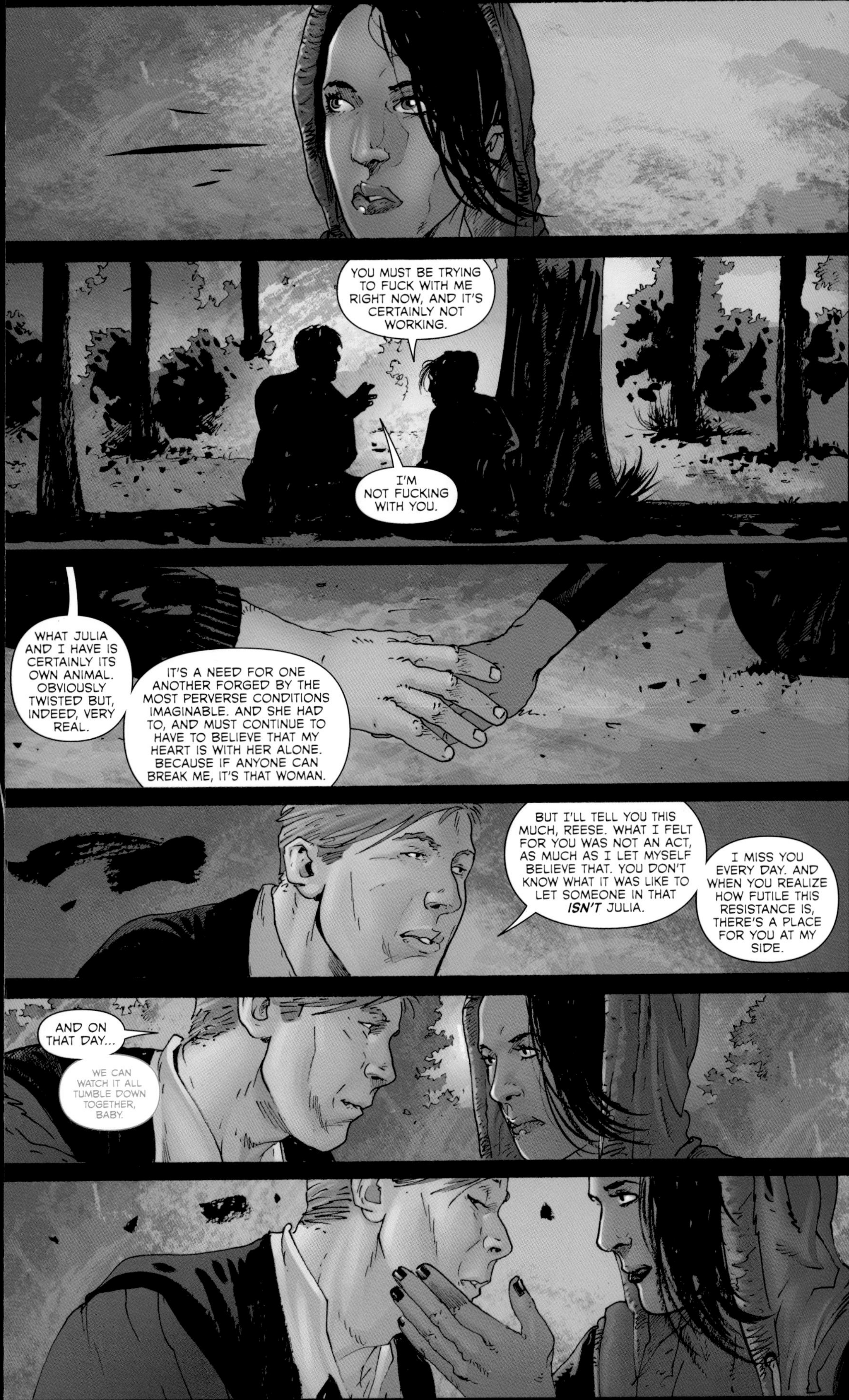
YOU MUST BE TRYING TO FUCK WITH ME RIGHT NOW, AND IT'S CERTAINLY NOT WORKING.
I'M NOT FUCKING WITH YOU.
WHAT JULIA AND I HAVE IS CERTAINLY ITS OWN ANIMAL. OBVIOUSLY TWISTED BUT, INDEED, VERY REAL.
IT'S A NEED FOR ONE ANOTHER FORGED BY THE MOST PERVERSE CONDITIONS IMAGINABLE. AND SHE HAD TO, AND MUST CONTINUE TO HAVE TO BELIEVE THAT MY HEART IS WITH HER ALONE. BECAUSE IF ANYONE CAN BREAK ME, IT'S THAT WOMAN.
BUT I'LL TELL YOU THIS MUCH, REESE. WHAT I FELT FOR YOU WAS NOT AN ACT, AS MUCH AS I LET MYSELF BELIEVE THAT. YOU DON'T KNOW WHAT IT WAS LIKE TO LET SOMEONE IN THAT *ISN'T* JULIA.
I MISS YOU EVERY DAY. AND WHEN YOU REALIZE HOW FUTILE THIS RESISTANCE IS, THERE'S A PLACE FOR YOU AT MY SIDE.
AND ON THAT DAY...
WE CAN WATCH IT ALL TUMBLE DOWN TOGETHER, BABY.

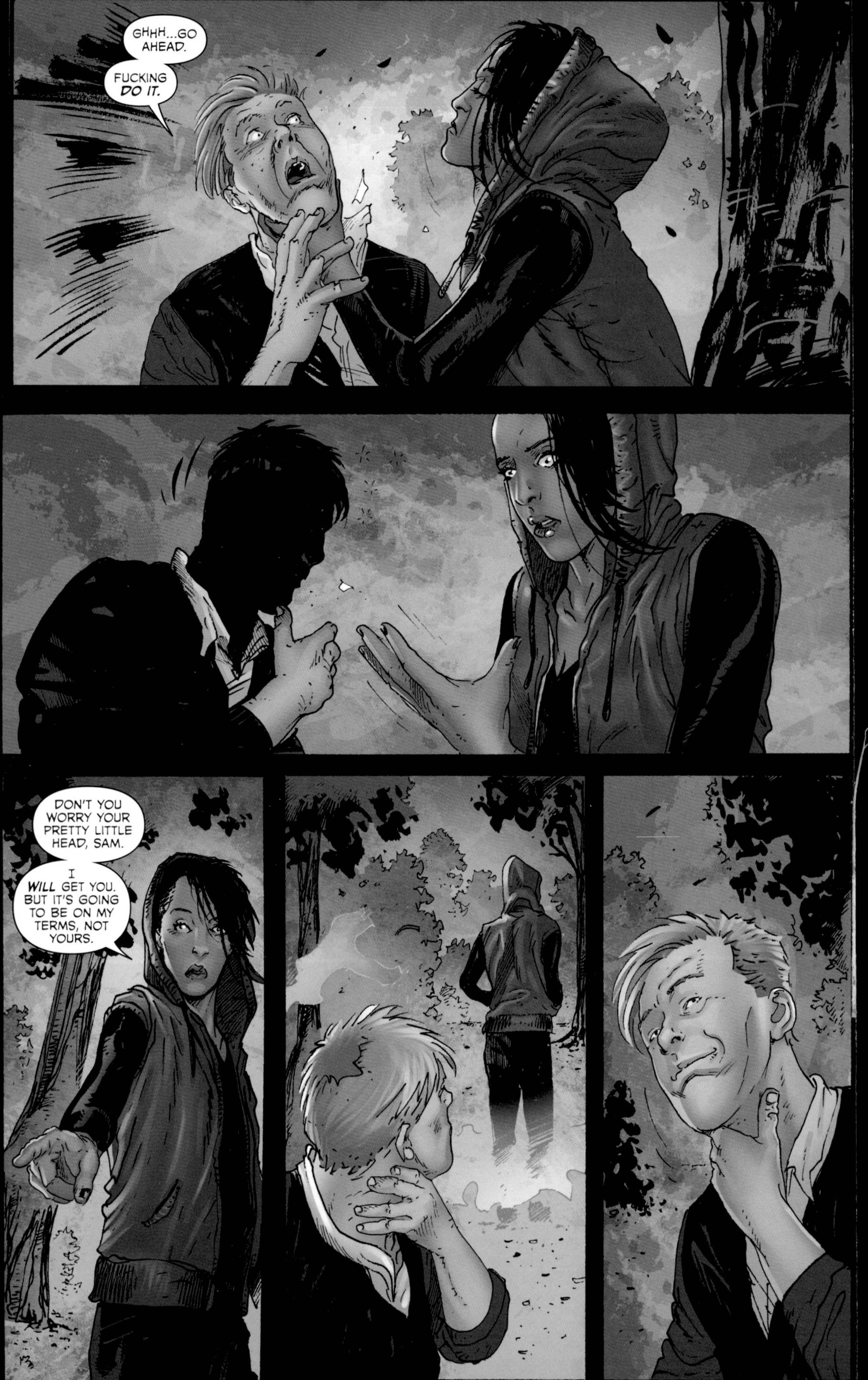
GHHH...GO AHEAD.
FUCKING *DO IT.*
DON'T YOU WORRY YOUR PRETTY LITTLE HEAD, SAM.
I *WILL* GET YOU. BUT IT'S GOING TO BE ON MY TERMS, NOT YOURS.

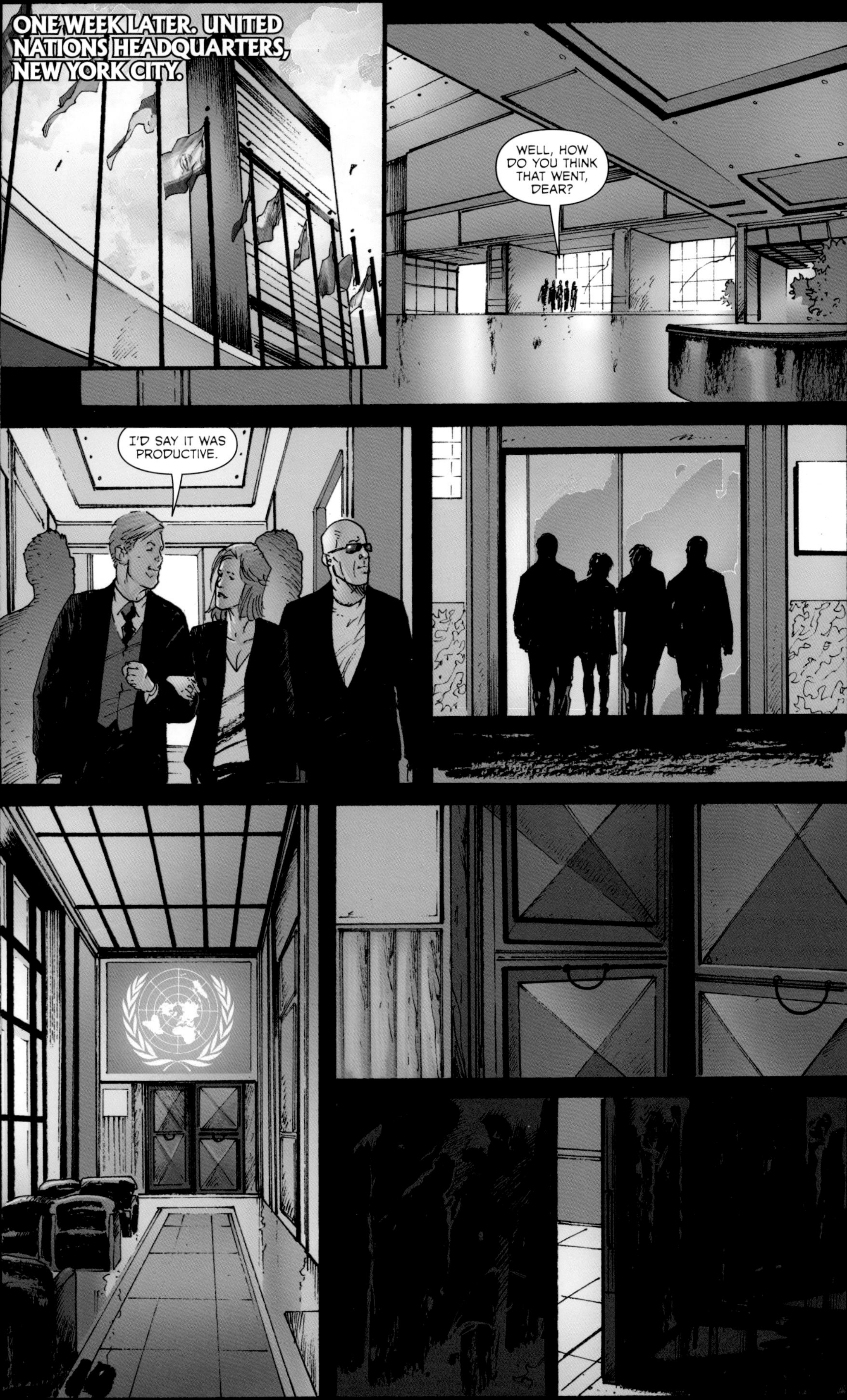
ONE WEEK LATER. UNITED NATIONS HEADQUARTERS, NEW YORK CITY.
WELL, HOW DO YOU THINK THAT WENT, DEAR?
I'D SAY IT WAS PRODUCTIVE.

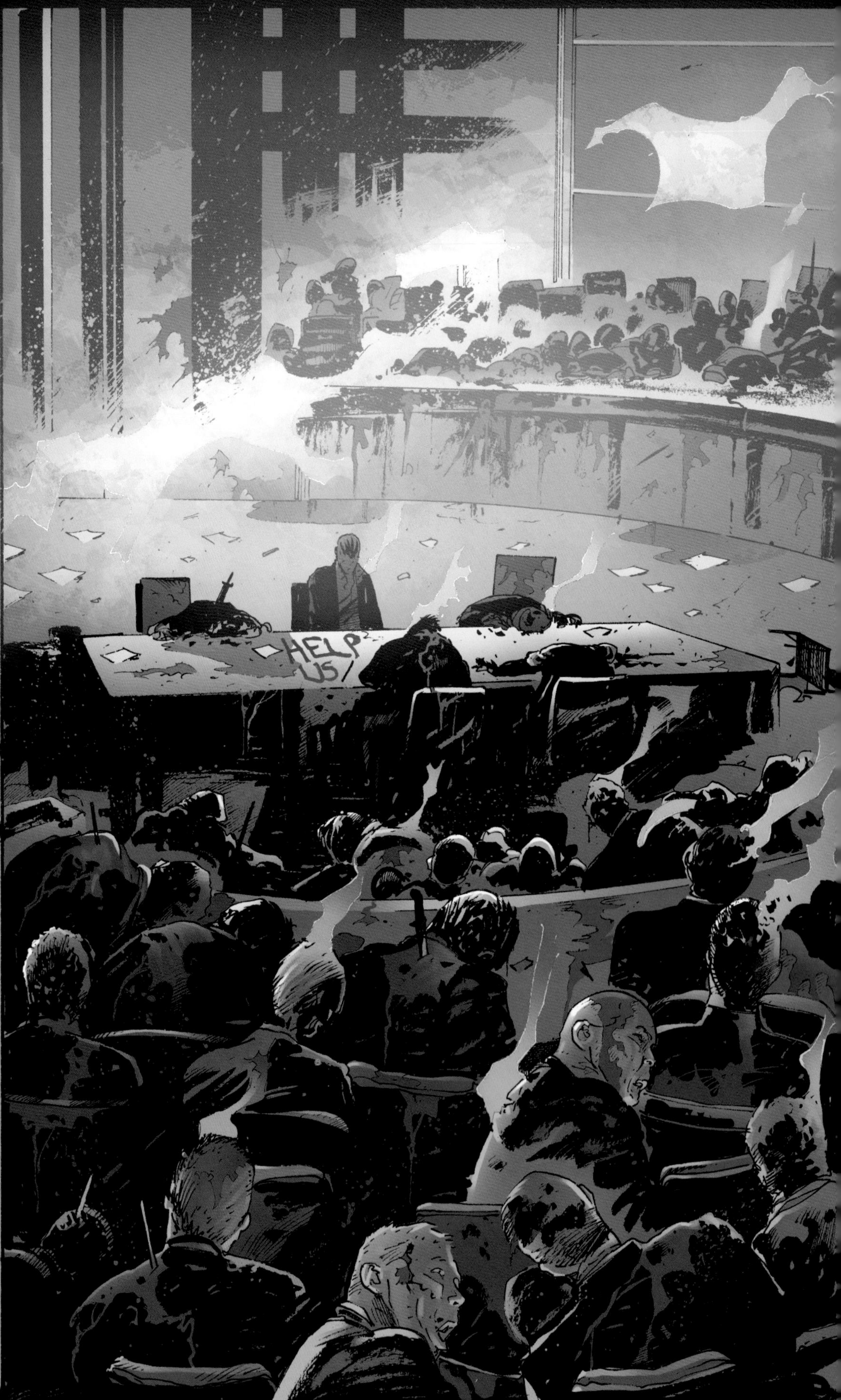
HELP US!

There are those who would oppose you, and we have righteousness on our side.
*Time is ticking down to a moment where you'll have to **fight back** or **pay the piper.***

exc. 4.0

CHAPTER
EIGHT

fig. 4

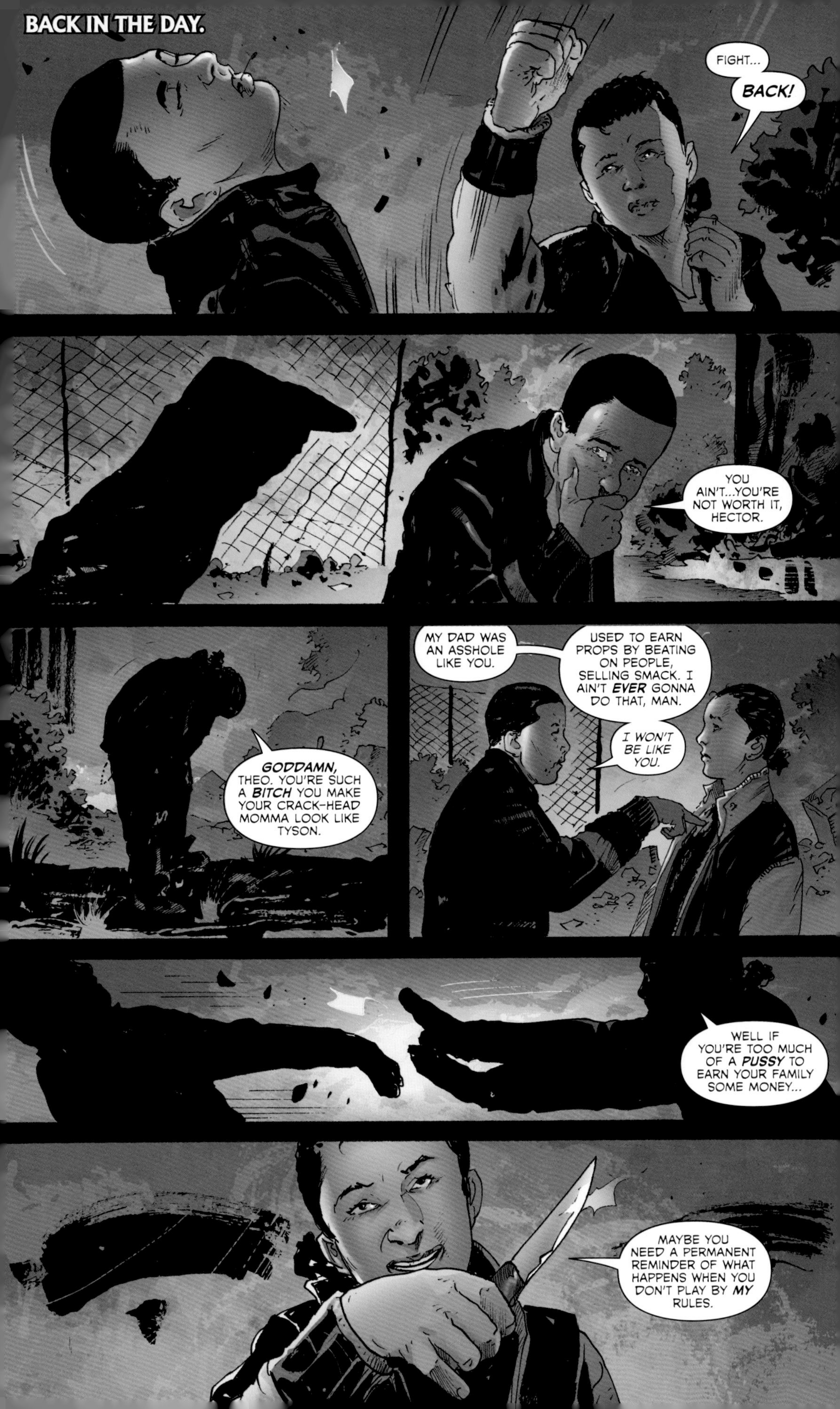
BACK IN THE DAY.
FIGHT... BACK!
YOU AIN'T...YOU'RE NOT WORTH IT, HECTOR.
GODDAMN, THEO. YOU'RE SUCH A BITCH YOU MAKE YOUR CRACK-HEAD MOMMA LOOK LIKE TYSON.
MY DAD WAS AN ASSHOLE LIKE YOU.
USED TO EARN PROPS BY BEATING ON PEOPLE, SELLING SMACK. I AIN'T EVER GONNA DO THAT, MAN.
I WON'T BE LIKE YOU.
WELL IF YOU'RE TOO MUCH OF A PUSSY TO EARN YOUR FAMILY SOME MONEY...
MAYBE YOU NEED A PERMANENT REMINDER OF WHAT HAPPENS WHEN YOU DON'T PLAY BY MY RULES.

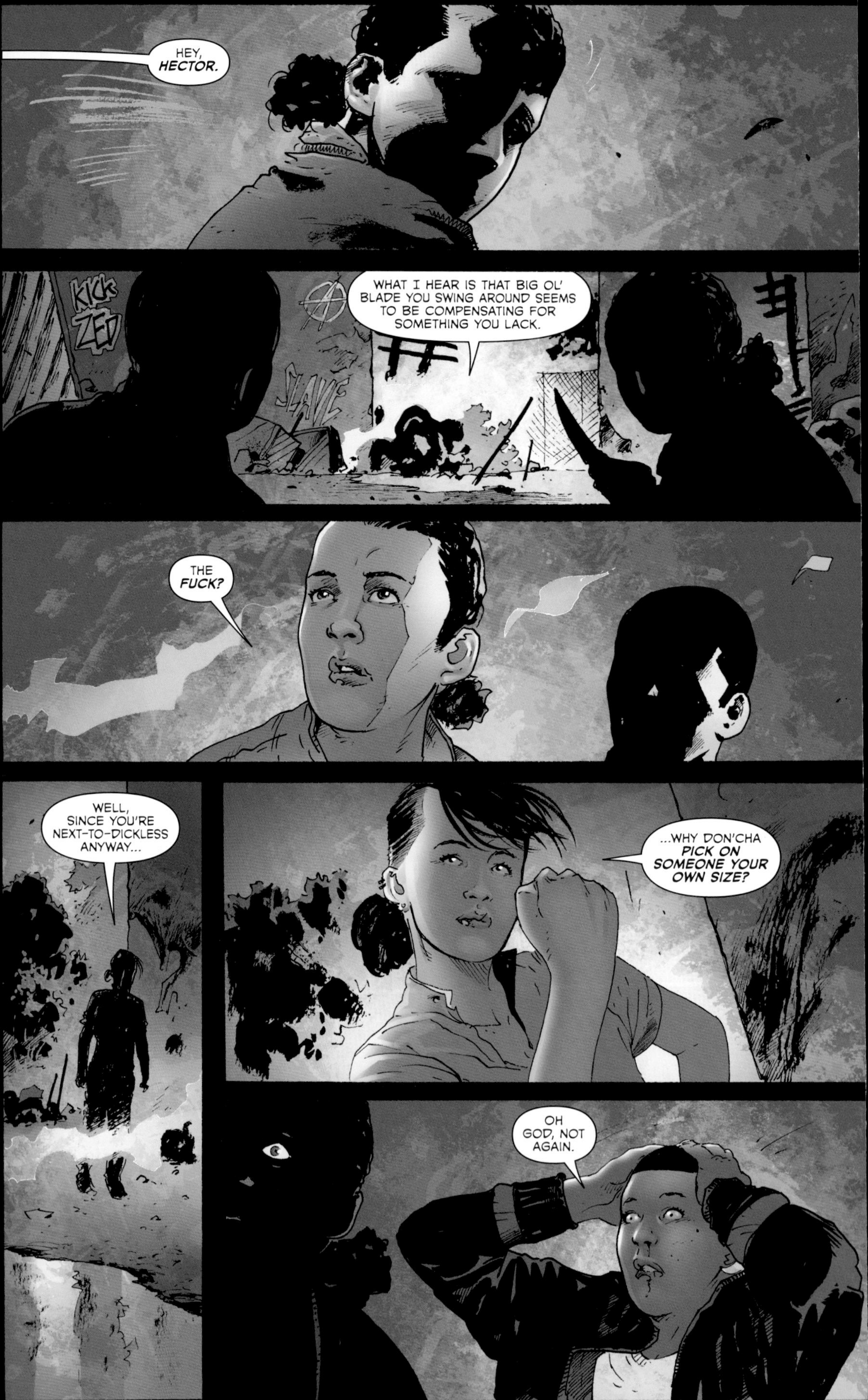
HEY, HECTOR.
KICK ZED
SLAVE
WHAT I HEAR IS THAT BIG OL' BLADE YOU SWING AROUND SEEMS TO BE COMPENSATING FOR SOMETHING YOU LACK.
THE FUCK?
WELL, SINCE YOU'RE NEXT-TO-DICKLESS ANYWAY...
...WHY DON'CHA PICK ON SOMEONE YOUR OWN SIZE?
OH GOD, NOT AGAIN.

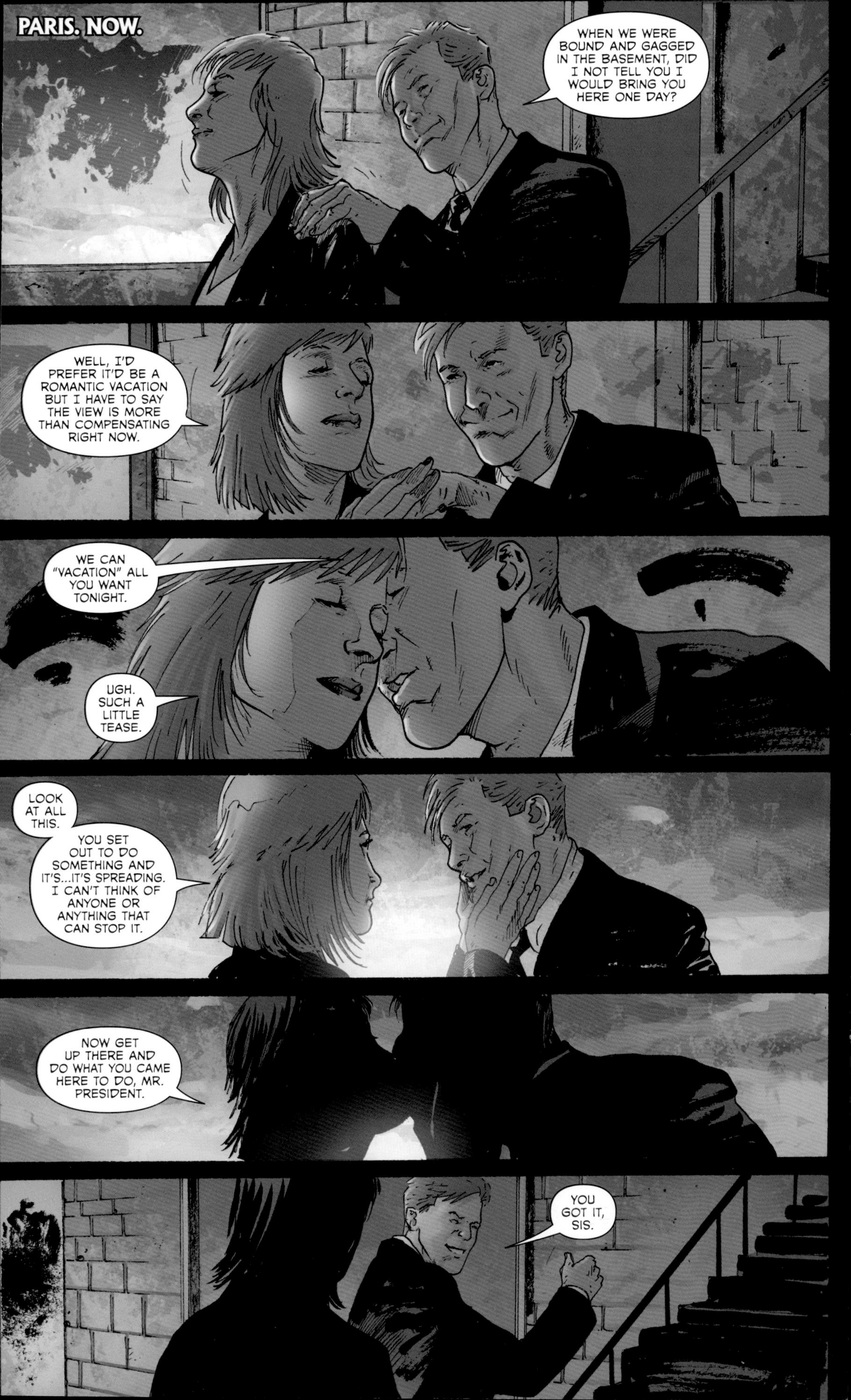
PARIS. NOW.
WHEN WE WERE BOUND AND GAGGED IN THE BASEMENT, DID I NOT TELL YOU I WOULD BRING YOU HERE ONE DAY?
WELL, I'D PREFER IT'D BE A ROMANTIC VACATION BUT I HAVE TO SAY THE VIEW IS MORE THAN COMPENSATING RIGHT NOW.
WE CAN "VACATION" ALL YOU WANT TONIGHT.
UGH. SUCH A LITTLE TEASE.
LOOK AT ALL THIS.
YOU SET OUT TO DO SOMETHING AND IT'S...IT'S SPREADING. I CAN'T THINK OF ANYONE OR ANYTHING THAT CAN STOP IT.
NOW GET UP THERE AND DO WHAT YOU CAME HERE TO DO, MR. PRESIDENT.
YOU GOT IT, SIS.

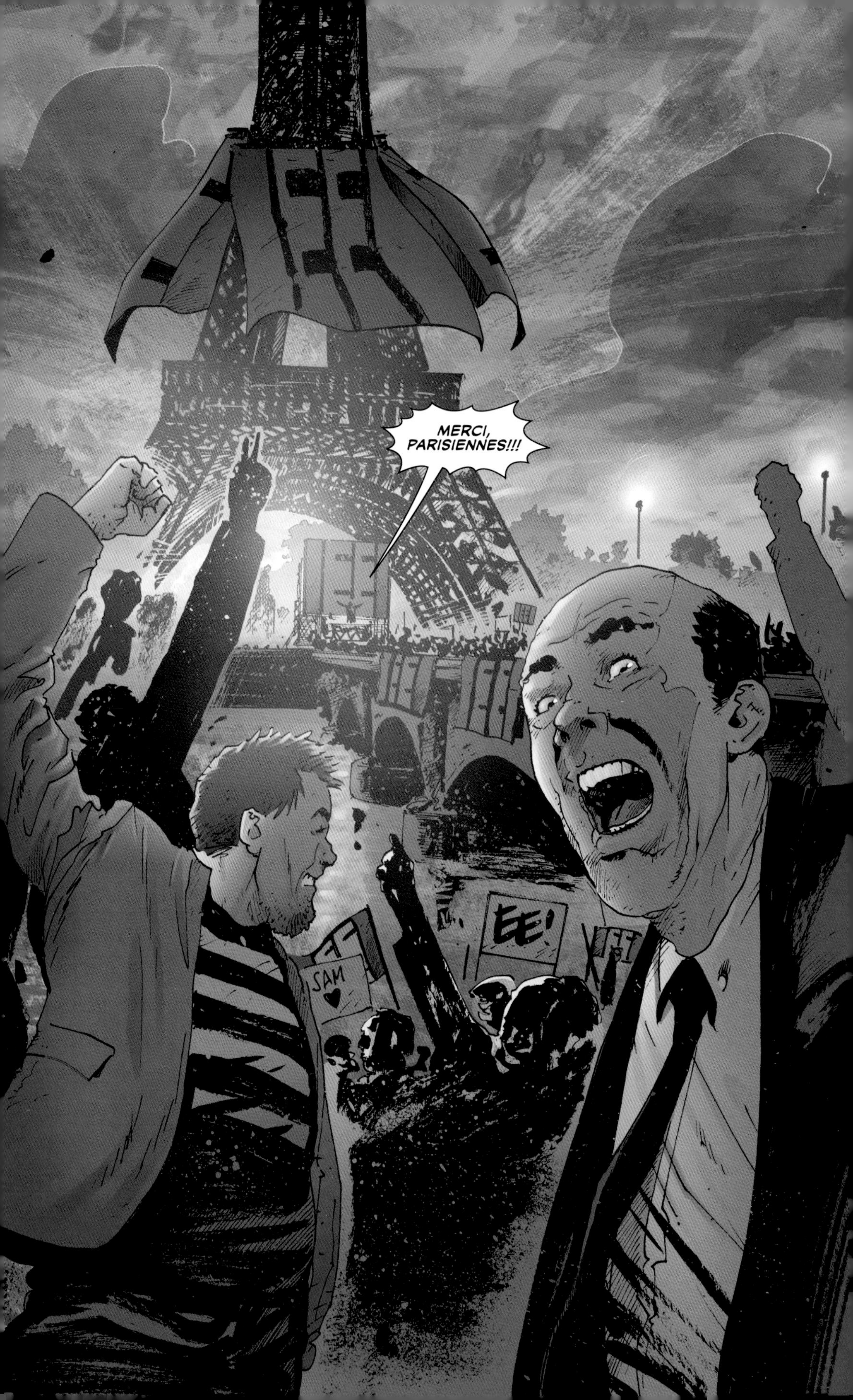
MERCI, PARISIENNES!!!
SAM

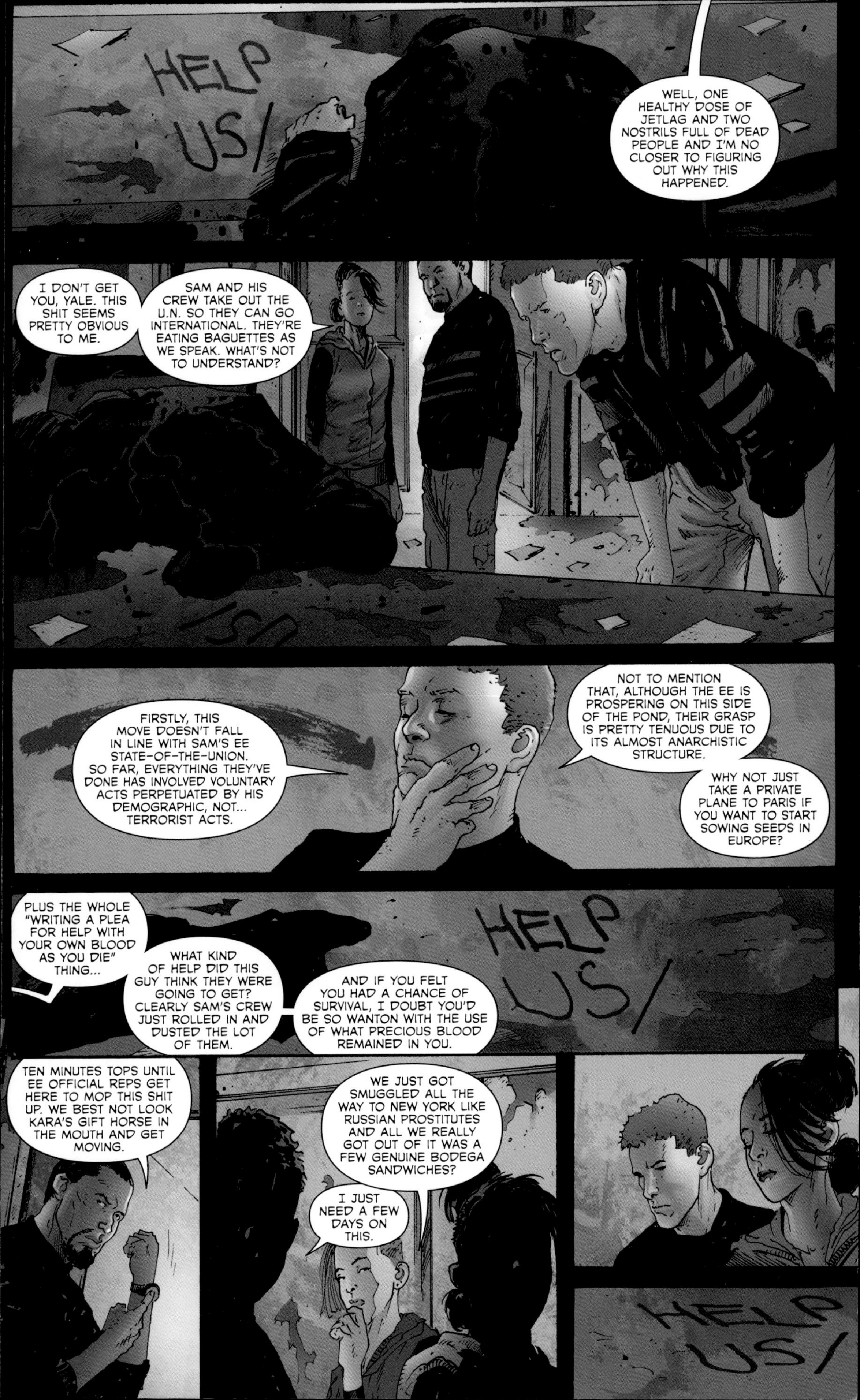
HELP US/
WELL, ONE HEALTHY DOSE OF JETLAG AND TWO NOSTRILS FULL OF DEAD PEOPLE AND I'M NO CLOSER TO FIGURING OUT WHY THIS HAPPENED.
I DON'T GET YOU, YALE. THIS SHIT SEEMS PRETTY OBVIOUS TO ME.
SAM AND HIS CREW TAKE OUT THE U.N. SO THEY CAN GO INTERNATIONAL. THEY'RE EATING BAGUETTES AS WE SPEAK. WHAT'S NOT TO UNDERSTAND?
FIRSTLY, THIS MOVE DOESN'T FALL IN LINE WITH SAM'S EE STATE-OF-THE-UNION. SO FAR, EVERYTHING THEY'VE DONE HAS INVOLVED VOLUNTARY ACTS PERPETUATED BY HIS DEMOGRAPHIC, NOT... TERRORIST ACTS.
NOT TO MENTION THAT, ALTHOUGH THE EE IS PROSPERING ON THIS SIDE OF THE POND, THEIR GRASP IS PRETTY TENUOUS DUE TO ITS ALMOST ANARCHISTIC STRUCTURE.
WHY NOT JUST TAKE A PRIVATE PLANE TO PARIS IF YOU WANT TO START SOWING SEEDS IN EUROPE?
PLUS THE WHOLE "WRITING A PLEA FOR HELP WITH YOUR OWN BLOOD AS YOU DIE" THING...
WHAT KIND OF HELP DID THIS GUY THINK THEY WERE GOING TO GET? CLEARLY SAM'S CREW JUST ROLLED IN AND DUSTED THE LOT OF THEM.
AND IF YOU FELT YOU HAD A CHANCE OF SURVIVAL, I DOUBT YOU'D BE SO WANTON WITH THE USE OF WHAT PRECIOUS BLOOD REMAINED IN YOU.
HELP US/
TEN MINUTES TOPS UNTIL EE OFFICIAL REPS GET HERE TO MOP THIS SHIT UP. WE BEST NOT LOOK KARA'S GIFT HORSE IN THE MOUTH AND GET MOVING.
WE JUST GOT SMUGGLED ALL THE WAY TO NEW YORK LIKE RUSSIAN PROSTITUTES AND ALL WE REALLY GOT OUT OF IT WAS A FEW GENUINE BODEGA SANDWICHES?
I JUST NEED A FEW DAYS ON THIS.
HELP US/

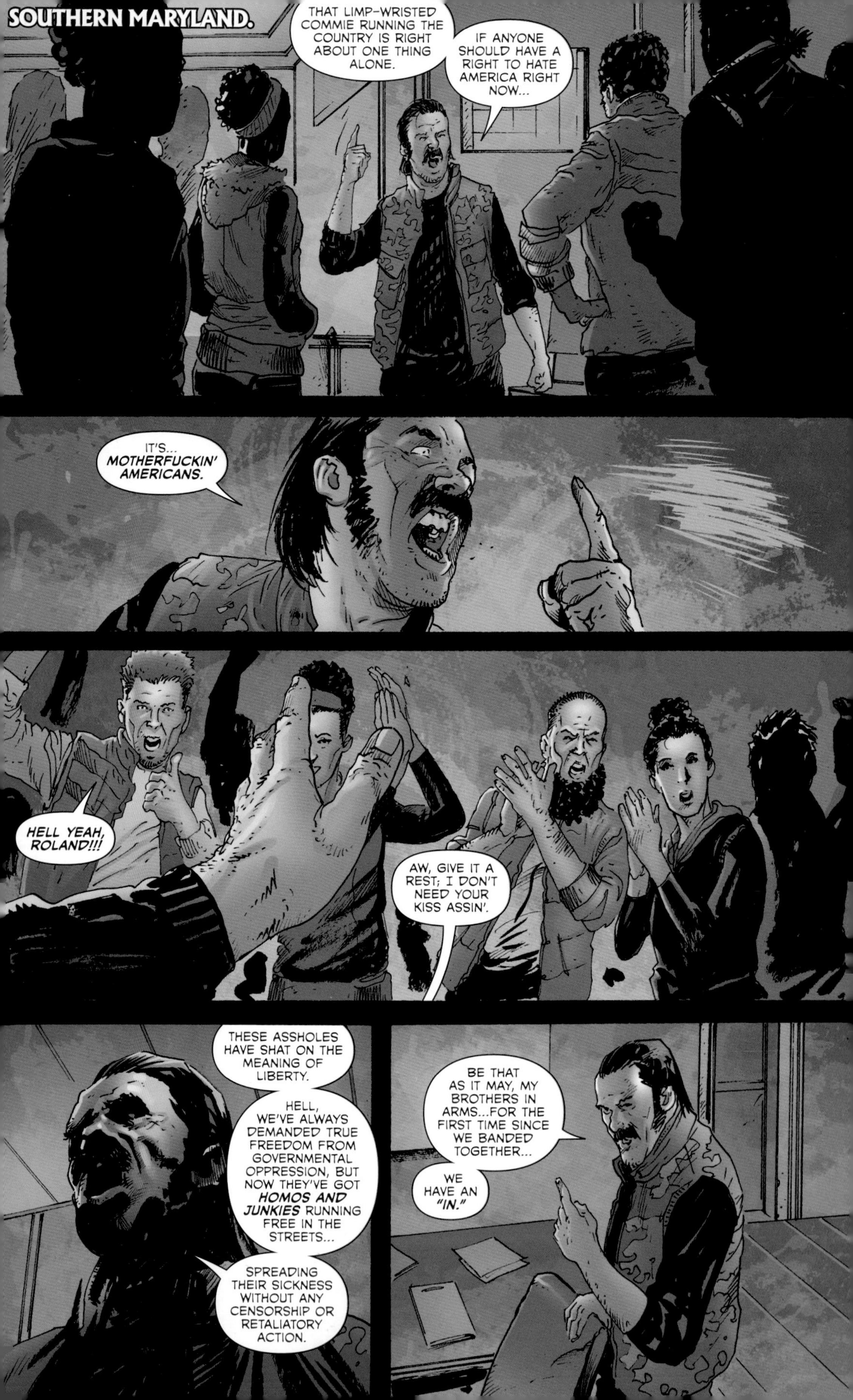
SOUTHERN MARYLAND.
THAT LIMP-WRISTED COMMIE RUNNING THE COUNTRY IS RIGHT ABOUT ONE THING ALONE.
IF ANYONE SHOULD HAVE A RIGHT TO HATE AMERICA RIGHT NOW...
IT'S... *MOTHERFUCKIN' AMERICANS.*
HELL YEAH, ROLAND!!!
AW, GIVE IT A REST; I DON'T NEED YOUR KISS ASSIN'.
THESE ASSHOLES HAVE SHAT ON THE MEANING OF LIBERTY.
HELL, WE'VE ALWAYS DEMANDED TRUE FREEDOM FROM GOVERNMENTAL OPPRESSION, BUT NOW THEY'VE GOT ***HOMOS AND JUNKIES*** RUNNING FREE IN THE STREETS...
SPREADING THEIR SICKNESS WITHOUT ANY CENSORSHIP OR RETALIATORY ACTION.
BE THAT AS IT MAY, MY BROTHERS IN ARMS...FOR THE FIRST TIME SINCE WE BANDED TOGETHER...
WE HAVE AN *"IN."*

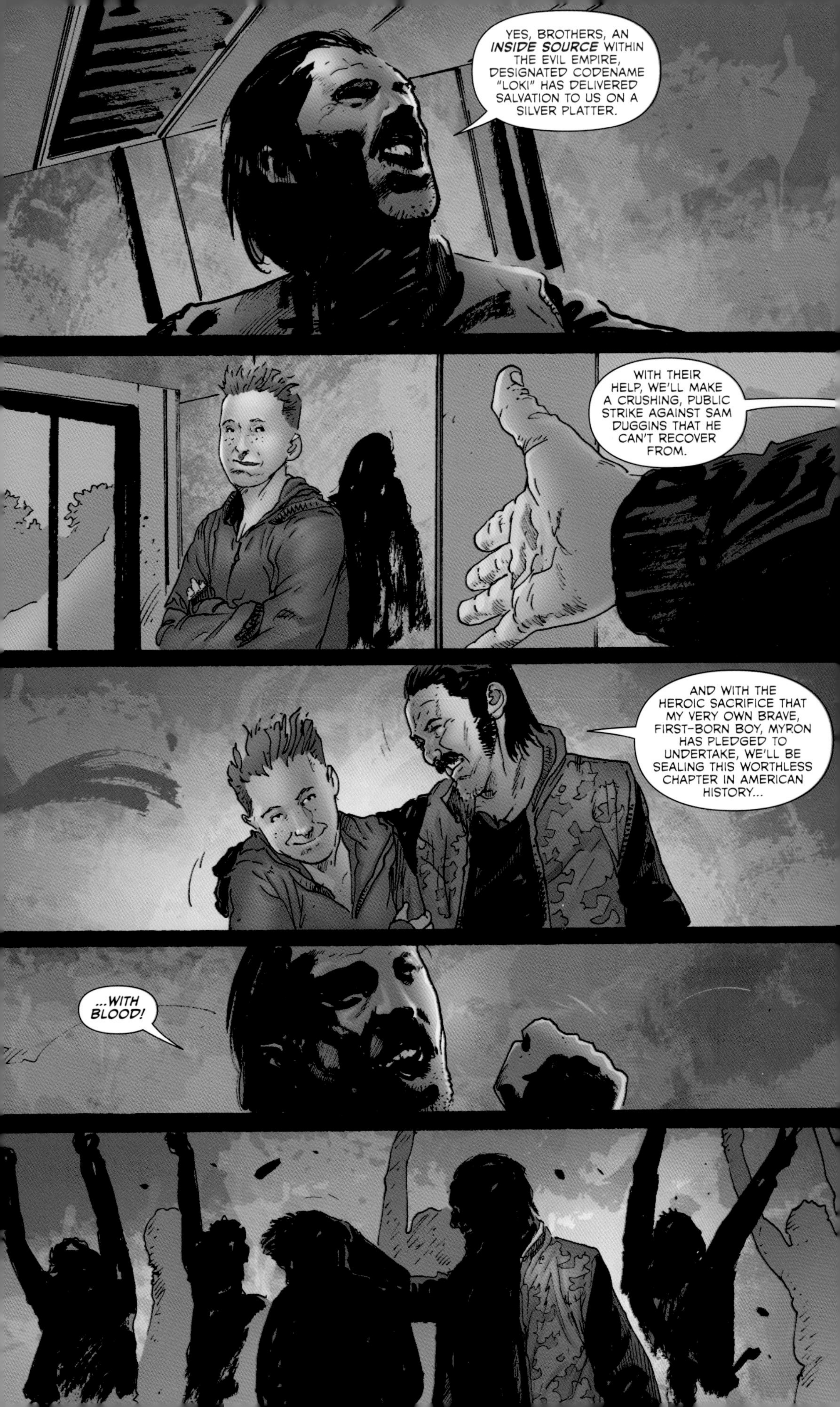
YES, BROTHERS, AN INSIDE SOURCE WITHIN THE EVIL EMPIRE, DESIGNATED CODENAME "LOKI" HAS DELIVERED SALVATION TO US ON A SILVER PLATTER.
WITH THEIR HELP, WE'LL MAKE A CRUSHING, PUBLIC STRIKE AGAINST SAM DUGGINS THAT HE CAN'T RECOVER FROM.
AND WITH THE HEROIC SACRIFICE THAT MY VERY OWN BRAVE, FIRST-BORN BOY, MYRON HAS PLEDGED TO UNDERTAKE, WE'LL BE SEALING THIS WORTHLESS CHAPTER IN AMERICAN HISTORY...
...WITH BLOOD!

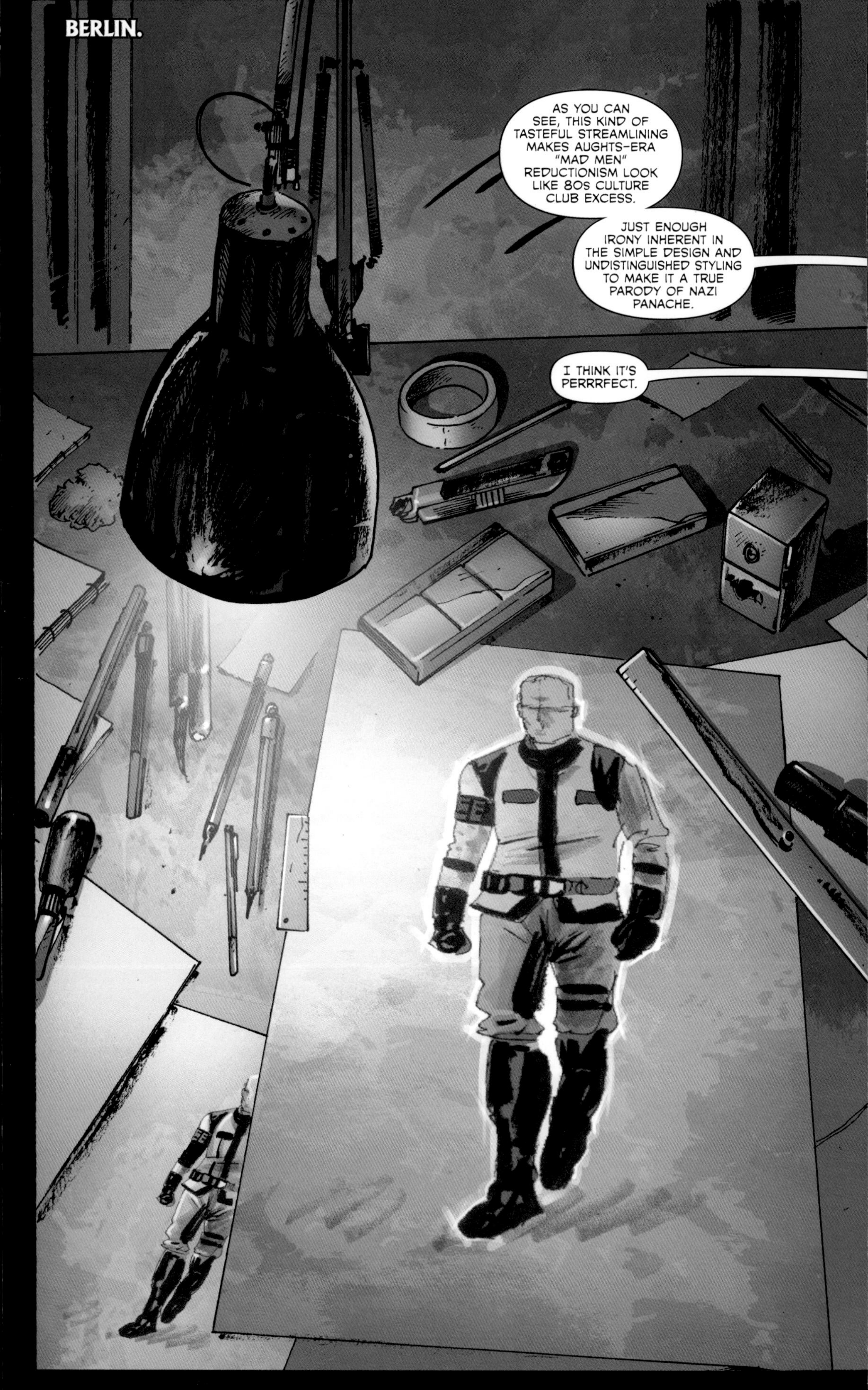
BERLIN.
AS YOU CAN SEE, THIS KIND OF TASTEFUL STREAMLINING MAKES AUGHTS-ERA "MAD MEN" REDUCTIONISM LOOK LIKE 80S CULTURE CLUB EXCESS.
JUST ENOUGH IRONY INHERENT IN THE SIMPLE DESIGN AND UNDISTINGUISHED STYLING TO MAKE IT A TRUE PARODY OF NAZI PANACHE.
I THINK IT'S PERRRFECT.

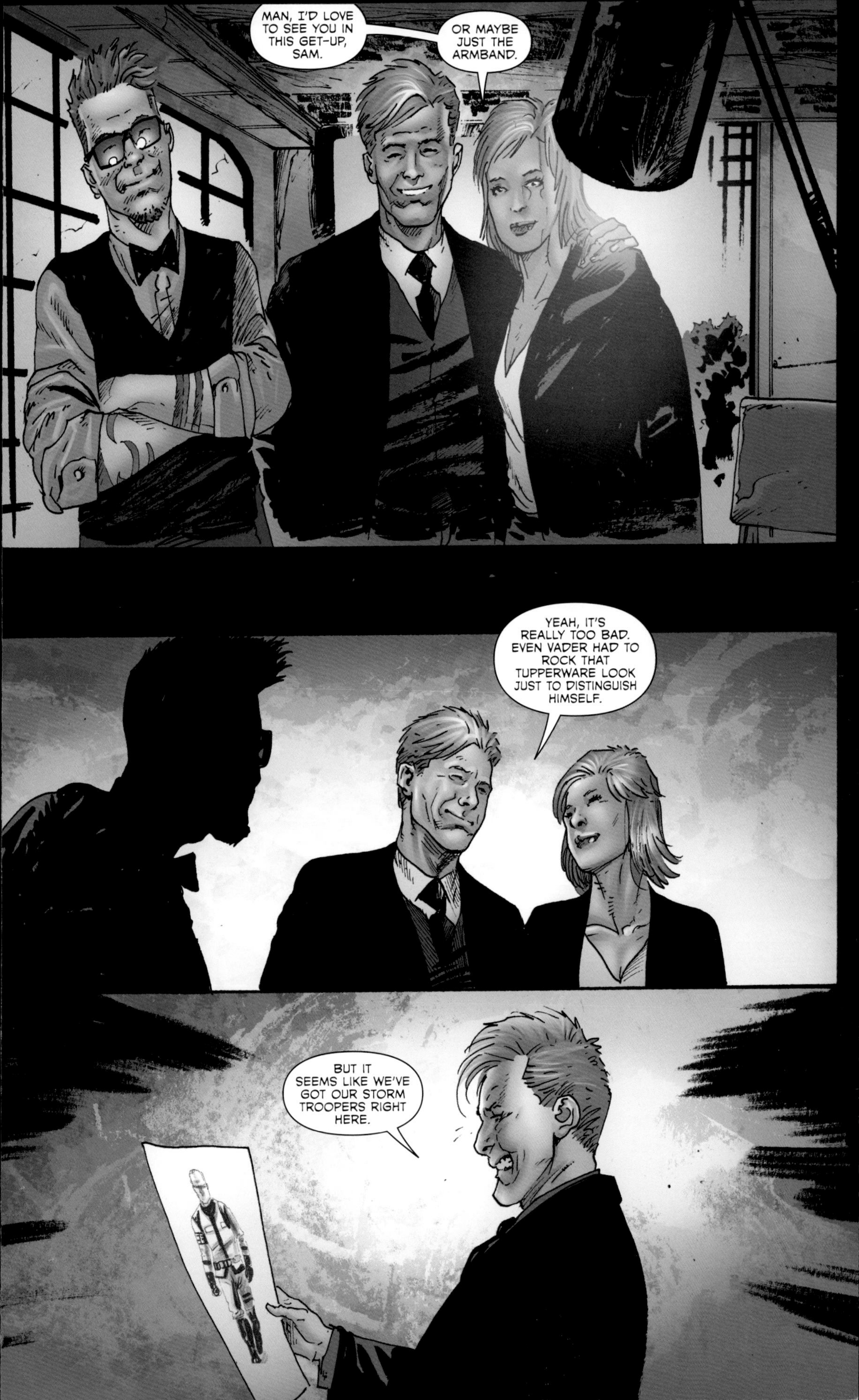
MAN, I'D LOVE TO SEE YOU IN THIS GET-UP, SAM.
OR MAYBE JUST THE ARMBAND.
YEAH, IT'S REALLY TOO BAD. EVEN VADER HAD TO ROCK THAT TUPPERWARE LOOK JUST TO DISTINGUISH HIMSELF.
BUT IT SEEMS LIKE WE'VE GOT OUR STORM TROOPERS RIGHT HERE.

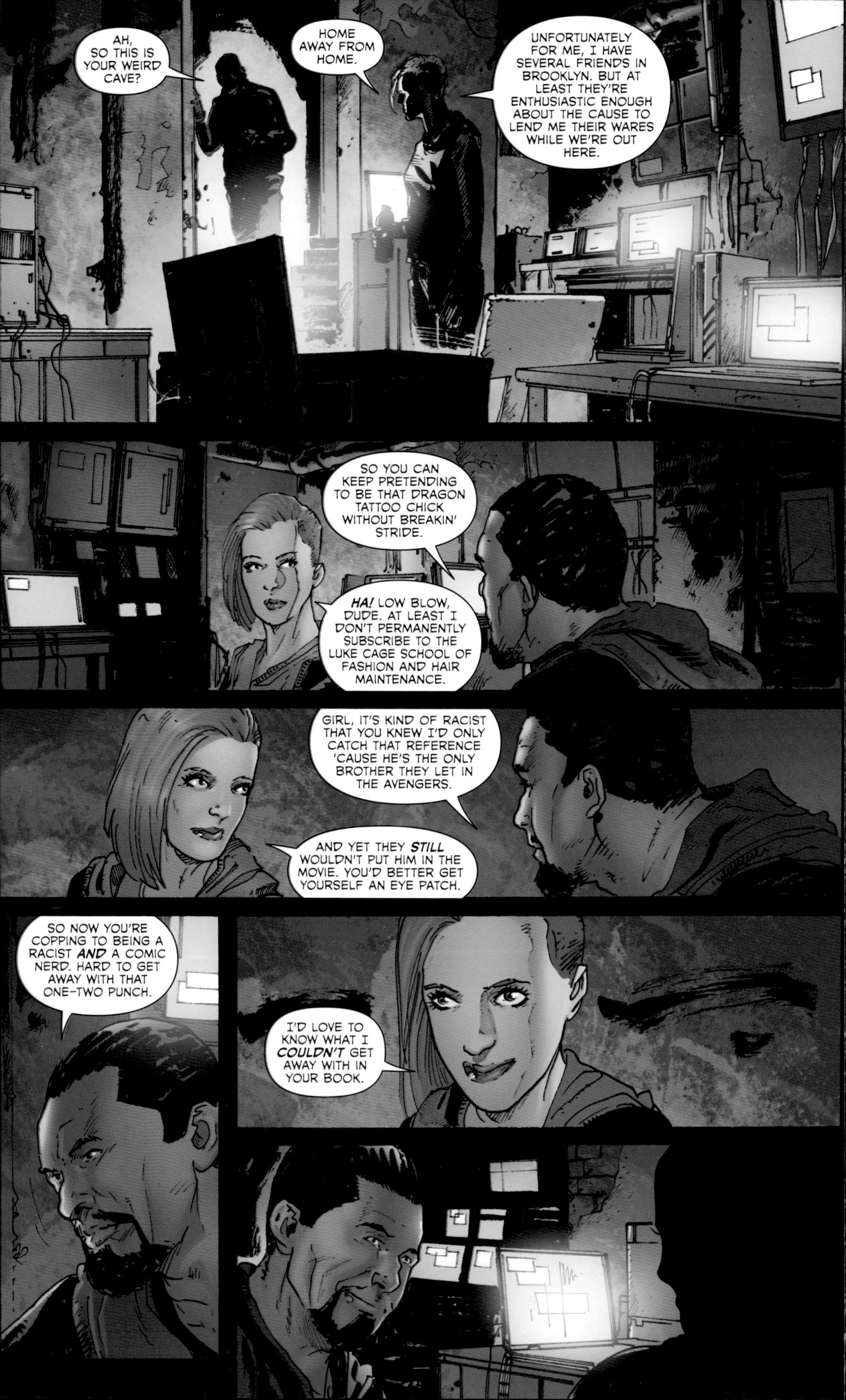
AH, SO THIS IS YOUR WEIRD CAVE?
HOME AWAY FROM HOME.
UNFORTUNATELY FOR ME, I HAVE SEVERAL FRIENDS IN BROOKLYN. BUT AT LEAST THEY'RE ENTHUSIASTIC ENOUGH ABOUT THE CAUSE TO LEND ME THEIR WARES WHILE WE'RE OUT HERE.
SO YOU CAN KEEP PRETENDING TO BE THAT DRAGON TATTOO CHICK WITHOUT BREAKIN' STRIDE.
HA! LOW BLOW, DUDE. AT LEAST I DON'T PERMANENTLY SUBSCRIBE TO THE LUKE CAGE SCHOOL OF FASHION AND HAIR MAINTENANCE.
GIRL, IT'S KIND OF RACIST THAT YOU KNEW I'D ONLY CATCH THAT REFERENCE 'CAUSE HE'S THE ONLY BROTHER THEY LET IN THE AVENGERS.
AND YET THEY STILL WOULDN'T PUT HIM IN THE MOVIE. YOU'D BETTER GET YOURSELF AN EYE PATCH.
SO NOW YOU'RE COPPING TO BEING A RACIST AND A COMIC NERD. HARD TO GET AWAY WITH THAT ONE-TWO PUNCH.
I'D LOVE TO KNOW WHAT I COULDN'T GET AWAY WITH IN YOUR BOOK.

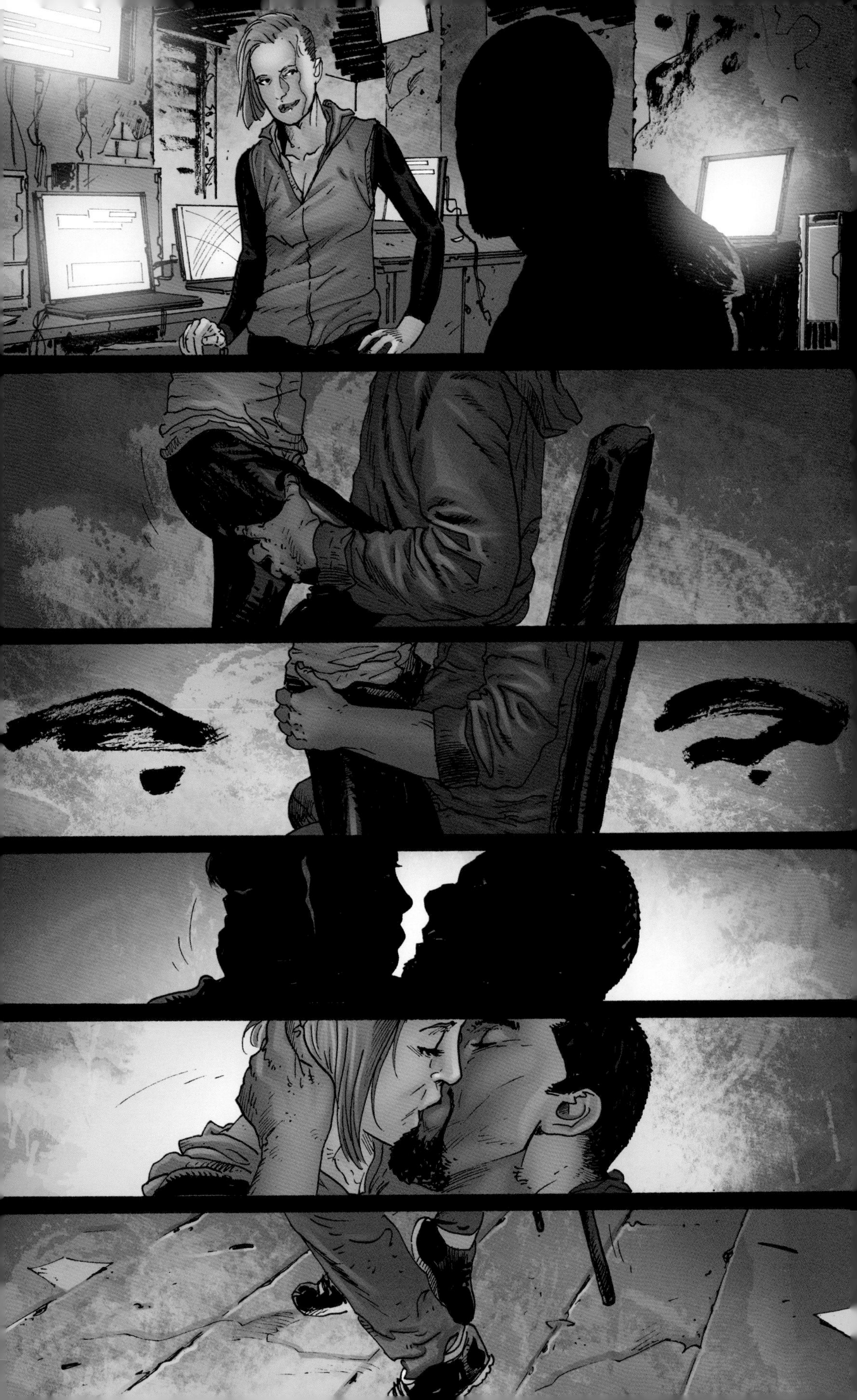

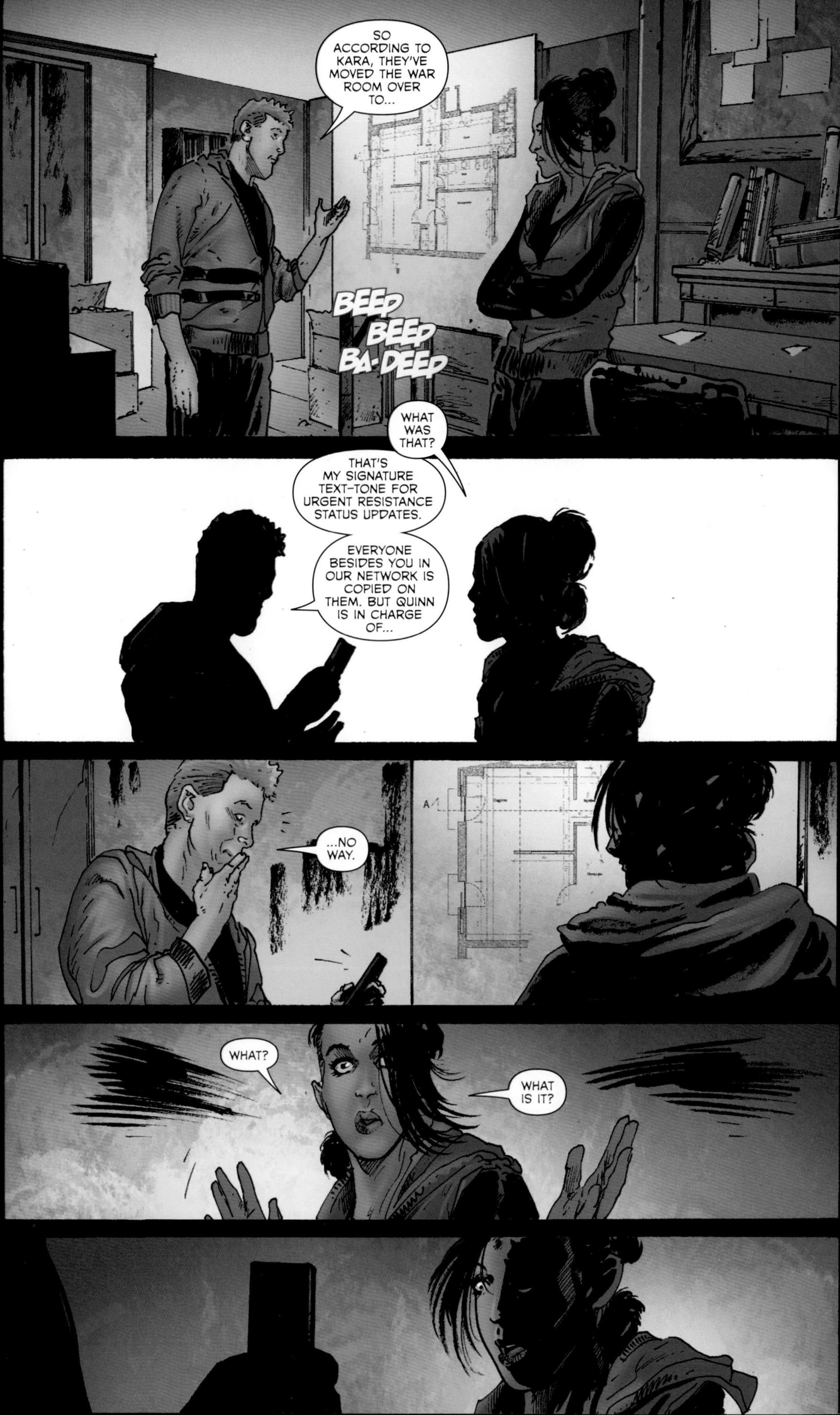

SO ACCORDING TO KARA, THEY'VE MOVED THE WAR ROOM OVER TO...
BEEP BEEP BA-DEEP
WHAT WAS THAT?
THAT'S MY SIGNATURE TEXT-TONE FOR URGENT RESISTANCE STATUS UPDATES.
EVERYONE BESIDES YOU IN OUR NETWORK IS COPIED ON THEM. BUT QUINN IS IN CHARGE OF...
...NO WAY.
WHAT?
WHAT IS IT?

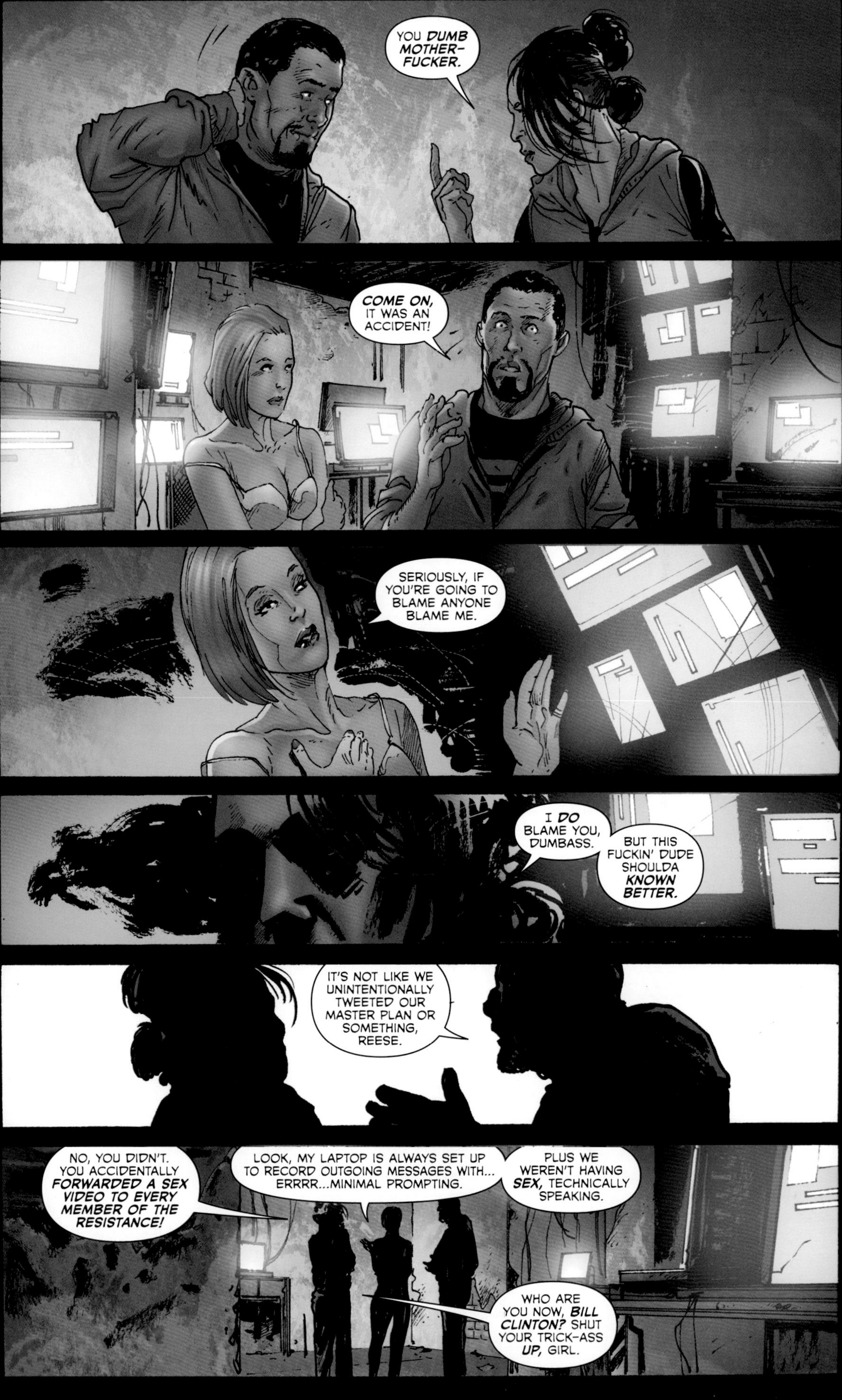
YOU DUMB MOTHER-FUCKER.
COME ON, IT WAS AN ACCIDENT!
SERIOUSLY, IF YOU'RE GOING TO BLAME ANYONE BLAME ME.
I DO BLAME YOU, DUMBASS.
BUT THIS FUCKIN' DUDE SHOULDA KNOWN BETTER.
IT'S NOT LIKE WE UNINTENTIONALLY TWEETED OUR MASTER PLAN OR SOMETHING, REESE.
NO, YOU DIDN'T. YOU ACCIDENTALLY FORWARDED A SEX VIDEO TO EVERY MEMBER OF THE RESISTANCE!
LOOK, MY LAPTOP IS ALWAYS SET UP TO RECORD OUTGOING MESSAGES WITH... ERRRR...MINIMAL PROMPTING.
PLUS WE WEREN'T HAVING SEX, TECHNICALLY SPEAKING.
WHO ARE YOU NOW, BILL CLINTON? SHUT YOUR TRICK-ASS UP, GIRL.

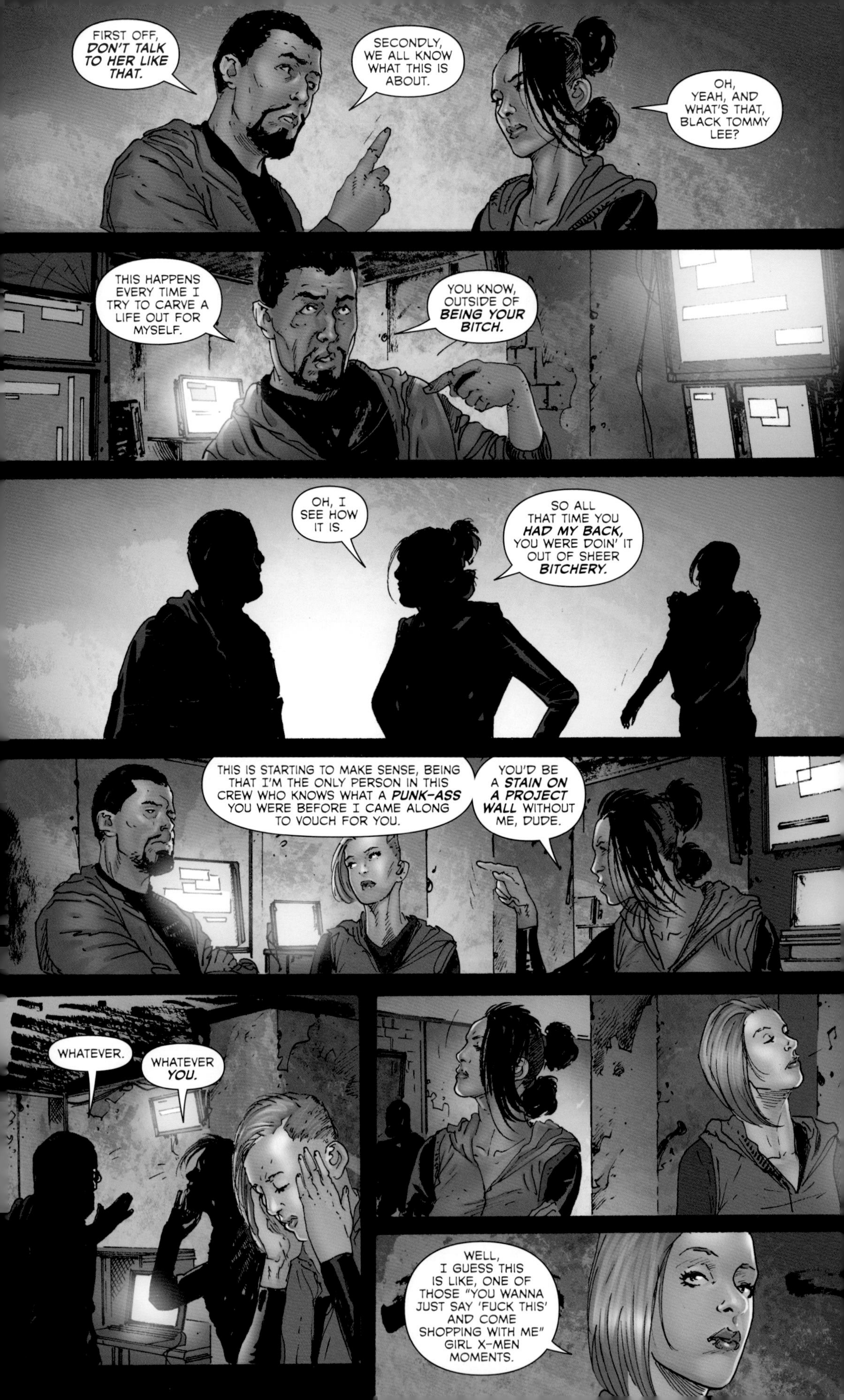
FIRST OFF, DON'T TALK TO HER LIKE THAT.
SECONDLY, WE ALL KNOW WHAT THIS IS ABOUT.
OH, YEAH, AND WHAT'S THAT, BLACK TOMMY LEE?
THIS HAPPENS EVERY TIME I TRY TO CARVE A LIFE OUT FOR MYSELF.
YOU KNOW, OUTSIDE OF BEING YOUR BITCH.
OH, I SEE HOW IT IS.
SO ALL THAT TIME YOU HAD MY BACK, YOU WERE DOIN' IT OUT OF SHEER BITCHERY.
THIS IS STARTING TO MAKE SENSE, BEING THAT I'M THE ONLY PERSON IN THIS CREW WHO KNOWS WHAT A PUNK-ASS YOU WERE BEFORE I CAME ALONG TO VOUCH FOR YOU.
YOU'D BE A STAIN ON A PROJECT WALL WITHOUT ME, DUDE.
WHATEVER.
WHATEVER YOU.
WELL, I GUESS THIS IS LIKE, ONE OF THOSE "YOU WANNA JUST SAY 'FUCK THIS' AND COME SHOPPING WITH ME" GIRL X-MEN MOMENTS.

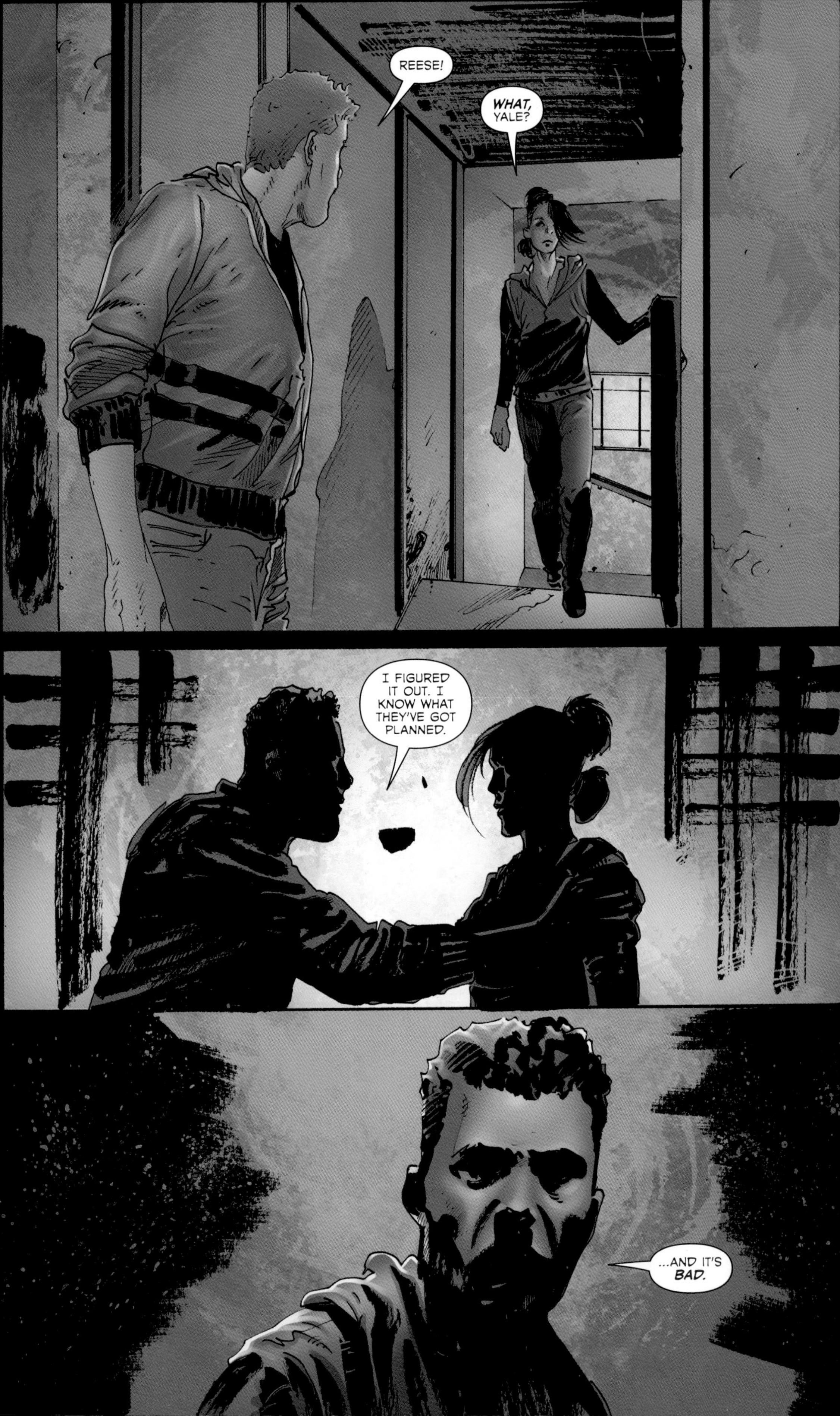
REESE!
WHAT, YALE?
I FIGURED IT OUT. I KNOW WHAT THEY'VE GOT PLANNED.
...AND IT'S BAD.

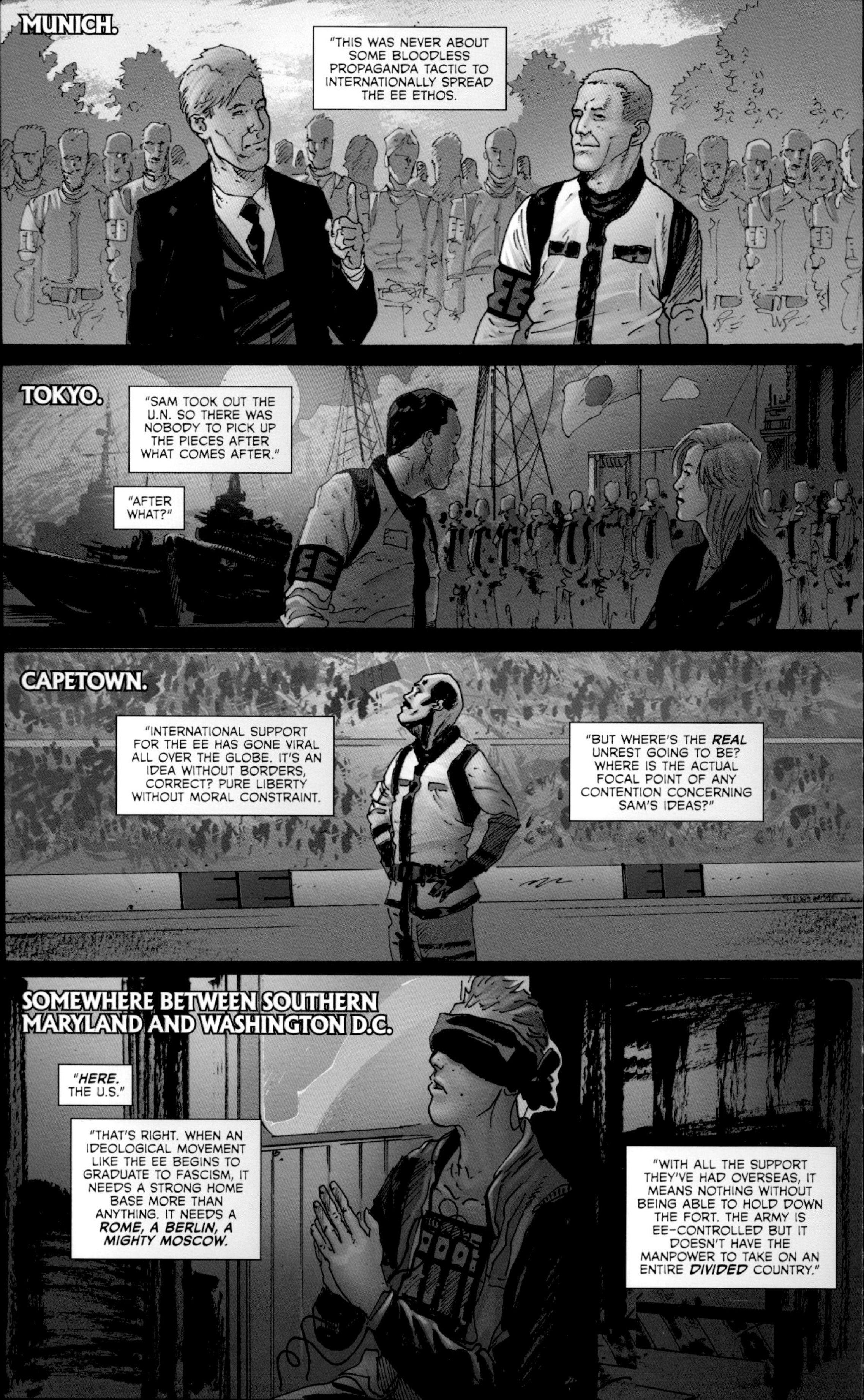
MUNICH.
"THIS WAS NEVER ABOUT SOME BLOODLESS PROPAGANDA TACTIC TO INTERNATIONALLY SPREAD THE EE ETHOS.
TOKYO.
"SAM TOOK OUT THE U.N. SO THERE WAS NOBODY TO PICK UP THE PIECES AFTER WHAT COMES AFTER."
"AFTER WHAT?"
CAPETOWN.
"INTERNATIONAL SUPPORT FOR THE EE HAS GONE VIRAL ALL OVER THE GLOBE. IT'S AN IDEA WITHOUT BORDERS, CORRECT? PURE LIBERTY WITHOUT MORAL CONSTRAINT.
"BUT WHERE'S THE *REAL* UNREST GOING TO BE? WHERE IS THE ACTUAL FOCAL POINT OF ANY CONTENTION CONCERNING SAM'S IDEAS?"
SOMEWHERE BETWEEN SOUTHERN MARYLAND AND WASHINGTON D.C.
"*HERE.* THE U.S."
"THAT'S RIGHT. WHEN AN IDEOLOGICAL MOVEMENT LIKE THE EE BEGINS TO GRADUATE TO FASCISM, IT NEEDS A STRONG HOME BASE MORE THAN ANYTHING. IT NEEDS A *ROME, A BERLIN, A MIGHTY MOSCOW.*
"WITH ALL THE SUPPORT THEY'VE HAD OVERSEAS, IT MEANS NOTHING WITHOUT BEING ABLE TO HOLD DOWN THE FORT. THE ARMY IS EE-CONTROLLED BUT IT DOESN'T HAVE THE MANPOWER TO TAKE ON AN ENTIRE *DIVIDED* COUNTRY."

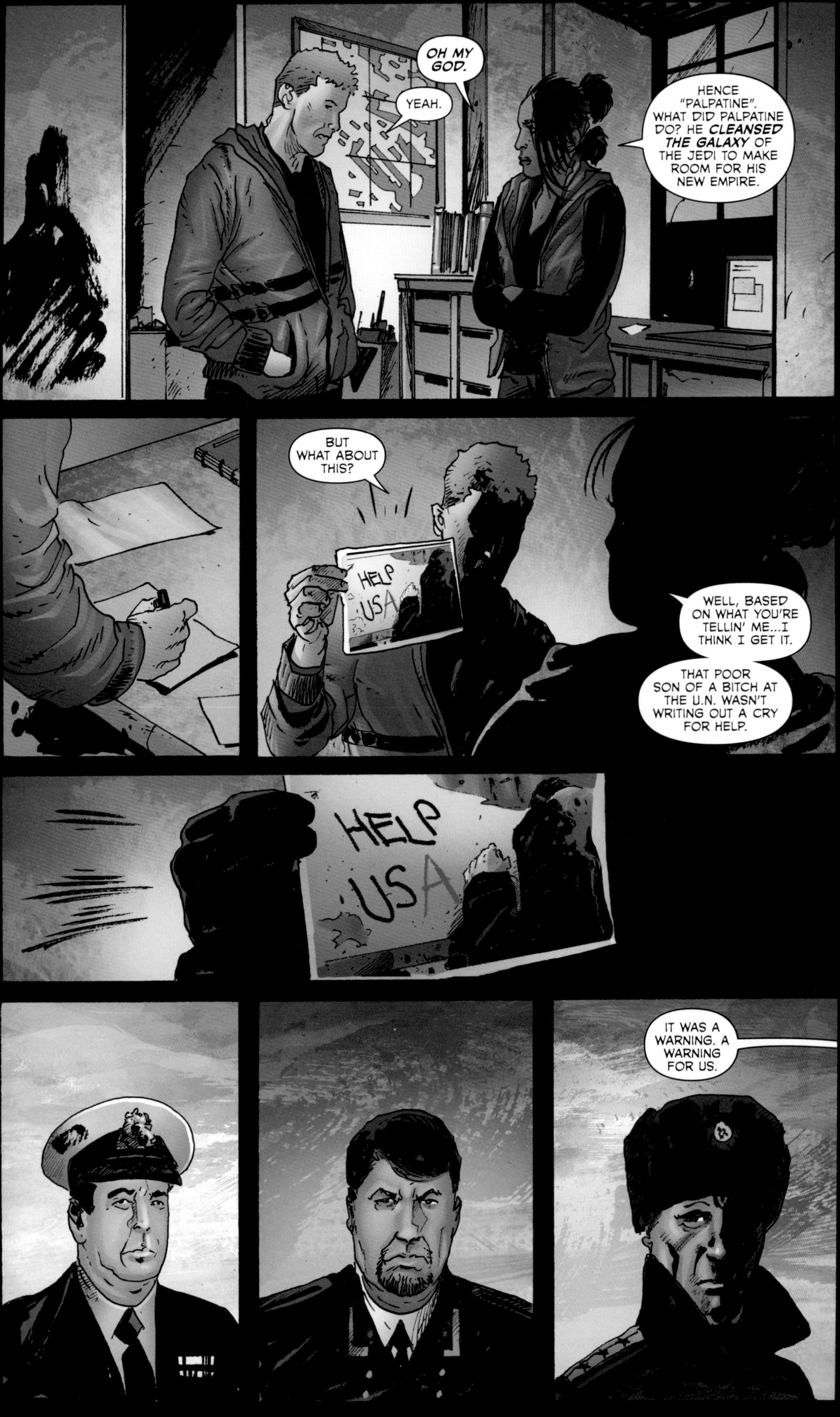
OH MY GOD.
YEAH.
HENCE "PALPATINE". WHAT DID PALPATINE DO? HE **CLEANSED THE GALAXY** OF THE JEDI TO MAKE ROOM FOR HIS NEW EMPIRE.
BUT WHAT ABOUT THIS?
HELP USA
WELL, BASED ON WHAT YOU'RE TELLIN' ME...I THINK I GET IT.
THAT POOR SON OF A BITCH AT THE U.N. WASN'T WRITING OUT A CRY FOR HELP.
HELP USA
IT WAS A WARNING. A WARNING FOR US.

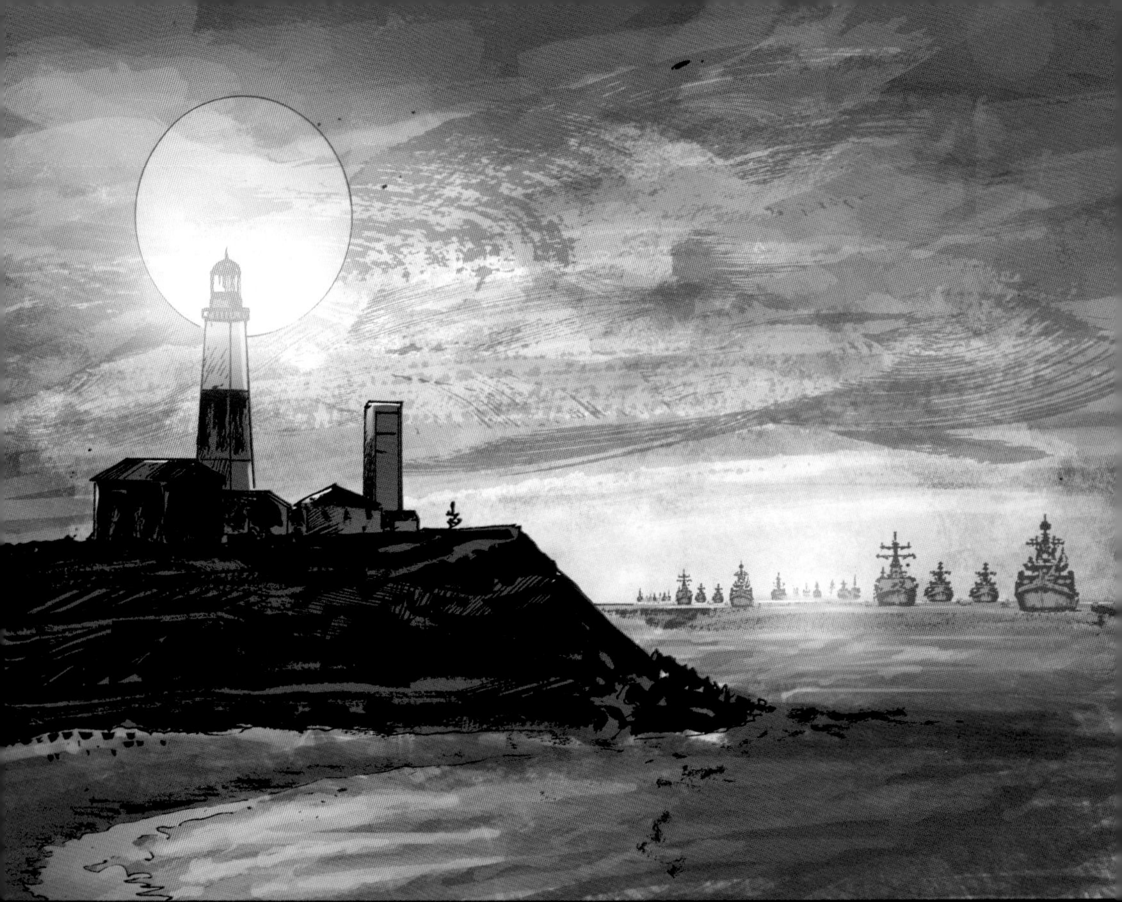
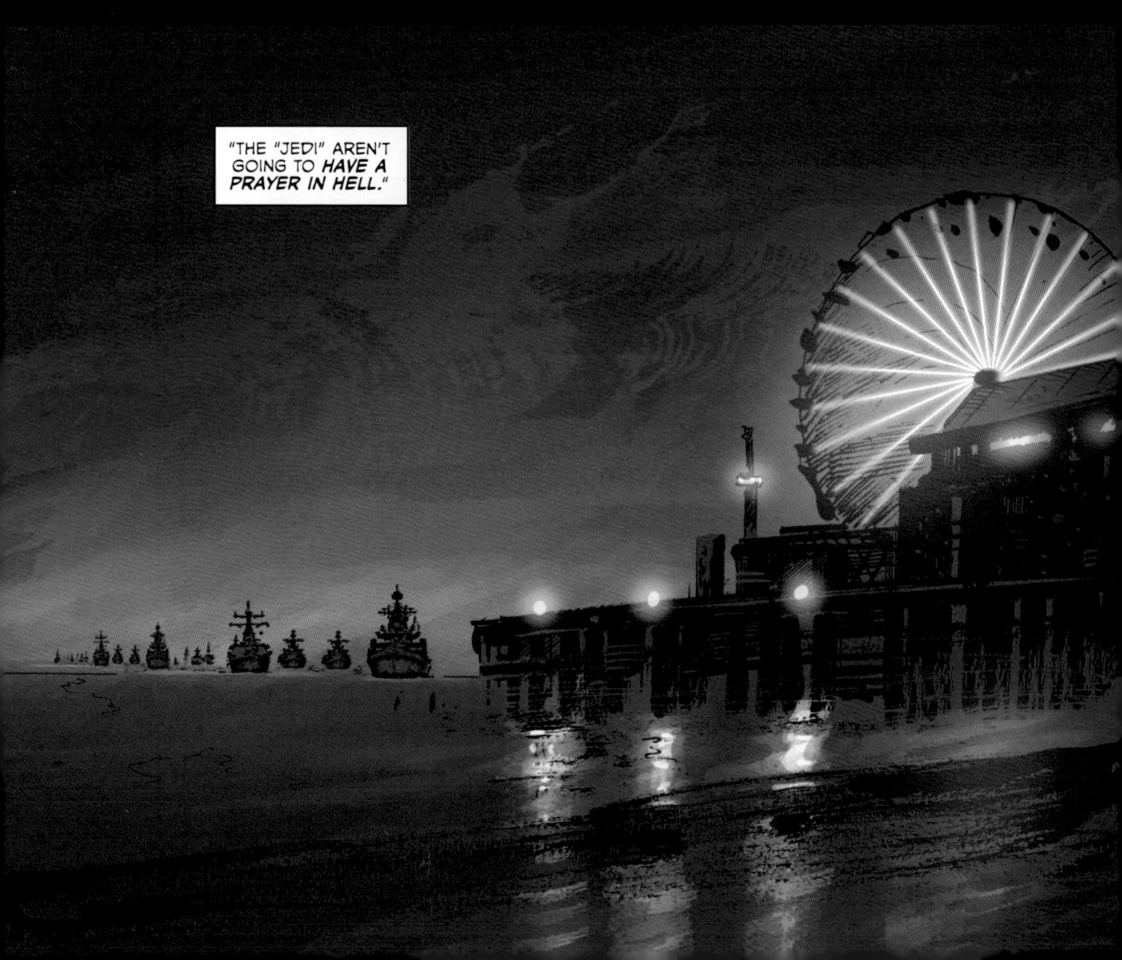
"THE "JEDI" AREN'T GOING TO HAVE A PRAYER IN HELL."

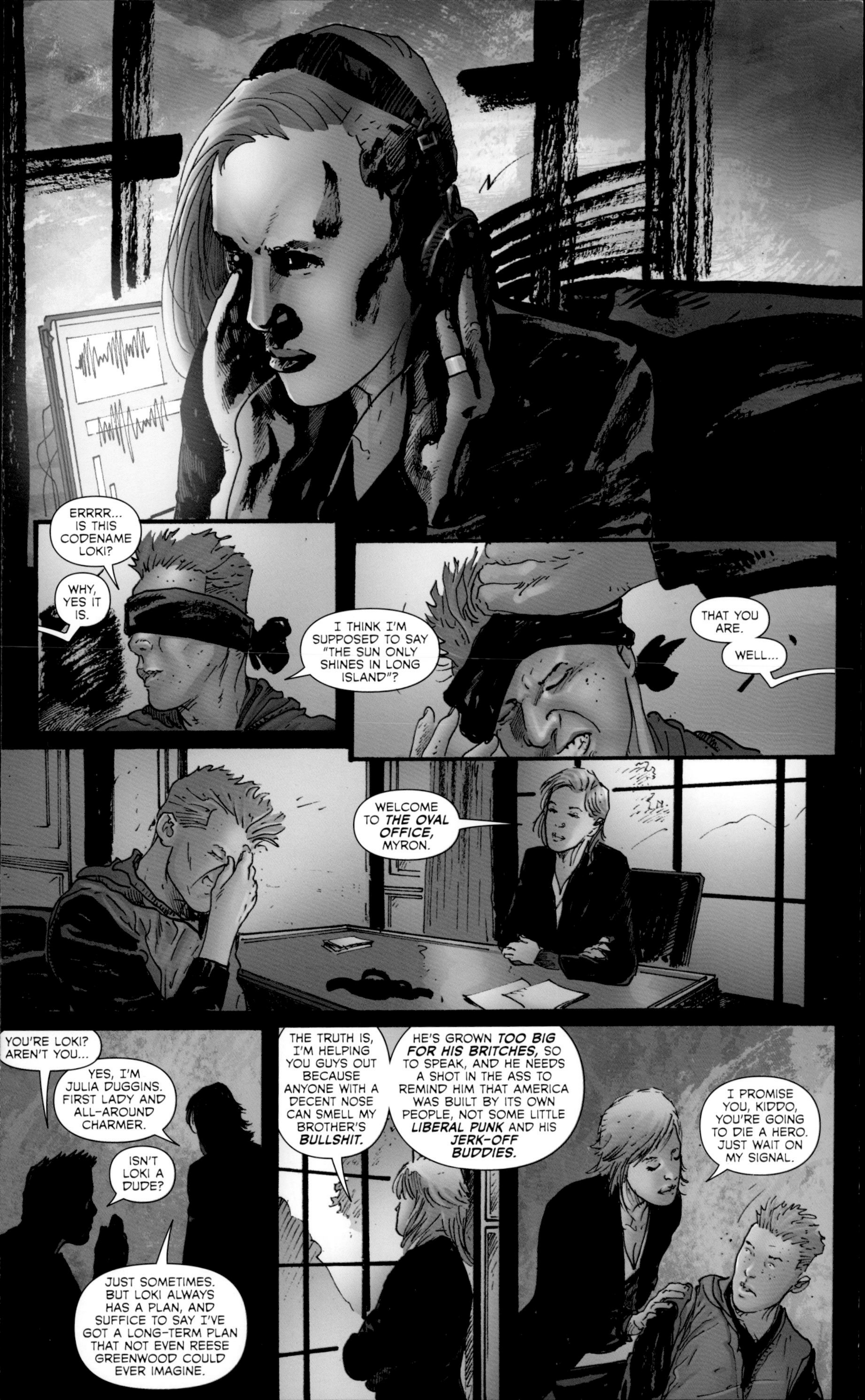
ERRRR... IS THIS CODENAME LOKI?
WHY, YES IT IS.
I THINK I'M SUPPOSED TO SAY "THE SUN ONLY SHINES IN LONG ISLAND"?
THAT YOU ARE.
WELL...
WELCOME TO THE OVAL OFFICE, MYRON.
YOU'RE LOKI? AREN'T YOU...
YES, I'M JULIA DUGGINS. FIRST LADY AND ALL-AROUND CHARMER.
ISN'T LOKI A DUDE?
JUST SOMETIMES. BUT LOKI ALWAYS HAS A PLAN, AND SUFFICE TO SAY I'VE GOT A LONG-TERM PLAN THAT NOT EVEN REESE GREENWOOD COULD EVER IMAGINE.
THE TRUTH IS, I'M HELPING YOU GUYS OUT BECAUSE ANYONE WITH A DECENT NOSE CAN SMELL MY BROTHER'S BULLSHIT.
HE'S GROWN TOO BIG FOR HIS BRITCHES, SO TO SPEAK, AND HE NEEDS A SHOT IN THE ASS TO REMIND HIM THAT AMERICA WAS BUILT BY ITS OWN PEOPLE, NOT SOME LITTLE LIBERAL PUNK AND HIS JERK-OFF BUDDIES.
I PROMISE YOU, KIDDO, YOU'RE GOING TO DIE A HERO. JUST WAIT ON MY SIGNAL.

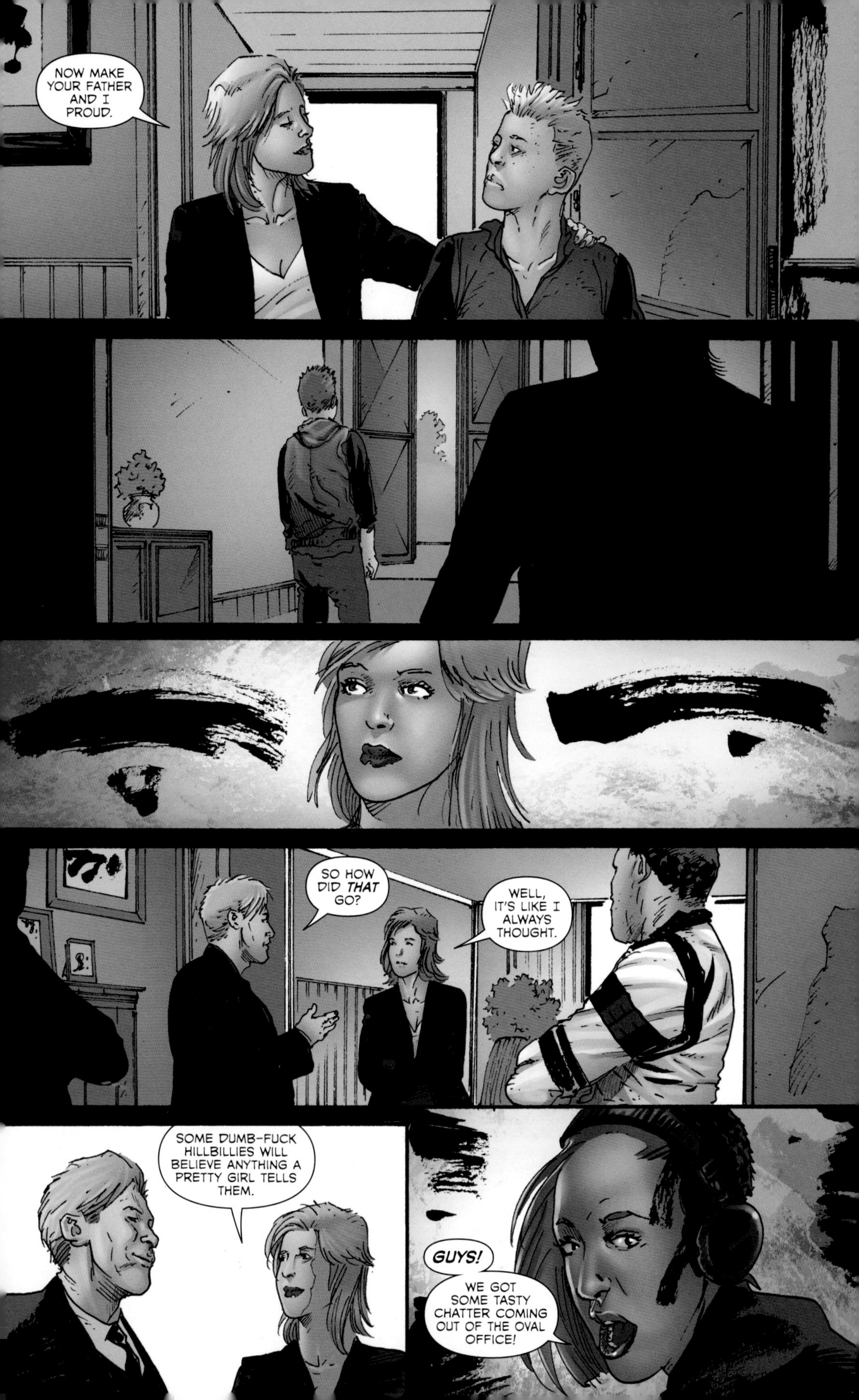
NOW MAKE YOUR FATHER AND I PROUD.
SO HOW DID *THAT* GO?
WELL, IT'S LIKE I ALWAYS THOUGHT.
SOME DUMB-FUCK HILLBILLIES WILL BELIEVE ANYTHING A PRETTY GIRL TELLS THEM.
GUYS!
WE GOT SOME TASTY CHATTER COMING OUT OF THE OVAL OFFICE!

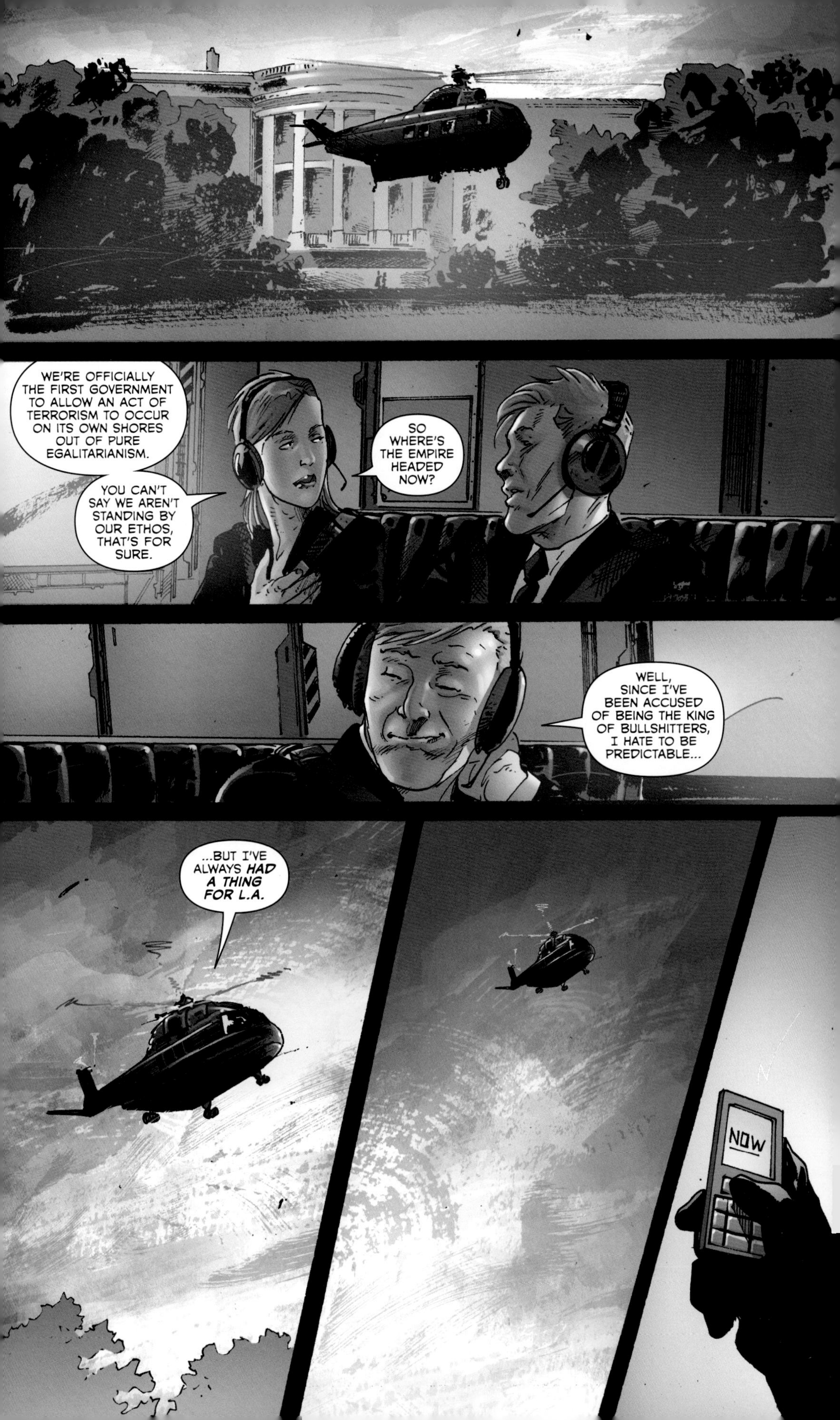
WE'RE OFFICIALLY THE FIRST GOVERNMENT TO ALLOW AN ACT OF TERRORISM TO OCCUR ON ITS OWN SHORES OUT OF PURE EGALITARIANISM.
YOU CAN'T SAY WE AREN'T STANDING BY OUR ETHOS, THAT'S FOR SURE.
SO WHERE'S THE EMPIRE HEADED NOW?
WELL, SINCE I'VE BEEN ACCUSED OF BEING THE KING OF BULLSHITTERS, I HATE TO BE PREDICTABLE...
...BUT I'VE ALWAYS *HAD A THING FOR L.A.*
NOW

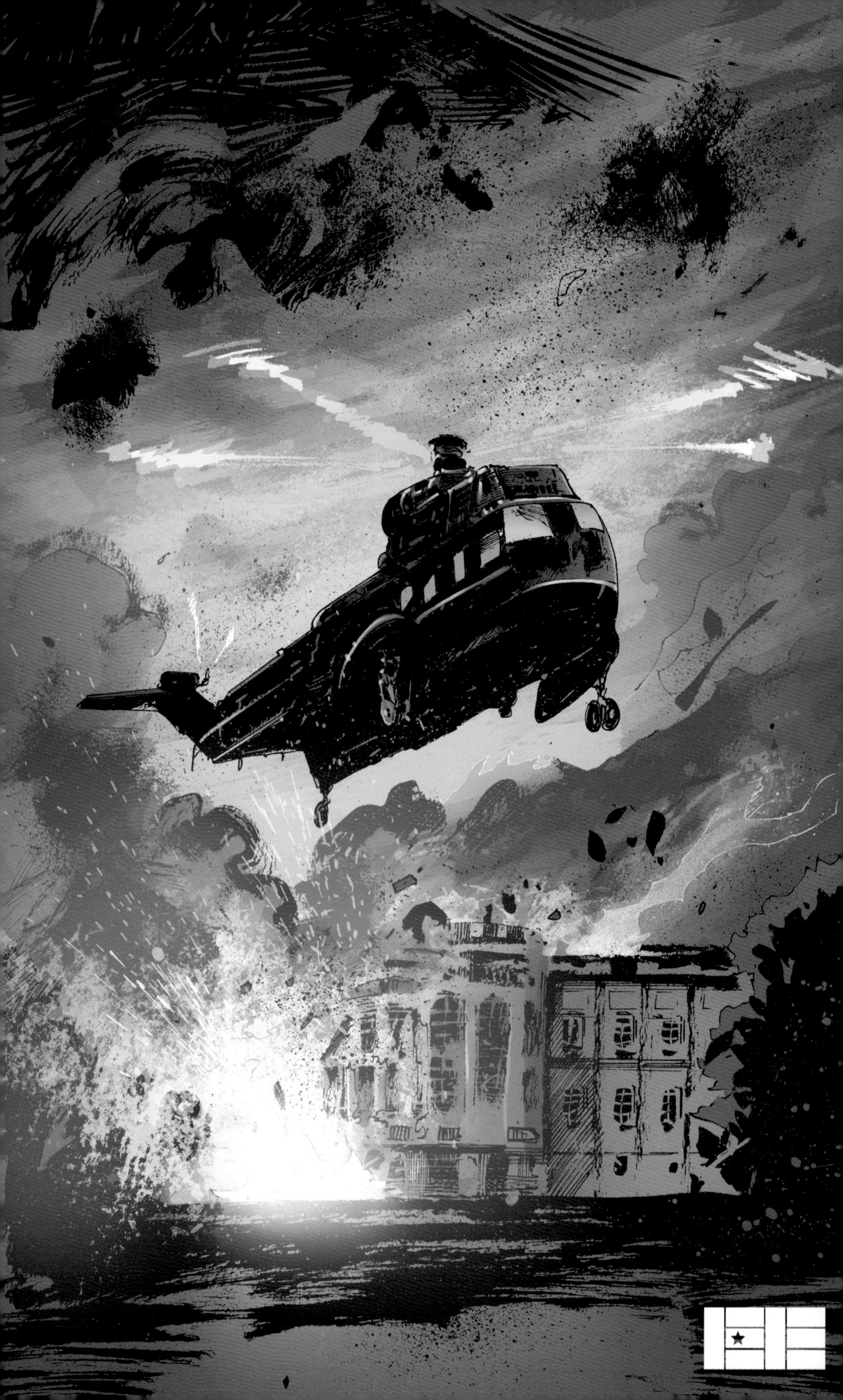

COVER GALLERY

........................*exc. 5.0*

I know damn well what we did, but…No one deserves this.

No one deserves this.

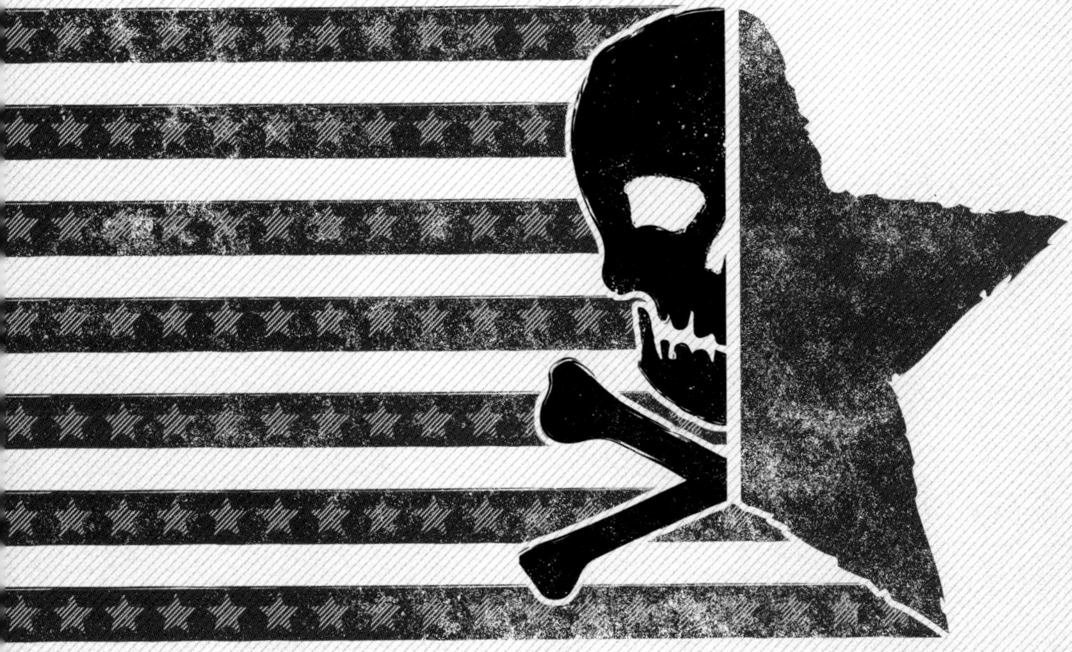

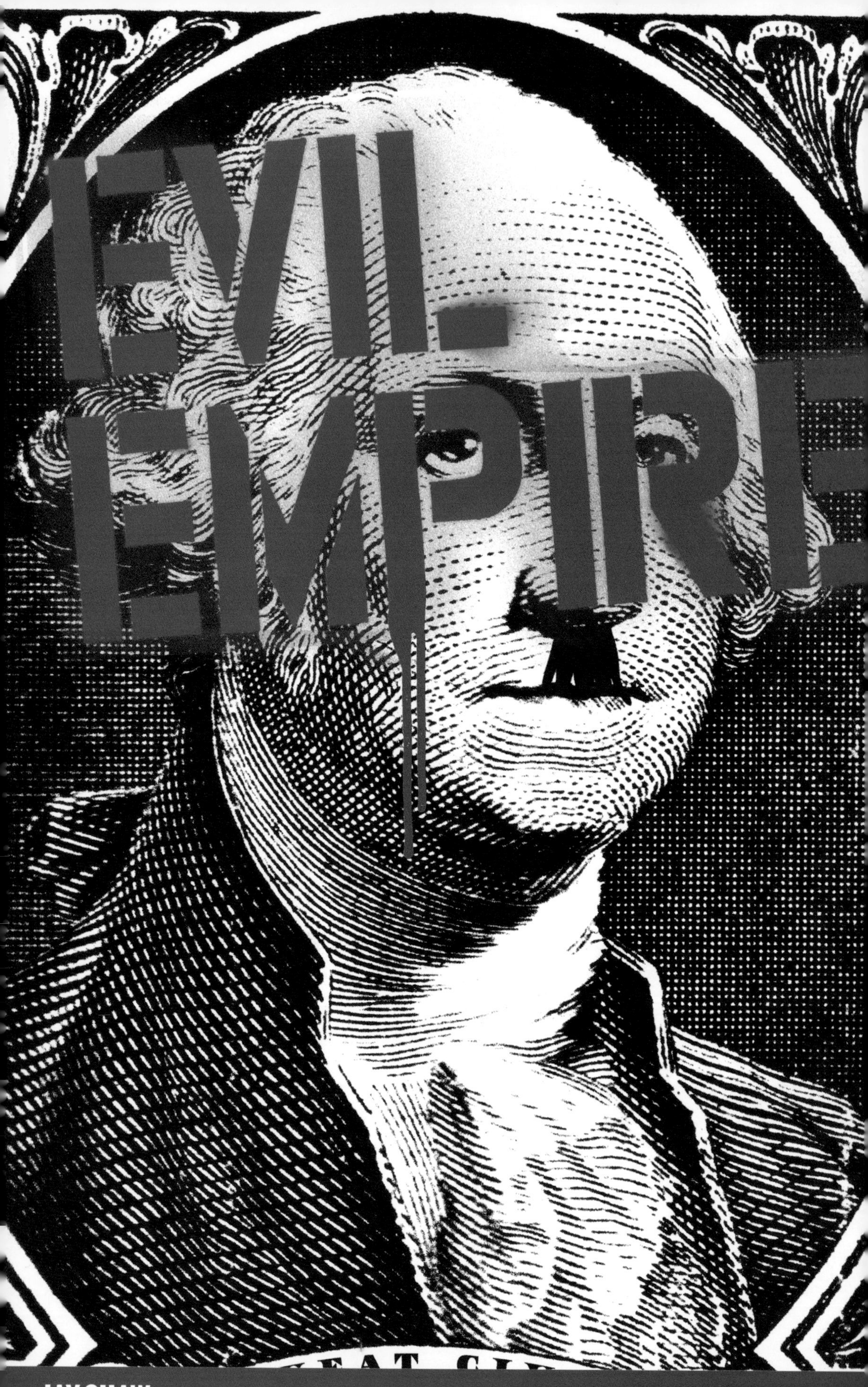
EVIL
EMPIRE

JAY SHAW ISSUE FIVE COVER

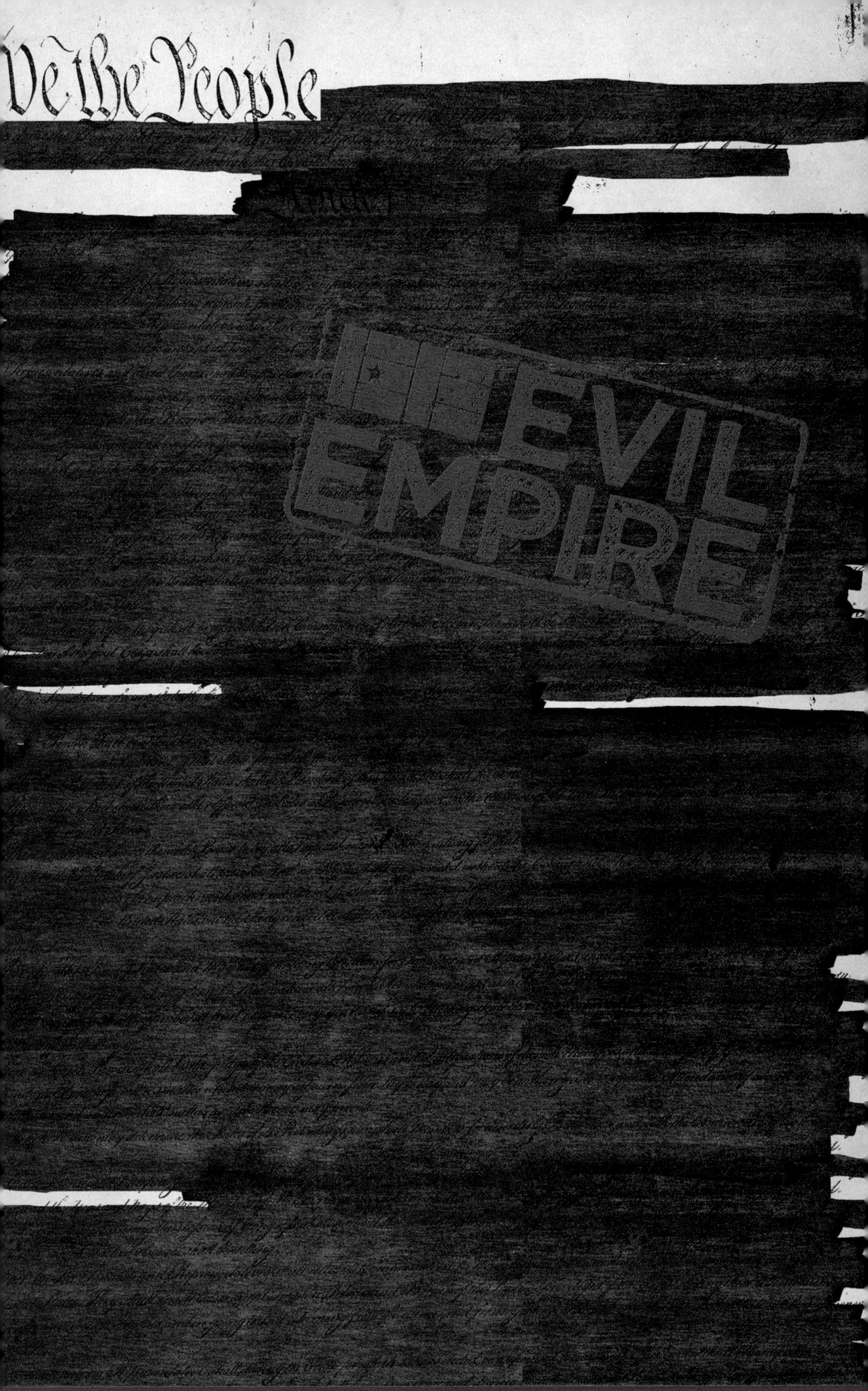
We the People
EVIL EMPIRE

ISSUE SIX COVER **JAY SHAW**

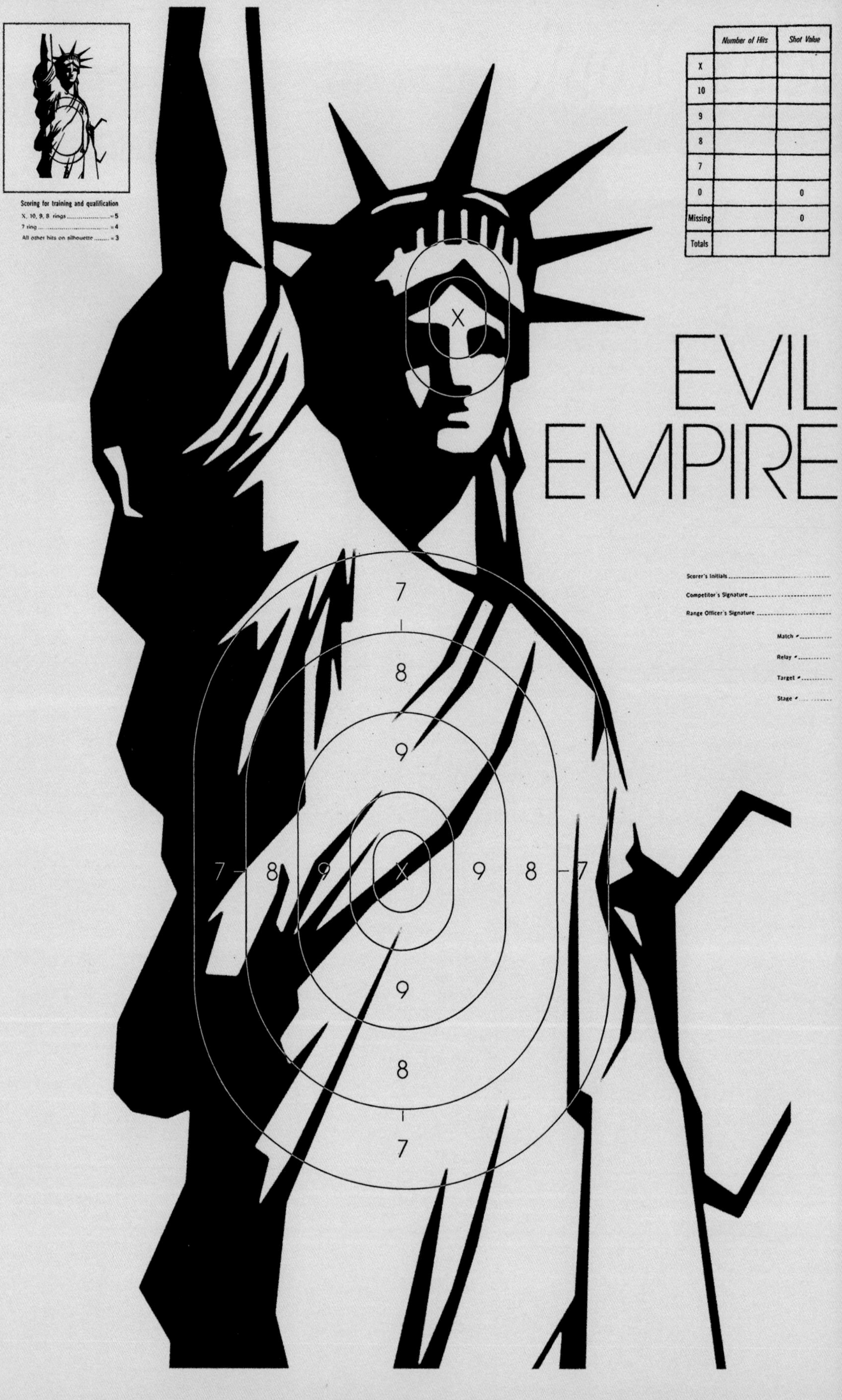
Scoring for training and qualification
X, 10, 9, 8 rings .... =5
7 ring .... =4
All other hits on silhouette .... =3
Number of Hits
Shot Value
X
10
9
8
7
0
0
Missing
0
Totals
EVIL
EMPIRE
Scorer's Initials
Competitor's Signature
Range Officer's Signature
Match
Relay
Target
Stage
7
8
9
X
9
8
7
7
8
9
X
9
8
7

JAY SHAW ISSUE SEVEN COVER

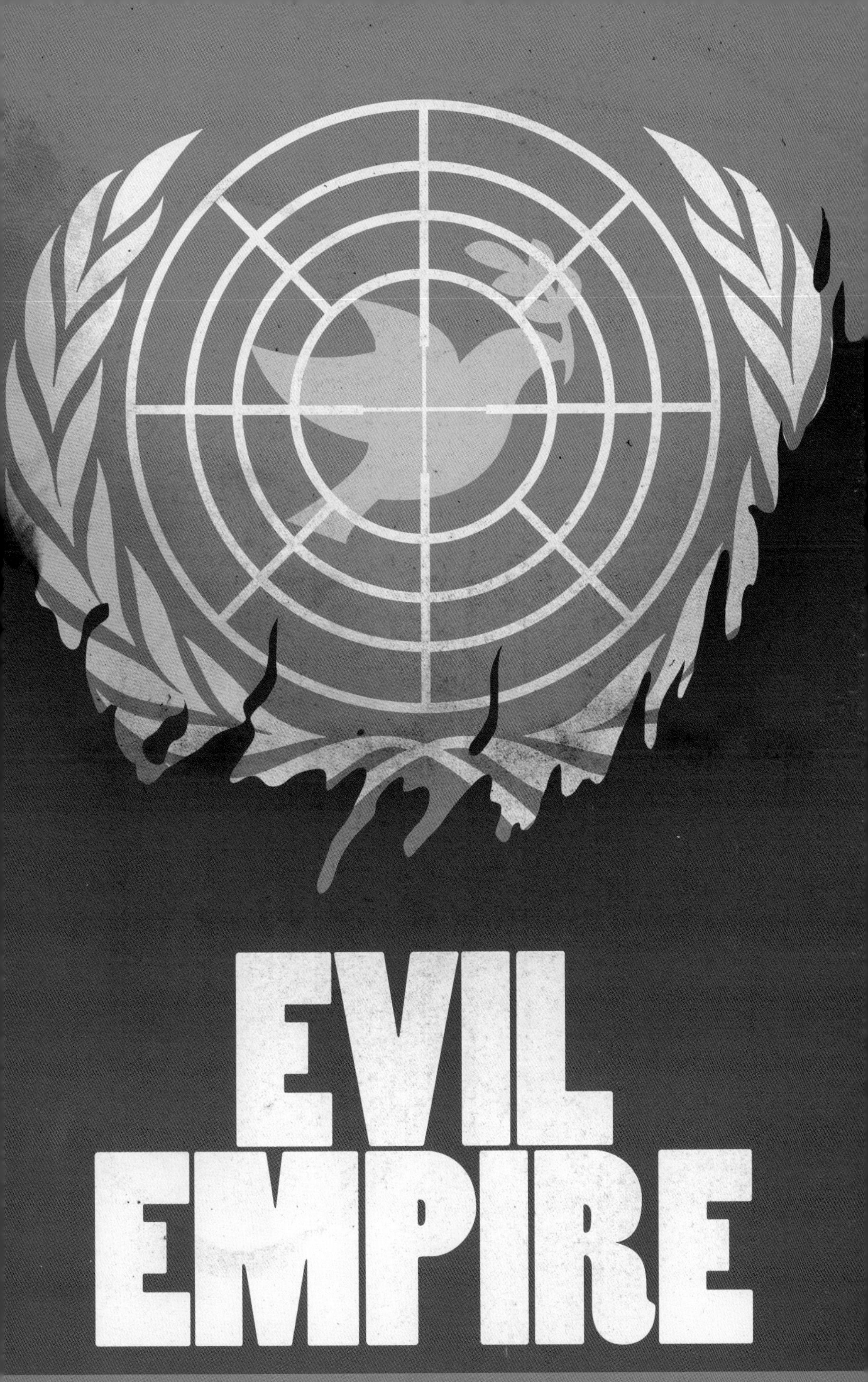
EVIL
EMPIRE

ISSUE EIGHT COVER **JAY SHAW**

SKETCH GALLERY

DESIGNS BY RANSOM GETTY

exc. 6.0

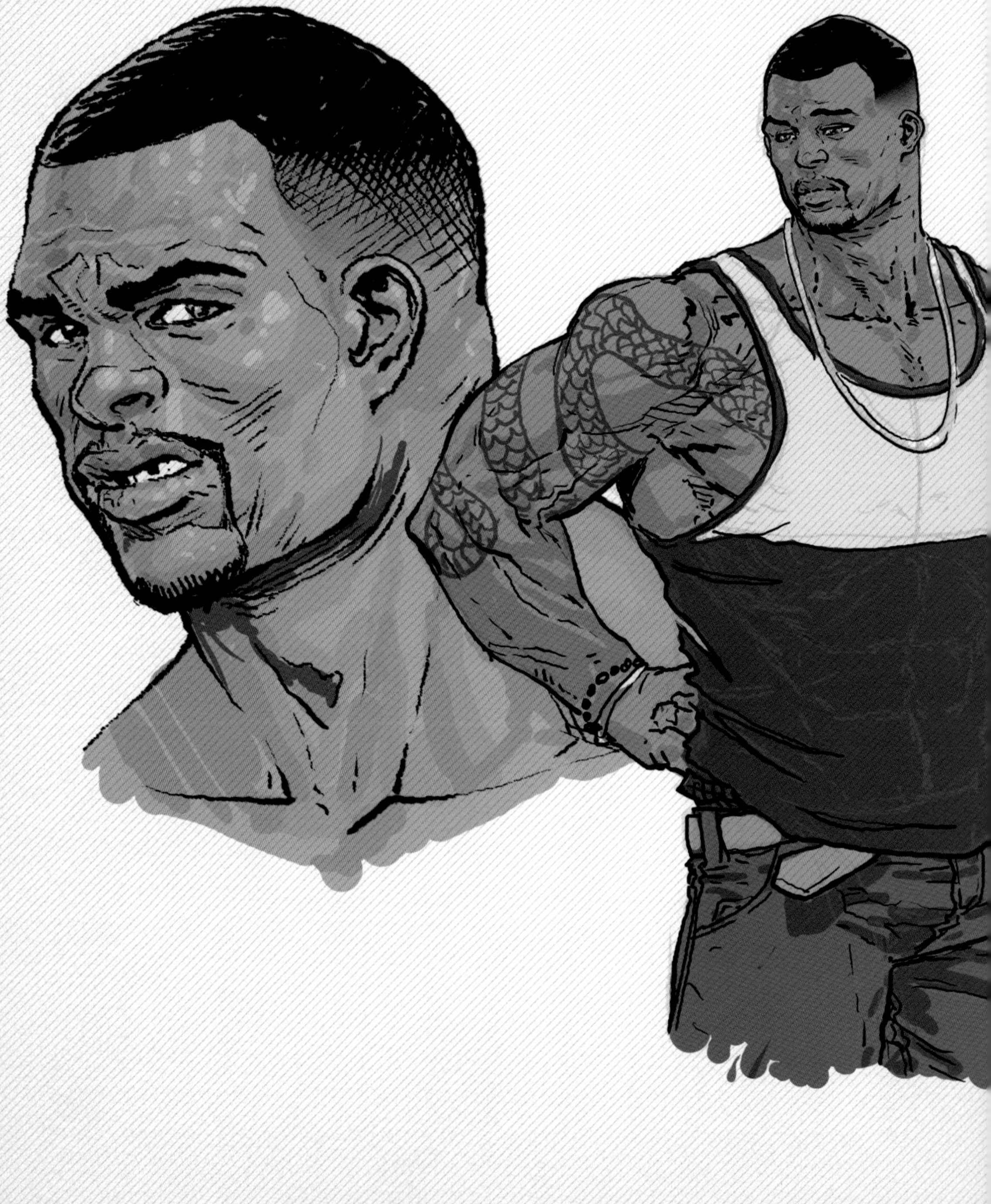

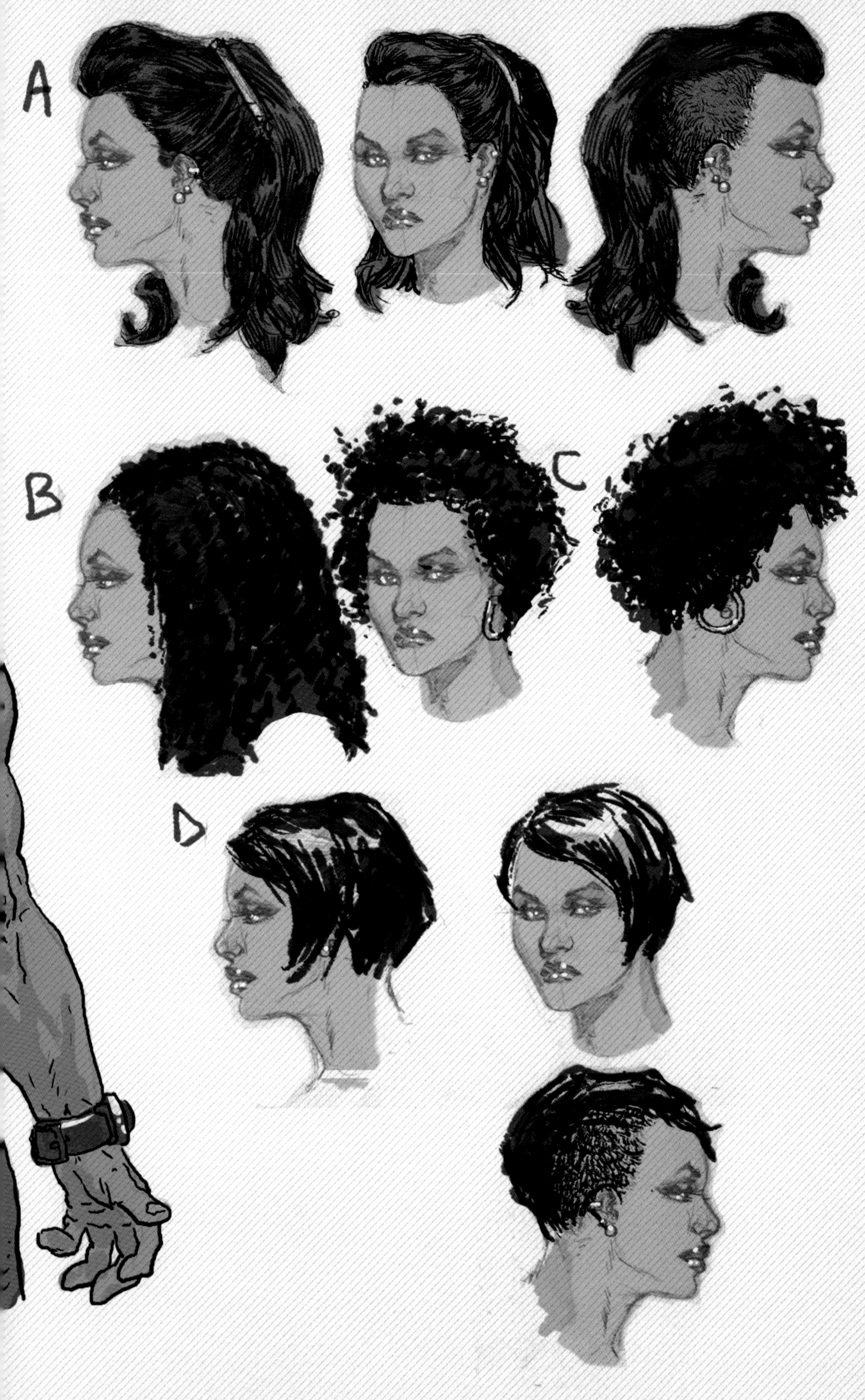
A
B
C
D

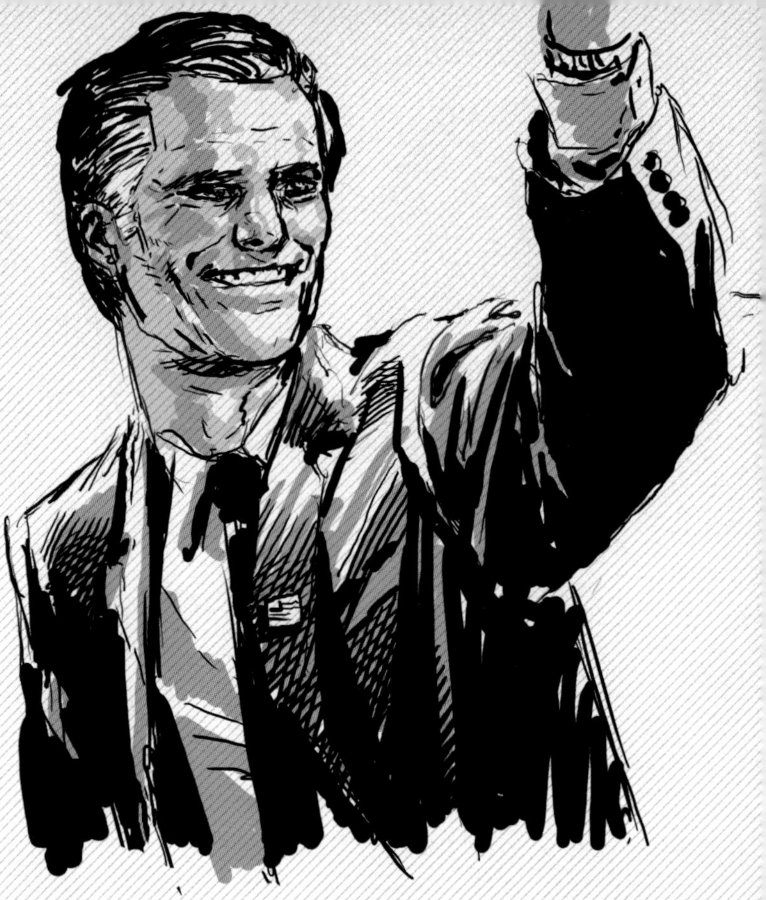
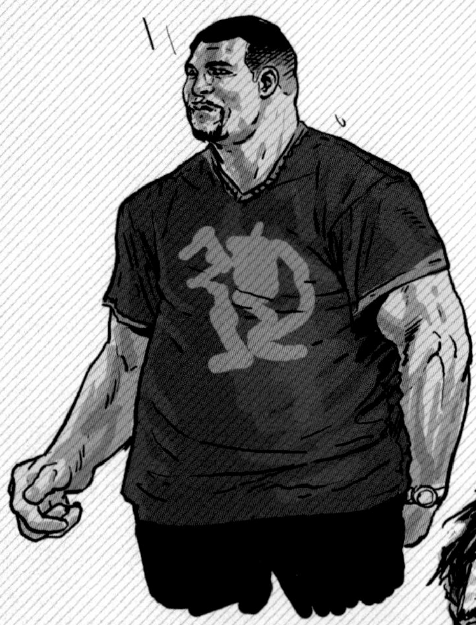
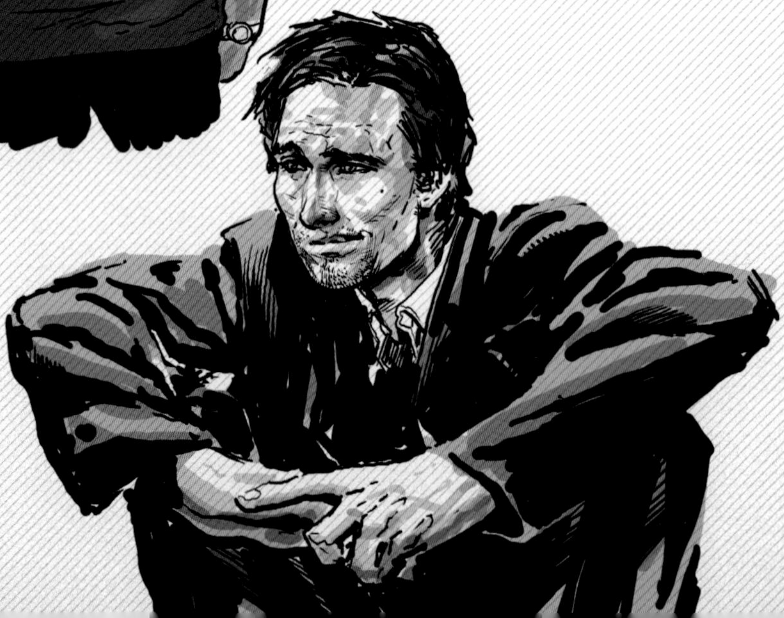

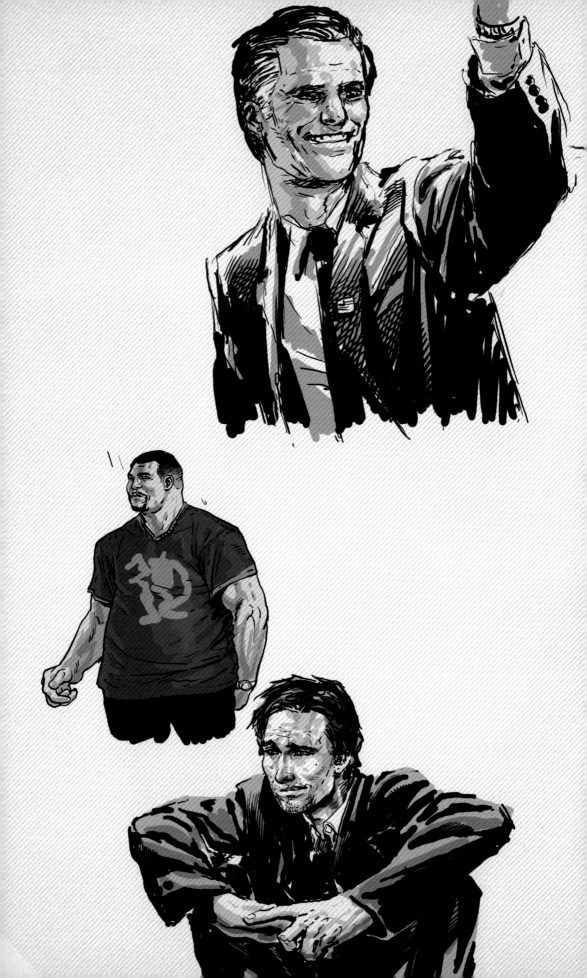

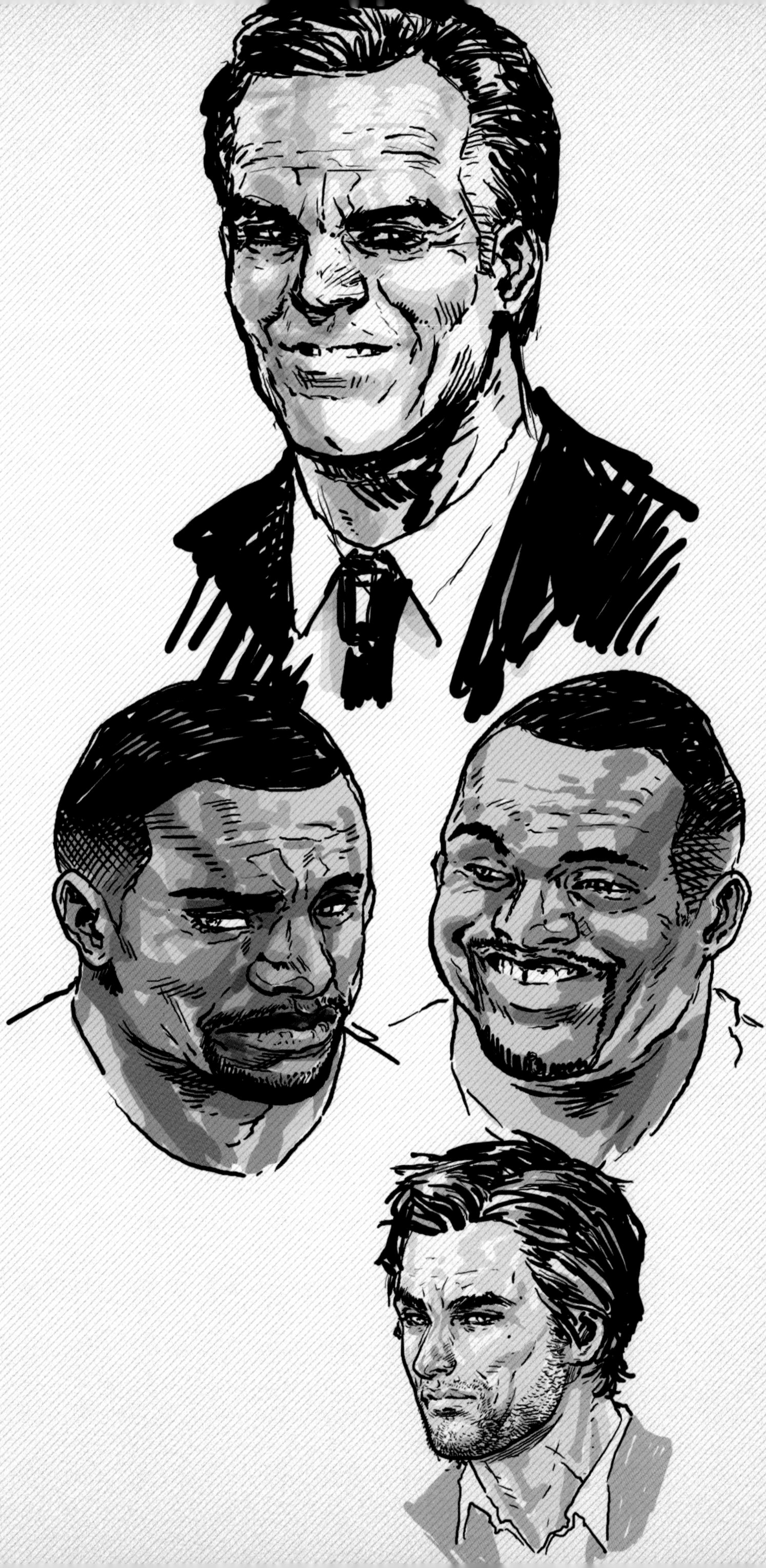

It was a warning.

.....exc. 7.0 *A warning for us.*